The voices got louder. The doorknob rattled. Cam stared into midnight blue eyes. He had to protect her. There was only one thing he could do.

"Lie down," he hissed, as he stripped off his jacket and flung it over the stolen laptop. "Lift your skirt."

Molly's eyes widened. "What?"

There was no time to explain. He pushed her down on the butterscotch sofa and climbed on top of her all in one motion. When the guy opened the door he'd see a couple humping like rabbits. Theft would be the last thing on his mind. Hiding in plain sight. It was the perfect alibi.

Praise for Ann Yost

EYE OF THE TIGER LILY
nominated for the Golden Heart award
~*~
ABOUT A BABY
Winner 2011 Phoenix Desert Rose Golden Quill Award
for best short contemporary
Finalist 2011 Gayle A. Wilson Award of Excellence
Finalist 2011 Wisconsin RWA
Write Touch Reader's Award
~*~
"I loved *ABOUT A BABY*. The characters breathe life right out of the pages!"

~Siren Book Reviews (5 Stones)
~*~
THAT VOODOO THAT YOU DO
Winner First Coast Romance Writers Published
Beacon Contest for romantic suspense
Finalist Wisconsin Romance Writer's
Write Touch Reader's award for romantic suspense
Long and Short Reviews Book of the Week
~*~
"Yost pens a story that's heavy on romance and suspense but with a comedic flair in the form of some elderly ladies who are convinced they are witches."

~Cindy Himler, Romantic Times

Eye
of the
Tiger Lily

by

Ann Yost

Eye of the Tiger Lily

Cover Art by *Kim Mendoza*

The Wild Rose Press
PO Box 708
Adams Basin, NY 14410-0706
Visit us at www.thewildrosepress.com

Publishing History
First Crimson Rose Edition, 2013
Print ISBN 978-1-61217-008-4
Digital ISBN 978-1-61217-963-6

Published in the United States of America

Dedication

To Pete, always

Chapter One

Molly Whitecloud squeezed her eyes to block out the stark overhead light in the treatment room. A burning sensation crawled up the back of her throat. She knew it couldn't be morning sickness. Not yet. Even if the procedure had worked she'd only been pregnant for about seventeen minutes.

Molly lifted herself off the table, shed the paper gown, tugged on her blue jeans and pulled her apple-red sweater over her head freeing her thick, black braid in the process.

If an acquaintance walked into the room she'd look like the same old Molly, the slightly sanctimonious, loud-mouthed crusader; the self-anointed guardian angel to the Blackbird Reservation and the Penobscot people. She'd look that way to her friends and neighbors. She'd look that way to her mother.

But the impression would be wrong. She wasn't the same. She'd let the halo slip. Molly wrinkled her nose. It was worse. She'd ripped off the halo and stomped on it. She deserved the quiverful of guilt that was already invading her bones. She knew it and accepted it. She'd bartered her self-respect for a chance to welcome Cameron Outlaw's baby during the Sewing Moon.

Molly imagined Cam's reaction to this betrayal and her lips thinned. He'd be furious to learn she'd helped herself to his sperm-on-ice. He no longer hated her.

She'd seen him a few times since his return to Eden and she'd experienced his indifference but under the smooth exterior of a sophisticated, buttoned-down financier there beat the heart of a lion.

Cam's fierce emotions were buried like the deadly rapids under the frozen Eden River and Molly Whitecloud had just drilled a hole in the ice.

She walked through the sparsely furnished lobby of Boston's Spotswood Fertility Clinic and into the brilliant blue of a late autumn morning. Normally she felt a surge of unalloyed freedom when she slid under the wheel of her ancient Jeep Wrangler. Not today. Molly felt no sense of relief that the hard decision had been made, that the die was cast, just a numbness and that stubborn, slender reed of hope.

Thirteen years ago she'd followed her head instead of her heart and she'd lost everything. It was too late now for love but a twist of fate had presented her with a last chance at motherhood. She'd jumped at the chance and she had no regrets. She couldn't afford to have any regrets.

****

Cameron Outlaw, Eden's golden boy, peered into his steam-clouded bathroom mirror. The fogged image reflected his uncharacteristic confusion. Normally he faced issues, took positions and solved problems with ease. Cam knew his success in business drew from his ability to make swift, accurate decisions. That ability had suddenly deserted him. He'd begun to dither and Cam despised dithering.

He glared at his dark visage.

Most of Eden's five thousand residents, from Ebenezer Whitfield, the oldest living inhabitant, to the members of the Chamber of Commerce, the bank's board of directors, and everyone in his family expected an imminent announcement of his engagement. And he had every intention of proposing to Sharon Johnson.

The owner/proprietor of the Garden of Eden Inn was perfect for him in every way. A striking redhead with porcelain skin and legs that wouldn't quit, Sharon was intelligent, kind, witty and, like Cam, committed to revitalizing Eden and the rest of western Maine.

Most importantly, she shared his desire to create a family. He knew Sharon would make an excellent stepmother for Daisy.

And yet he was dithering.

Turned out that contemplating the murky waters of matrimony from the safe shore of widowerhood was not the same as actually flinging himself into the drink. Cam shuddered. Sharon's perfection paled before the memory of his past mistakes. He considered himself a two-time loser in the sweepstakes of the heart and he found himself extremely reluctant to cast his lot again.

Cam frowned into the mirror and started to scrape his straight razor over his lathered cheeks, aware that his problems were not limited to the incipient engagement. He'd been a fool to get involved with the Penobscots. Blackbird Reservation, for him, was the dark side of the moon and yet he'd developed and funded the casino and spa.

He gritted his teeth and dropped his head. He'd tried to ignore recent rumblings about disappearing profits, mismanagement and worst of all, exploitation of some of the native staff. None of it concerned him. His part—building and paying for the casino—was finished. The resulting problems weren't his business.

Hell, the rez wasn't his business. That had been well established more than a dozen years ago. An annoying sense of responsibility niggled at the back of his mind but he shook it off. He wanted nothing more to do with Blackbird Reservation or its residents. Not now. Not ever.

A noise outside his door prompted him to set down his razor, hook a fluffy cocoa-colored bath towel around his waist and jerk open the door.

"Hi Daddy," Daisy said.

Cam took a step forward but instead of thick carpeting under foot, he felt rough bristles and quivering flesh and an irritated squeal rent the air. He pitched forward.

"What the hell..." he barked, as his arms wind-milled and he landed on something warm and scratchy. He cursed again as he peered into tiny, reproachful red-rimmed eyes of a pot-bellied pig.

"Daddy, you got a white beard," Daisy chirped, apparently unconcerned with the fate of either her sire or her pet. "You look like Santa."

A pang of remorse made him vow to clean up his language.

"Daze," he asked, "why are you and that pig in my room?"

She moved closer and pressed a small finger into the foam on his chin.

"Do you shave inside that hole?"

He grinned in spite of himself and kissed the tiny finger. He hoisted his lean frame off the floor.

"Yeah, I do."

"I wanna watch."

She followed him back into the bathroom and

4

perched on the closed toilet seat like a curious, curly-haired gargoyle. Cam noticed that, for once, Wilbur didn't follow her. He was a smart guy, that pig. Probably headed back to the safety of his headquarters, the kitchen.

"I went to Hallie's yesterday," Daisy chattered. Cam knew the child spent much of her time at the veterinary clinic run by his brother, Basil and Baz's wife, Hallie. He knew, too, that Hallie frequently took the little girl with her on house calls throughout Eden County.

"Did you have a good time?"

Daisy nodded. "'Cept for that dumb baby."

Cam hid a smile. He knew his daughter didn't like sharing the adult attention with the newest Outlaw.

"Hallie says me and her can go some places without that baby."

"She and I. What places?"

"The Black Bird. Molly's been gone but now she's back."

Cam's heart lurched and his razor slipped. Damn. He'd have to go to the office with toilet paper stuck on his face.

"I know she missed me," Daisy continued, with the confidence of extreme youth.

Cam knew about the friendship between Molly Whitecloud and Daisy. On the one hand he wanted to warn his daughter to guard her heart against the faithless midwife. On the other, he knew in his gut Molly wouldn't deliberately hurt the child the way she'd hurt the child's father. He didn't like the association but he wouldn't officially object as long as he could stay out of it.

He was finished with the rez and he was finished with Molly. The girl with the raven's wing hair and indigo eyes was nothing to him now.

"Daddy?"

"Hmm?"

"Hallie said you might get married."

Cam made a mental note to speak to his well-meaning but meddling sister-in-law.

"What would you think about that? Are you ready to have a mommy?"

Sky blue eyes met their match in the mirror.

"I been ready a long time."

Of course. Elise Outlaw had died a few years after their child's birth. That was why Cam had ultimately returned to Eden. He'd wanted to give Daisy aunts and uncles. He'd wanted to give her a normal family. Hell, that was why he'd courted Sharon in the first place. He wiped the remnants of shaving cream off his face.

"Do you like Miss Johnson?"

"She's nice."

"Yeah. Pretty, too."

"I guess."

Cam nodded and slapped on some aftershave. The tangy citrus stung the scratch on his cheek.

Daisy sniffed the air like a curious dog.

"You smell like lemonade," she said. She leaned closer. "Hallie said you might marry Miss Johnson."

"That okay with you?"

She eyed him, solemnly. "Could my new mommy be Molly?"

Cam's heart squeezed and he growled at the child.

"Tell Asia I'll be right down. I've got to get dressed."

"But what about Molly?"

Her name caught in his throat as he caught a quick mental picture of the graceful curve of Molly's jaw and the dark circles beneath her fine eyes when he'd seen her several weeks earlier. She didn't look much older than she had at eighteen but she'd lost that effervescence he'd loved. He had no sympathy for her. She'd made her choice. If life had been hard for her it was no one's fault but her own.

"Miss Johnson will be a perfect mommy. You wait and see."

The words hung in the air like the canned peaches Asia put in lime Jell-O. They staked his claim, sealed his intentions. He glanced at the mirror. The steam had cleared. He could see the grooves in his lean, tanned cheeks. He could see the future, too. Whatever he said in this moment, Daisy would tell Asia and Hallie and by noon all of Eden would know. Including Sharon.

It struck Cam that he'd been born in the wrong century. For the second time in his life he would marry an "appropriate" woman.

This time, though, he was prepared. This time his expectations had changed. He knew happily ever after belonged in the pages of Daisy's fairytales and he was glad. He no longer craved a soul-mate. He wanted someone he could count on, someone he could trust with his child and his life.

Sharon Johnson would make him the perfect wife.

****

Molly turned off Highway 31 onto Rural Route 2. The air had changed somewhere between Hartford and western Maine. It was clearer here, fresher, more invigorating.

She loved the portage from the steamy dog days of late summer to the Moon of Ripening Berries. She turned onto the unnamed main drag on Blackbird Reservation, home of the Penobscot Nation. The late afternoon sun hovered above the horizon like a benediction bathing the rez in golden warmth. Molly saw the bone-deep poverty but she also saw the proud tradition. When she looked at the shabby modern-day trailers she saw rows of tidy longhouses, too. Grass-less front yards filled with rusting automobiles were replaced with neat fire rings and the worn-out, toothless old men camped out in cheap plastic chairs watching the infrequent traffic became young braves, broad-shouldered hunters and skilled fishermen.

The Penobscot people were made of the same heroic stuff as their ancestors, but times had changed. She'd worked hard to help them find their place in the present. It was her mission and, for a long time, she'd thought it was enough. Not anymore. She deflected the arrows of guilt and fear that pricked her with thoughts of the Penobscot foremothers Molly Mathilde, the peacemaker, Molly Ockett the healer, Molly Spotted Elk, the dancer. Molly herself, as a fifteen-year-old foster child, had borrowed the ancestors' name. Many times over the past thirteen years she'd leaned on their courage. She squared her shoulders and took a deep breath. It would be okay.

Her buzzing cell phone interrupted her thoughts. She slid it out of the leather satchel that served as her purse and spoke.

"*N'nonon*." Mother.

"How did you know it was me?" Muriel Whitecloud asked.

"The same way you knew I was back."

Her foster mother hooted. Molly pictured Muriel's cherub cheeks jiggling with good humor.

"How did everything go?"

"All right."

"Did the uh, thing work?"

Muriel was as real as Mother Earth and just as blunt.

"You mean the artificial insemination?"

"Yeah. That."

"I won't know for awhile."

Muriel hadn't approved of the plan but her reaction was typically supportive.

"I hope it will make you happy, *nizwia*." Sweetheart. "You've been so…" Her voice trailed off.

"Bad tempered?" Molly finished for her. "Irritable? Witchy?"

"Sad," Muriel replied. "You've been sad."

Molly couldn't speak around the lump in her throat.

"I have bad news, though. Lenaya Dove is pregnant."

Molly's heart sank. Lenaya was barely sixteen. She was one of the teens Molly had worked with to emphasize the importance of education and birth control.

"How could that happen?"

"I'll tell you how," Muriel said, indignation in her voice. "She's working up at the resort. There's orgies going on up there."

Molly breath caught.

"She wasn't…raped?"

"The girls need money."

9

The simple explanation tore at Molly's heart. She'd been instrumental in getting the tribe to build a resort and gambling casino. From the beginning she'd known it was a risk. It was impossible to bring in jobs and improved living conditions without exposing the People to the dangers and temptations of the outside world.

"How do you know this?"

"I heard it from Connie Black Squirrel who got it from Tanya Stillwater. The maids and waitresses up at the resort go to parties in the bathtub."

"You mean the hot tub?"

"That's it. After, they get paid for s-e-x."

It never occurred to Molly to doubt the ever-reliable reservation grapevine. She wondered, briefly, if Cam knew about this business. Since he'd founded the Eden Community Bank two years earlier, he'd had a finger in nearly every local financial pot including the resort and casino. She felt certain he'd be heartsick about the exploitation. But Molly couldn't rely on Cam to handle this newest problem. He'd stayed away from the project since it had opened six months earlier and she knew why. He hadn't wanted to bump into her.

Now she didn't dare bump into him.

"I'll take care of this," Molly told Muriel.

"This isn't your fault, daughter. You just wanted to help."

Molly wondered. She'd hoped to bring in funds for a maternity clinic, a childcare center, and more businesses but it appeared she'd failed to protect the tribe's vulnerable youth as she followed her own agenda.

She turned onto the single-lane path that led to her cottage. Fresh white paint gleamed in the last rays of early evening and the blue morning glories that framed her front door had closed up for the night. It took her a moment to recognize the brown sedan in her driveway. When she did, she let out a cry.

Daniel was home.

The tall man with arrow-straight posture, flowing gray hair and a profile lifted from the face of an Indianhead nickel met her at the door. He held out his arms and Molly felt emotions well to the surface as her ex-husband pulled her into a comforting embrace.

"*Doni gedowiozin*?" How are you?

There were only a few fluent speakers of Penobscot left on the rez. Molly and Daniel and a handful of others tried to keep what was left of the language alive.

She smiled at him even as she contrasted the man she adored with the man she loved. Daniel was a wise and circumspect chief. Cameron Outlaw, without a drop of Native American blood, was a warrior, passionate and proud.

"*Newowlowzi*." I'm fine.

Tears leaked out of the corners of her eyes and Daniel made a sound of sympathy. His affection sent her over the edge.

"*Nizwia*."

More tears fell. This time they were for Daniel. He'd connected her to the Penobscot Nation, given her a home and status in the community, rescued her from the humiliation of an unwed pregnancy and she'd given him nothing but loneliness.

His unbound hair flowed around her, comforting her, protecting her. He continued to hold her but he loosened his grasp.

"You didn't go through with it."

She thought about the months of injecting herself with fertility drugs, the letter to the Boston clinic outlining the exact characteristics she was looking for in donor sperm, the prayers she'd offered that Cam's sperm wouldn't have been discarded or marked as private-use only and this morning's appointment for the insemination that she'd almost canceled.

"I did."

Daniel like Muriel had not approved of the devious plan. It offended his strong sense of fair play.

"Conscience bothering you?"

"A little. But I want that baby so much."

"I know." He did know. He'd been there to pick up the pieces when she'd lost Cam's baby all those years ago. "Come have some tea."

Daniel drew her into the small kitchen and settled her in one of the hand-hewn wooden chairs. He moved quietly, efficiently, heating water, pouring it through loose tea leaves creating a heartening brew. Then he set the mugs on the table and took the opposite chair. His dark eyes held hers. Molly hoped he wasn't going to talk about her recent actions.

"Actually," he said, "I'm here on business. And to bring you some news."

She relaxed a little. She and Daniel had remained close after their divorce ten years earlier, but she seldom saw him since he'd moved to Washington, D.C., to work with the Indian Gaming Commission.

"I'm coming home."

She grinned. It was the best possible news. "*Oligun*. It is good. Have you quit the commission?"

He shook his head. "Not yet. There's unfinished

business."

Molly remembered Muriel's words and she felt the hairs stand up on the back of her neck. "It's about Blackbird Casino, isn't it?"

He took a sip of the fragrant tea before he answered. "The projected profit isn't there," he explained. "We're getting the numbers, but not the income."

"What do you suspect?"

"Skimming. Theft."

Molly gasped. This was a far cry from the exploitation of the girls. It was a different problem. An additional problem.

"But who?"

He shrugged. "There's no proof yet but, you know what they say. Follow the money."

"And where does the money lead?"

"Well, Davey just purchased a new Porsche."

Davey Tall Tree, middle-aged, pudgy, the original never-met-a-stranger kind of guy had recently been elected Sagama in a popularity contest. As chief he spent his days working at the community center, organizing computer classes, bingo tournaments, basketball games for very little money. Molly knew he was the tribe's liaison with the syndicate that had partnered with local bankers, including Cam, to fund the casino. The gambling syndicate, Trimerica, was now running both the casino and resort.

There was no way Davey Tall Tree could have afforded an expensive sports car on his own.

"Surely he isn't using casino profits for himself."

"Not directly. But there are a hundred ways the syndicate can find to 'pay' him for services rendered."

"This isn't fair! The Tribal Council promised we'd use the first profits to build a clinic. I can't believe Davey would cheat us. Maybe the car's a loaner."

Daniel shrugged. "He's got that new wife. I imagine he's trying to impress her."

Sandra Tall Tree was a generation younger than her forty-five-year-old husband. She was stylish, sophisticated and she didn't mix well with the other women on the rez. Like Molly, Sandra was only part Indian and an import to the Penobscot Nation. Sandra came from a small Maliseet reservation in Canada. When the casino opened she'd taken a job as personal assistant to the resort manager and since then her nose seemed to ride even higher in the air.

"Even if, for the sake of argument, Davey's getting a kickback, it wouldn't account for the shortfall. Eddie DiMarco is behind this," Daniel said, referring to the casino manager. "He claims he hasn't had the traffic to generate more money. My sources say he's lying."

Molly knew Daniel, a reservation native, was still well connected. Much of the staff of both the casino and resort was Indian.

"Can you investigate in your official capacity?"

He pushed a hand through his long hair.

"The commission has no guts and no teeth. I need hard evidence to turn this over to the FBI. DiMarco showed me the records he wanted me to see. The trouble is, these days you can move money electronically. There's no paper trail."

Molly pondered that.

"Even so wouldn't there be a record on a computer?"

He nodded. "Sure. I saw the official computer.

14

Examined it. Everything on it supports DiMarco's claims. There has to be another one somewhere. Probably a laptop. But my hands are tied. Without some kind of tangible proof, I can't run a search."

Molly understood Daniel's frustration. His agency was under-funded and it didn't pack the legal muscle to push these casino operators to the wall even though everyone suspected they were often operating on the edge of the law and sometimes on the other side of it.

"What do you think is going on?"

"We believe Trimerica has ties to the Calabrese family in L.A."

Molly felt the world caving in. "We've hired a mobster to run the casino? Good grief. When the Tribal Council hired DiMarco we thought we were getting someone with experience."

"He's got experience all right. Most of it in fraud."

Molly studied him with brooding eyes. She hated to be the bearer of even more bad news. She sighed. There wasn't really any choice.

"Daniel, are you ready for the other shoe to drop?"

He looked at her with dark eyes.

"Muriel says someone, probably DiMarco or that resort manager, Dwight Winston, is using our girls as an-an escort service. Lenaya Dove is pregnant."

Daniel shook his head but he didn't look surprised. It occurred to Molly that he'd seen nearly every kind of exploitation in his forty-eight years.

"We thought the casino would ensure sovereignty and fiscal health. We should have tried something else. The Choctaws in Mississippi make circuit boards, the Wisconsin Chippewa operate a pizza chain and the Eastern Cherokee own a mirror company."

"You know we did our research, Daniel. Maine is a tourist state. This seemed like the best option at the time."

"I know."

He sounded hopeless.

Molly shivered. For a moment Daniel reminded her of her father. She'd watched as a combination of disappointment and disillusionment had propelled John Wind down a path to drink and self-destruction. She didn't really believe that would happen to Daniel. He was strong. But Molly had to be sure. She owed Daniel and she owed the tribe. She made a quick decision.

"I'm going to find out," she said. "I'll get a job up there and get the proof you need to shut the casino down until the mob guys are weeded out. I can be a maid or a masseuse. That'll give me a perfect opportunity to check out these hot tub orgies and to hunt for the laptop."

He shook his head but she forestalled his protest.

"Don't try to talk me out of it. I'm perfect for the job. I haven't been near the resort or casino since they opened. Neither DiMarco nor Winston knows me. And you know I can take care of myself."

His black eyes narrowed on her. He shook his head. "You're known to the staff, Molly. Don't you think people will wonder why a busy midwife is moonlighting for minimum wage?"

"I'll say I need the extra money to take some on-line classes. Everybody will understand that."

He looked at her for a long moment. "What will you do when some guy propositions you?"

She blinked. Their marriage had been a rescue mission. Sex was not a subject Molly usually discussed with Daniel.

"I don't imagine anyone is forced. I'll just say no."

"Is this atonement? Do you feel guilty about the insemination?"

Unbearably guilty. Even though she hadn't broken any laws. She'd asked for a sperm donor that matched Cam's characteristics, right down to and including, "plays piano by ear."

Molly knew she had no moral right to this baby but she wanted him or her enough to abandon her strong sense of right and wrong, enough to betray the man she still loved, enough to live with guilt for the rest of her life. Second only to the baby and the baby's father, Molly loved the tribe.

"I want to do this for the rez," she said, quietly. "This is my home, Daniel. This is where my life is."

"A lonely life."

"Maybe that will change."

"You should marry someone else, Molly. You need a husband as well as a child. Cameron Outlaw is not the only man in the world."

"He is for me." She said it simply, unemotionally, but it was true. She knew it and Daniel knew it.

Daniel made an exasperated sound and switched back to the other subject. "I don't like this plan. It isn't your job to take care of the tribe."

She shook her head. "I never do anything I don't want to do. You, of all people, should know that."

"You'll be alone up at the casino," he warned.

"You'll be a phone call away." She was ready to talk about something else. "Will you live here, with me, when you move back?" Her cottage belonged to Daniel.

"We'll talk about that later," he said.

"That sounds mysterious."

He cocked his head to the side. "Maybe you aren't the only one with secrets."

Her eyes widened and she gaped at him.

"Daniel! Have you met a woman?"

"Not in the way you mean. As I said, we'll talk later. You're tired now and so am I."

Molly's mind spun with plans for her project. It could be a little sticky but she was grateful for the diversion. It would keep her from dwelling on the insemination and her guilt. She had no proof the sperm belonged to Cam, but she knew it did. She knew it in her heart, just as she knew the insemination would be successful. She would get her dark-haired, blue-eyed baby. She just knew it. A short time later she fell asleep with a smile on her lips

****

Cam's cell phone buzzed the minute he'd forked a sizeable bite of syrup-soaked pancake into his mouth.

Figured.

"Want me to answer it?"

He smiled at the elegant woman seated on his left. Sharon Johnson's fresh complexion and dark auburn hair reminded him of strawberries and cream. They were in the midst of a breakfast meeting with Eden's would-be micro-entrepreneurs. Cam had just set up a lending circle to allow Nellie Smith to start a wedding cake business, Seth Digby, a car detailing shop, and Mrs. Eulalie Catteridge, a computer website through which she could sell her hand-knit sweaters.

The air in the Garden of Eden's dining room hummed with excitement. The small business people of Eden were getting a new lease on life and Cam was happy to be part of it.

"'Ats okay," he spoke around his food. Cam intended to put off the caller. He wanted Nellie, Seth and Mrs. Cat to know they were important to him. He chewed fast and punched the phone without bothering to leave the table. "This is Grey Wolf. I need to talk to you."

The voice though previously unknown to him, sent a jolt of electricity screaming through his body. Every nerve stood on end.

Daniel Grey Wolf. Molly Whitecloud's husband. The man she'd married when she'd chosen her heritage over Cam. The delicious food turned to cardboard in his mouth.

"I'm busy."

"It's about Molly."

Naturally. Cam clenched his teeth even as he intercepted Sharon's concerned look. "She isn't my business."

"Then you don't care if she is in danger?"

Cam bit out a curse that halted the breakfast table conversation. He angled his body away from the group and lowered his voice.

"You help her."

"I can't. Not this time."

Cam's heart jerked. Damn the man. Damn the woman, too.

"Do you know where the spinney is in the woods near Blackbird Pond?"

The spinney. His mind spun back thirteen years to another September day. Under the canopy of lush brown leaves he and Molly Whitecloud had made love for the first and last time just before he left for college.

Even now he could hear the squawking cicadas and feel the drumming of his eighteen-year-old heart. She'd kissed him and, overcome with a sense of love and impending loss, he'd slipped his arms around her waist. They'd kissed before, but this time was different. This time Cam couldn't control his hunger. He'd tugged her to the ground, his hands moving urgently. At the first taste of her resilient flesh he'd lost track of the insects and the grass, the clear blue sky, the light breeze. He'd lost touch with reality as he'd kissed Molly and stroked her. He'd nearly exploded when she'd touched him with eager, shy hands. Mindless with excitement, he'd buried himself in her softness. It had never been like that again and Cam had long accepted the grim truth. He'd loved the girl he'd nicknamed Tiger Lily. Some part of him, damn his soul, still loved her.

Cam caught sight of Sharon's curious brown eyes and he forced himself to relax. Molly was no longer part of his life. He had a bright, new future with a woman who would be loyal. He loosened his death grip on the phone and lowered his voice.

"I know where the spinney is," he bit out, "but I'll be damned if I meet you there or anywhere else."

"Forty-five minutes," Grey Wolf said. He hung up.

Cam held very still for a moment before he pocketed his phone. He forced himself to smile at Sharon. He forced himself to continue the business meeting. He tried to force himself not to get in his late model Mercedes to go meet with the man who had married his woman. His heart.

He failed.

Chapter Two

Well, hell. He was trapped in a sugar cube.

Cam paced the snow-hued carpet and glared at the vanilla walls.

Normally he didn't pace any more than he dithered, but, dammit, nothing about his life was normal anymore. Especially not the prospect of meeting up with Molly.

Tiger Lily.

It had taken him years to stop dreaming about her, years to stop hating her, years to recover his equilibrium and now he was risking his hard-won contentment. He still couldn't believe he'd agreed to play her escort. *What the hell was wrong with him?*

He sucked in a deep breath and reminded himself this was temporary. He had a bright new future, a new woman. And he had a purpose for this masquerade. He'd built the casino. He was responsible for the welfare of the employees and the honesty of the operation. He really had no choice but to investigate. It was just too damned bad that Molly Whitecloud was part of the deal.

Cam measured the length of the room again with his long strides. Finally he forced himself to stop. He pulled an unopened package of cigarettes out of his breast pocket and frowned at it. He hadn't smoked in the years since college, not until Daniel Grey Wolf had interrupted his breakfast meeting three days earlier. He didn't intend to smoke the pack in his pocket. It was a prop because this was a charade.

Cam squinted at the cream-colored upholstery on the antique sofa. He could almost imagine he was sitting on a cloud in heaven about to meet up with the angel who'd betrayed him. Only the blood-red roses in a milky vase on the white marble console broke the pale canvas of the room. They stood out like a bloodstain on a freshly laundered sheet. A faint shiver trickled up his spine. Panic gripped him and he fought it with anger.

Dammit all. He didn't want to be in this saccharine hell. He was no damn knight in shining armor. If DiMarco was defrauding the tribe he had to be stopped. But not by him. And not by Molly.

He snorted in derision. Of course by Molly. The woman would do anything for the tribe. It had always been her first, greatest love. This time, at least, her interests and his overlapped. Not only did he feel responsible for the casino, his own reputation was at stake. He wondered, briefly, if she'd feel grateful for his help and decided she wouldn't. He'd been a blip on her radar screen, an alien experience that she, no doubt, regretted as soon as he'd gone away to college. When he'd seen her around during the past year she'd looked composed, serene, older than he remembered but contented. It was clear she didn't regret giving him up. He no longer regretted it either.

Would she bail out when she discovered he was here? Would she insist on handling the undercover assignment alone? His stomach clenched at the thought. She was a tiny woman. It would be David facing Goliath minus the slingshot.

Cam glanced into the room that contained a heart-shaped bed. Frothy, whipped-cream drapes around it provided a veil of intimacy. He felt an unwanted stirring beneath his belt. He'd have to work fast. He'd have to make sure they were miles away from here before night. Otherwise he faced hours of lying on the white sofa with visions in his head of Tiger Lily's black hair spread on the heart-shaped bed's pillow, her long, black lashes half-hiding her indigo eyes.

He'd always thought those eyes contained magic. And love.

Of course, he'd been wrong.

Cam cleared his throat, straightened his bow tie, tugged the black jacket of his tux and checked his Rolex. She was due in forty-five minutes. He'd make short work of this, then he'd return to his real life. And Molly Whitecloud could return to the mists of memory like the ghost she was.

****

Molly took a deep cleansing breath, the kind she instructed her patients to use during labor. She let it out slowly. It didn't help. She made a face. No wonder her instructions always earned her that look of disbelief.

A moment later she stepped off the glass-enclosed elevator on the eleventh floor and smoothed her hands over her form-fitting black cocktail dress. The halter-top left most of her back bare and her borrowed push-up bra left most of her breasts exposed. She looked like a hooker. She felt like a hooker.

She had to remind herself that was okay.

For tonight, she was a hooker.

Dwight Winston, the tall, slick-looking hotel manager with dark hair rendered stiff by an overuse of products, and a shark-like smile that included more gum than teeth, had been happy to hire her. He'd barely listened to her trumped up resume. He'd offered her the job of masseuse and, as soon as she'd accepted it, he'd asked if she'd be willing to serve as a dinner companion for a male guest.

Even though she was expecting it, Molly was shocked. Was this what all the female employees faced? Was it possible she was supposed to be just a dinner companion? Or would she get the implicit proposition sometime during the evening?

She half hoped the guest would proposition her. After all, that's why she was here. The other half of her hoped the intelligence was wrong, that Lenaya Dove was the exception that proved the rule or that the young girl had succumbed to her own hormones.

Molly shook her head. She knew she couldn't count on that. She'd get the come-on, she'd turn him down and she'd make a note of everything that had happened. She didn't kid herself that she'd get more than one chance. Word would get back to Dwight and she'd be canned. She planned to plead for a second chance, a second night, to give herself a chance to search the manager's office for the laptop Daniel was so certain existed.

She hoped, too, to observe other staff members and find out what their patterns were.

All in all, she had a lot to accomplish in a small window of time and, in spite of Daniel's warnings, she'd dismissed the idea of danger to herself. She was used to being on her own and she had Daniel's number on speed dial. All she had to do was press a button and he'd show up in his war paint and the full authority of the BIA and the Eden County sheriff's department. Still, she hoped there was no truth to the rumor of mob involvement. She could handle an amorous guest but she wasn't in a big hurry to meet a hit man.

Molly reached her destination, room 806, and her lips twitched.

The Honeymoon Suite. Winston had neglected to mention that. She wondered, briefly, if the client waiting for her recognized the irony. She lifted her fist and knocked once and the door swung open.

Molly's jaw dropped, her carefully planned introduction forgotten.

Cam. She'd seen him a number of times since he'd returned to Eden, but never at point blank range. She hadn't been close enough to count his individual eyelashes or to inhale his masculine scent. Her insides twisted with longing.

With the memory of longing, she reminded herself. Cam was part of the past. She smoothed a palm over her abdomen and sucked in a breath as she gazed at the lean, powerful physique. He'd filled out some since high school. A pleated tuxedo shirt failed to conceal the hard muscles of his arms and chest. The black pants, with their crisp crease and perfect break did nothing to civilize the narrow hips and long legs. He should have looked like an executive in evening dress clothes. To Molly, he looked like a wolf on the scent.

For the gazillioneth time she wondered what it was about him that made every other man in the world fade to gray. He was striking rather than conventionally good looking, his carved nose slightly hooked, a Cary Grant dimple in his strong chin, the cheekbones high in his narrow face. His eyes, sky blue fringed with sinfully long lashes contrasted with the natural tan and the straight, black hair. Yes, he was good-looking enough and full of masculine energy but her fascination with Cam Outlaw lay in the inner intensity reflected in his piercing gaze. He had a fierce passion for everything he did—although he'd have hated the word. She felt her lips tilt into a faint smile until she remembered how it had felt to have that passion directed at her. Incandescent. All consuming.

Frightening. He'd never doubted they could make a life together in his world.

"Come in," he said, jerking her back to the present. There was no smile in the blue eyes, neither was there a sense of surprise. He'd expected her. Was it possible she wasn't at the resort at all? Was this just another of her dreams?

He read her mind just as he'd always done in the old days.

"You're not asleep," he said.

The low, gritty tone of his voice, so different from that of the enthusiastic teenager, so adult, so blatantly sensual, set her blood on fire. She wanted to touch his hard lips with her fingertips. Naturally she didn't. She had to remember that things had changed. There was no connection between them anymore.

She felt a wave of sadness so profound that she trembled.

"Molly?"

The unwilling tenderness in his voice made her want to weep. With an effort she shook off the nostalgia. It was time to get down to business.

"What are you doing here?"

His unblinking stare sent her pulse racing and her

heart pounding. His silence gave Molly her answer.

He was here to rescue her.

In spite of the past, the bitterness, the resentment.

Her throat ached with unshed tears.

"Come inside, Tiger Lily."

The nickname was like a match to dynamite. It carried with it all the first flush of love, the anticipation of youth, and the misplaced belief in happy-ever-after. She couldn't seem to move. Cam took her arm and led her into the suite. He touched her lightly, briefly, a white-hot sensation on her bare skin. And then he let her go.

"Grey Wolf sent me."

Ah. This was not really about her after all. Daniel had, no doubt, appealed to Cam's overdeveloped sense of responsibility, the same quality that had driven Cam to rescue her from the curious crowd on her first day at Eden Consolidated High. They'd wound up making an odd couple, Eden's favorite son and the orphaned half-breed who belonged to no one. The acquaintance blossomed into a friendship and then so much more. With an effort Molly cut off the painful memories.

Cam indicated a sofa upholstered in a nubby fabric that reminded Molly of oatmeal and she sat. He handed her a drink full of clear bubbles. Champagne?

"It's ginger ale."

He'd remembered her preference. Amazing since he'd had no reason to think about it for the past dozen years during which time he'd graduated from college, started a career as a financier, married and become a father. And a widower. The recollection stung Molly into speech.

"I was sorry to hear about your wife."

Even as she spoke she realized the hypocrisy of the words and she braced herself for a blistering set-down. He didn't look at her, keeping his focus on the whiskey he was pouring into a glass, his long fingers, nimble and efficient. He crossed the room and sat opposite her with the easy coordination she remembered so well.

"Thank you."

She marveled at his ability to block any discernible emotion while, at the same time, making it clear he had no intention of discussing his late spouse. It had to have been hard, Molly reflected, to have lost a wife, the mother of a much beloved daughter. She had the most absurd desire to go back several years to comfort him at the time of Elise's death.

"This whole thing," she said, surprising herself, "is my fault."

He looked at her for a long minute. Did he think she was talking about this mess at the casino or the sins of the past? He shook his head and his reply indicated his only interest was in the present. Molly was conscious of a certain disappointment.

"I supported and promoted the casino and resort," Cam said, oblivious of her thoughts. "There's always a risk with investors. Normally I employ a healthy amount of distrust until all the returns are in. I bailed out on this too soon, let go of the reins."

Because he was avoiding her? It seemed likely.

"This was a big, complicated project," she pointed out, "with lots of people and varied interests involved. It wouldn't have been possible to control everything."

Cam's eyes held hers for a long moment.

"I hear you're planning to build a maternity clinic."

She held very still until her rioting emotions

settled. Maternity was not a topic she wanted to discuss with this man. "It's really a general health clinic," she said, eventually. "Most people on the rez don't have insurance or regular healthcare."

She concentrated on her soda hoping the soft effervescent crackle of the bubbles would create enough of a zen effect to distract her from Cam's nearness and the danger of the situation. She'd never expected to be alone with him again. She hadn't hardened her heart against him and she felt frighteningly vulnerable. Why, she wondered, not for the first time, was it like this with only him? Was there something to the myth about the one true mate? Were people like timber wolves and ducks and loons?

If they had met a few years later would they have made it? At seventeen she'd been afraid to leave the rez and she'd known Cam was too young to assume the responsibility of fatherhood. Should she have told him about the baby? She looked at his harsh face. No. She'd made the right decision there.

"What?"

Molly flinched, inwardly. As had been the case all too often, she'd been lost in the past and the past was dead. Unless one of those sperm was successful. She curled her fingers into fists and told herself to get a grip. They were here on a mission.

"Cam," she said, "I need for you to leave. I can't play the role of a companion with you hovering over me like a big brother."

His sculpted lips twitched.

"I'm playing a role, too. Your official escort."

Suddenly she understood.

"Oh, no. You're the guest who's hired me?"

"You don't have to sound so horrified. I wouldn't ravish you if you were the last woman on the planet."

The words stung but she didn't let him see that.

"Of course not. But I don't need you. I can do this better alone."

He squinted, his eyes cat-like slits.

"Grey Wolf said you're planning to break into DiMarco's office to search for a laptop. You think Winston will roll over because you're a beautiful woman? This operation's a cash cow. They'll protect it with their lives. And they won't hesitate to sacrifice your life, Lily."

She didn't hear anything after the word "beautiful." He still thought she was beautiful?

"By the way, I had to bribe Winston to get your services for tonight. He'd already booked you with someone else."

"Who?"

"Himself."

"Oh." It was a sobering piece of intelligence. Apparently she did need a protector. She'd never get the information she needed if she had to spend her time fighting off a lecherous Dwight Winston.

"DiMarco's office is isolated," Cam continued. "It's at the end of a corridor behind the casino. He's in and out most of the night except between two and four a.m. when he takes a break."

"How do you know all that?"

His blue eyes leveled her. "I did my homework."

She didn't miss the implied criticism, which was, unfortunately, deserved. He was right. She hadn't thought this through. She'd been preoccupied with her other secret. For a long time now she'd thought of little else than her quest for a child. His child. But she wasn't about to try to explain that. Her best bet was to accept his help. If they could find evidence indicating there'd been fraud it wouldn't matter whether the girls were being used. The whole place would be shut down and before it reopened Molly would make sure the staff was protected.

She nodded. "We should be able to do this tonight."

"If everything goes like clockwork."

Her gaze locked on his beautiful eyes. The color was familiar and not just because of the past. She'd used it on her living room walls. *Morning-glory blue.*

"What if we hit a glitch?"

He shrugged. "We'll take another shot at it tomorrow night."

Molly's heart nearly stopped. "You don't expect me to spend the night here."

He emptied his glass. "Like I said," his tone was dry, "you'll be safe with me."

Her body, maybe, but what about her heart?

"If necessary, you can have that monstrosity," he nodded toward the heart-shaped bed. "I'll bunk out here."

"Fine."

His indifference hurt but she was expert at masking pain. But Cam had always been able to see through her. It was one of the reasons she shouldn't be here with him now. He moved close to her and she could feel his warmth, his strength and his reluctant tenderness.

"We're here to do a job, Lily. Let the past rest."

She nodded. He was right.

"We'll clean up the mob and get rid of that maggot

Winston, too. Kill two birds with one stone."

He made it sound so easy.

"I'm surprised Grey Wolf left you alone to handle this."

"He didn't leave me alone. He called you."

His eyes seemed to harden for an instant before they were once more impassive. "We'll look less suspicious if we fake being lovers. Think you can handle that?"

Her heart jerked.

"Of course. What about you?"

"Piece of cake," he said. "I'm a hell of an actor."

Was that a dig at her?

"That wasn't personal," he answered her silent question. "Just a joke. What happened to your sense of humor, Molly?"

She wasn't going to tell him that nothing much had seemed funny in the past twelve years. Thirteen.

"Have you got a plan for getting into Eddie's office?"

His lips tilted in a familiar grin and she felt her heart kick hard. He pulled a ring of headless keys out of his pocket.

"Pick locks."

"Very James Bond."

He made a face at her. "Yeah."

At least they could still laugh together. This would be okay. She watched him gather the glasses and deposit them on the bar. I *can* handle this. I can do it. At least I can do it if I get stinking drunk.

But she couldn't get drunk.

She might be pregnant.

****

Pretending Molly was a generic female wasn't working

Cam's imagination wasn't that good.

Even after twelve years and the sexual encounters he'd experienced with other women, her body seemed so familiar. When her small, high breasts pressed against his chest, Cam remembered exactly how they'd felt. That sensation alone had been enough to drive him wild in the old days.

Things hadn't improved.

Cam fought to restore a few molecules of air between them. Beads of sweat broke out on his forehead. He was hot and hard and pissed off at himself. He shouldn't have insisted on dancing.

He tried, again, to pretend she was someone else. His ex-wife. His future fiancée. Nicole Kidman. Anybody.

It was no good. He breathed in her unique scent, a combination of herbal soap and sunshine. *Tiger Lily.* She still fit under his chin the way she had all those years ago, as if she'd been molded just for him. Tonight she'd worn her long, thick braid coiled around her head. Cam itched to tear out the pins, to spread the black silk over her graceful shoulders, to bury his hands in it while he kissed her full lips. He'd forgotten her special gift, her ability to make him feel as though he was her universe. Every drop of his blood rivered south.

It's just chemistry. He chanted the reminder. This wasn't the past, when he'd wanted her heart as well as her body. *This is just chemistry.*

Unfortunately, he wasn't able to keep his desire secret.

Each time she swayed against him she had to feel

the hard length beneath his fly and to hear the sharp intake of breath. And she did feel it. Her slight form stiffened again and again and she flattened her small hand against his shirt front as she tried to create some distance between them.

The movement enraged him and he hauled her against his rigid body, pressing his own palm against her butt.

Jesus.

"Cam."

"Sorry," he muttered. He waited for a lecture that didn't come. Instead, she slid her slim fingers behind his neck and up into his hair and he shuddered.

"Don't," he hissed.

He felt her shift against him, a move that created an unbearable friction.

"It's just an act," she said, lightly. "We're supposed to be lovers, remember?"

He arched back and narrowed his eyes at her. Was she taunting him? The damn woman was asking for it. He ground himself against her.

"This 'act' is about to turn embarrassingly real," he warned.

Two spots of bright color lit her cheeks and tiny beads of sweat embroidered her delicate upper lip. The soft sound her breath made went right to his groin and her next words practically sent him into a coma.

"You feel good to me, too."

He wasn't going to make it. He struggled against the almost unbearable need to push her up against a wall and shock the hell out of the rest of the room. He fought to ignore the rush of sensation and emotion. He fought to withstand her heat. He found a shield in the hurts of the past.

"A likely story. I know you, Molly. I know your passion's as false as your loyalty."

She said nothing. Just returned his glare with a level look of her own. He knew he'd hurt her. He wanted to lose himself in her indigo eyes. He wanted to apologize. Instead, he buried the flare of remorse in an avalanche of memories. She'd promised to wait forever and the minute his back was turned she'd married someone else. One of her own. It scarcely mattered that the marriage hadn't lasted. She hadn't just rejected him, she'd protected herself against any future advances. She couldn't have made her feelings more plain if she'd taken out an ad in the *Eden Excelsior.*

He tightened his grip on her waist and felt, again, that unnerving sense of coming home.

"It's just chemistry," she said, dryly.

His answering grunt turned into a moan as a whirling couple bumped into them, knocking her against his agonized body. Heat exploded as he felt the imprint all the way to his soul. *Mother of God.*

"Get a room," the man cracked.

Cam didn't respond. They already had a room.

And if they had to use it tonight, they'd have a very big problem.

Chapter Three

Cam checked his watch and realized it was time for phase two of his plan. He ushered Molly off the dance floor and across the mezzanine to the glass elevator that transported guests to their rooms. He kept his arm around her shoulders. It was important for anyone paying attention to believe they were headed for a night of lovemaking in the marshmallow honeymoon suite.

At the eighth floor they got off and as soon as the elevator doors closed, Cam piloted Molly to the stairwell.

"We're gonna walk back down?"

He sent her a brief look.

"The alternative is to let Dwight Winston et al see us head down the hall toward DiMarco's office."

"Oh. Right. It's just that it's kind of hard to manage the steps in these spikes."

"You could take them off."

An unfortunate choice of words since his body was still tense from the dance floor. He got a quick mental image of Molly Whitecloud with her shoes off, her legs wrapped around his waist, her voice in his ear. He must have made some kind of bovine noise because she threw him a sharp glance.

"It's fine. I can make it."

She tottered a little but held onto the railing. He stayed in front of her. In case she fell he'd prevent her from getting hurt. As a bonus this position meant he didn't have to touch her. Or even look at her. It should have been a relief.

He reminded himself of his two-pronged goal: Find the laptop and avoid the image of Molly stretched out in that heart-shaped bed.

The stairs ended in a deserted back corridor behind the casino floor. They hurried toward the manager's office. Cam hoped Big Eddie would stay occupied long enough for them to find the laptop and get out. He quickly picked the lock.

"Not bad," Molly whispered. "Apparently this isn't your first breaking-and-entering."

Cam didn't laugh. He was well aware of the brigade of well-armed security guards posing as casino workers, It seemed like overkill for a small-time, Indian-owned casino in the Maine woods and there was no doubt that if they caught the intruders in Big Eddie's inner sanctum they'd been instructed to shoot first and ask questions later.

There was no time to lose.

Shadows filled the empty room except around the desk where a single bulb glowed through a stained-glass dragonfly on a tiffany-style lamp. An oversized, butterscotch faux leather sofa anchored one wall and faced a pink marble fireplace stacked with fake wood. A reproduction of dogs playing poker above the mantelpiece was a curious counterpoint to what was, otherwise, an elegant room. He watched Molly gaze at the picture.

"Interesting choice of art work," she murmured.

Cam wasted no more time. He picked the locks on all the desk drawers and those of the tall, metal file cabinet that stood in one corner while Molly shadowed him rifling through files and papers. The search turned up nothing. She scanned the room.

"What about a safe?"

It was a good idea. He should have thought of it. Since he hadn't, he reacted defensively. "Do you see a safe?"

"No."

There was short silence while Cam rubbed the back of his neck. Every passing second brought them closer to getting caught. Every passing second brought them closer to the need to spend the night in the honeymoon suite. His head felt like someone was turning a screw into it. He'd always suffered from headaches, even as a teenager. Unwillingly, he recalled the way Molly's talented fingers had worked his temples and the base of his neck. He wished he could commandeer those fingers now. *Damn.* He needed to get her out of here.

"Let's go."

"We haven't found the laptop."

"We've run out of places to look."

She headed for the sofa and lifted the cushions.

"What're you doing?"

"Sometimes people hide things in the most obvious places. You know, like money in your mattress or a gun beneath your pillow."

"You think he left the laptop under a cushion where someone could sit on it?"

She didn't get a chance to answer. Voices in the hall reached their ears at the exact same moment. Apparently Eddie had cut his break short.

"It's too late," she whispered. Molly looked at him, her dark blue eyes a pair of giant bruises in her heart-shaped face. A wave of fierce protectiveness slammed into Cam as his eyes strafed the room. There was no place to hide. No floor-length drapes to offer a kind of sanctuary. His eyes lit on the butterscotch sofa. There couldn't be much more than a foot between it and the wall. There was no choice. He didn't mind facing Eddie but he wanted to do it alone. He wanted Molly out of the way.

He grabbed her waist, lifted her easily and deposited her behind the sofa. She didn't cry out or struggle. Instead she shocked him by sinking her fingers into his arm and pulling him down on top of her. His big body pinned hers and they were wedged so tightly they could barely breathe, a couple of goddam fish in a barrel.

He could feel her lungs, trapped and smashed by his weight, struggling for air. He couldn't push away from her. There was no place to go. Worse, his back was literally to the enemy. Eddie could take them both out with one well-placed bullet. He heard the key in the lock and knew there was no longer any choice. All they could do was hold as still as death and pray the fat man would have no reason to look behind his couch.

And that neither of them had to sneeze.

Almost immediately Cam realized he had another quickly developing problem, the same one that had plagued him on the dance floor. The feel of Tiger Lily's soft curves was triggering a familiar reaction. His violent arousal was most unwelcome to him. She seemed to find it amusing. Their eyes met as they heard the door opening and she winked. Cam's body jerked and he scowled at her.

"It better be here, Dwight." The voice was

distinctly feminine, high-pitched and querulous. "I want my money. Now."

"All in good time, baby. First, there's a little something I can do for you." Dwight Winston's voice was thick, his intention clear. Cam bit back a groan.

"Not here," the woman said. "We could get interrupted. Just give me my reward."

Cam felt more than heard the hitch in Molly's breathing. He didn't recognize Dwight Winston's companion but he felt certain Molly did. Her body tensed beneath his and questions tumbled through his mind. Was it someone from the rez? Was she a prostitute or a partner in the alleged fraud? Would her wishes prevail? Or was he doomed to listen to another man do what he, Cam, longed to do right now? He shuddered. The last would be intolerable. He prayed for the sound of disappearing footsteps and the close of the door.

"I'm gonna give you a reward, princess," Winston said. His words were slurred, as if he'd already passed the point of no return. *Shit.*

"How's that feel, baby?"

Her opposition seemed to collapse because her voice slowed to a smooth drawl.

"Hot and heavy. God, Dwight. You been carrying that thing around all night?"

"Savin' it for you," he murmured. "Help yourself."

Cam stared into Molly's indigo eyes and prayed the guy was talking about a candy bar but even before he heard the unmistakable sound of a zipper, he knew his prayers would go unanswered.

The butterscotch sofa jerked as Winston and his companion fell onto it, crushing the couple into the wall.

Goddammit all to hell.

"One quick blow," she said.

A heartfelt male groan triggered a rush of blood into Cam's groin and his arousal flexed against Molly's stomach. He saw her lips part, felt her chest expand and knew she was about to let out a gasp. Instinctively, he covered her lips with his.

It was a mistake. A huge mistake. His temperature shot up and his heart slammed against his ribs as his body prepared to launch. She tasted incredible, like mint and coffee, wine and memories. She tasted like Tiger Lily and the worst of it was that she didn't understand he'd done it just to silence her.

She kissed him back.

Her tongue, sweet and supple and tantalizing slid along the roof of his mouth, behind his teeth, probing, inciting, driving him insane. Cam stopped breathing, unwilling to interrupt the moment of pure joy.

After a moment he became aware of her own wildly beating heart and he tried to shift to give her some breathing room. Another mistake. The movement, like a rushing stream with a small rock, dislodged one of her hands which drifted between his legs. He felt her palm against his hard-on and his whole body surged with desire. He forgot about the present danger, the bitter past and the unprotected future. All he wanted to do was jerk their clothes out of the way, to bury himself in her tight warmth. All he wanted, in that moment, was Tiger Lily.

"Yeah," Dwight Winston's voice was hoarse. "Oh, God, yeah. Harder, baby. Tighter."

Cam fought his awareness of her hand and of the

desperate groans of the man separated from him by a few inches of faux leather. He stared into the indigo eyes but it was too dark to read her expression and, anyway, he was in no condition to read. He dropped his head, intending to relieve the strain on his neck but as soon as his lips touched the gentle mound of her breast he drew it into his mouth, surprising another gasp.

Cam froze but Winston was too far gone to hear anything but the throbbing of his own blood.

"I'm almost there," Winston croaked. "I'm coming, baby."

God. A play by play.

"Then it's as good a time as any to take a break," the woman said.

There was brief, shocked silence before he let out a stream of curses. Winston sounded mad enough to slap her around and Cam wondered if he'd be called upon to rescue the tease.

"Hey," she said, "chill. I'm not gonna leave you like that but I want my money, Dwight. Is it in the safe?"

Safe. Cam was so aroused he could barely get his mind around the word but he knew it was important. It took all his compromised brainpower just to refrain from sliding his tortured organ into Tiger Lily's warmth.

Except she wouldn't be warm or welcoming, not for long. Despite her apparent willingness she'd made it clear, long ago, she didn't want him for keeps. He needed to keep that in the front of his mind. Her body might want him now. Her heart never had.

The fierce need receded enough for him to search her face and, despite the darkness of the room, despite the danger they were in, despite the arousal that had him on the rack, he saw that she was different. Thirteen years earlier, Tiger Lily's indigo eyes had welcomed him unconditionally. Now there was a barrier in place, a wall. He might take her body. He would not be given access to her secrets.

Cam's body was still hard and hot but the fierce drive to join with Molly began to subside.

The sofa shifted and creaked and Winston let out a series of harsh curse, which turned into footsteps and the sound of a tumbler somewhere across the small room. Was the safe behind the picture of the dogs playing poker? He must have extracted the money and handed it to the woman because the next thing Cam heard were Winston's growled words.

"Here. You happy?"

"Real happy, baby. And now I'm gonna make you happy." The unknown female gasped. "Hey, wait a minute."

"I'm done waiting," the man hissed. Cam heard the sound of cloth ripping followed by a shriek. *Shit.* He might have to be Sir Galahad after all. He couldn't let Winston rape her. Cam prepared to shove the sofa back and jump to the rescue but Molly shook her head.

"You're dripping wet," Winston's voice was thick with passion again. "You're ready for me, doll. C'mon now. Tell me how much you want it." He grunted and the sofa slammed against Cam. The feel of the feminine curves sent an electric shock of need through him and he could barely hear the companion's assent.

"Come for me big boy," she cooed. "Come like a bull moose."

The sofa slammed into him again and again as

Winston, apparently took her advice. Cam tried to protect Molly from the worst of the jackhammering and he tried to still the rejuvenated demands of his own body. He tried to empty his head and just endure until the nightmare was over and he was back in Eden, with his daughter and his family and the woman he intended to marry.

Moments later the other couple left the room. Cam leaned his shoulder into the back of the sofa and created a few more inches of space but before he could get to his feet he felt something light feathering his cheek. It was her fingers. Cam's heart clenched in his chest and he felt an absurd wish to cry.

Clumsily he got to his feet and held out a hand to help her up. He didn't know what to say. He made a lame attempt. "Thank God they finally finished."

She straightened her dress and looked up at him. Her braid had begun to unravel and her cheeks were flushed. "He finished. She was faking it."

He squinted at her.

"How d'you know that?"

She shrugged. "She didn't really want him. It was just a business thing for her."

"Just a business thing, huh? I suppose you know the difference."

She stared at him solemnly. "I suppose I do."

****

The safe was, in fact, located beneath the poker playing dogs but Cam couldn't open it. His picks had no impact on the combination lock. There was, Cam said, another kind of a tool that he'd pick up the next day.

The next day.

Molly's heart sank.

They were going to have to spend the night in the Romanov's winter palace that was the honeymoon suite.

She'd rather be shot than sleep in that heart-shaped bed. She'd bunk out in the bathtub.

They didn't discuss the compromising position they'd found themselves in behind the butterscotch sofa. They didn't discuss anything and Molly's heart was heavy as they trudged up the stairs.

"Feet hurt?"

She tried for a lightness she didn't feel.

"I knew there was a reason I didn't become a lawyer. Moccasins and Dr. Scholl's are not good practice for spying in high heels."

He let out a forced chuckle and she felt a slight uptick in mood. This wasn't easy for him, either. It was undoubtedly awkward to be thrown together with someone from the past. Awkward and uncomfortable but at least he wasn't carrying a burden of guilt. She'd done what she had to do all those years ago but she couldn't bear to think about the way she'd betrayed him earlier this month. What had she been thinking? How had she thought she'd be able to keep something so crucial from him? And what about the child, if there was one? Would she deny the father his baby and vice versa? She'd complicated the life of an innocent man and she'd practically destroyed her own.

"Molly? You okay?"

They'd reached the door of their suite. She dredged up a faint smile.

"It's like you said," she lied. "My feet hurt."

Once inside the door he headed straight for the bar,

poured a drink and brought it to her.

"Sit down and drink this," he said. "I guarantee it'll help."

Damn. She couldn't drink the brandy and she couldn't tell him why.

"No. Thanks." She knew she sounded like a prude. "Some ginger ale, maybe?"

His blue eyes were hard, like a couple of marbles but he said nothing. A moment later he handed her another glass. He pulled a pack of cigarettes out of his pocket and lit one.

"There's no smoking here."

He regarded her with a complete lack of interest, inhaled and blew out a stream of smoke.

She realized, suddenly, she'd never pictured him with a cigarette. It didn't seem to fit the image she had of him as a lean, fit athletic type of guy.

"When did you start to smoke?"

The blue eyes narrowed.

"When did you start to care about what I do?"

She deserved the bitterness. She knew it derived from the unexpected intimacy they'd shared earlier but it still hurt. She wanted to tell him she didn't blame him for turning her into a pancake of smoldering desire down in Big Eddie's office. She wanted to tell him she knew his arousal had been because of the situation and had nothing to do with her. She wanted to tell him she was sorry for everything and that she did not consider him vulnerable in any way. She couldn't seem to come up with the words.

"I just figured you were still a runner," she said, lightly. "And a health nut."

"I was never a health nut," he said, indignant.

"Oh, I guess that guy who carried trail mix in his backpack and refused to eat Twinkies was someone else."

He wasn't interested in her pathetic attempt at snack-cake humor.

"Tomorrow we'll hang out together. Then we'll have dinner again and spend some time gambling."

She noticed he didn't mention dancing. Probably a good thing.

"You'll leave around midnight. I can take care of the safe alone."

Her spine stiffened. "This is my investigation. If one of us is going to leave it will be you."

"Forget it. I promised your husband I'd look after you. I don't break my promises."

His words rankled.

"And I do."

He shrugged again.

"It might surprise you to know that a lot of people on the rez count on me," she said, defensively. "And I'd like to point out again that Daniel isn't my husband."

"Tell him that."

"He's a friend. A good friend."

Cam rolled his shoulders as if trying to shrug off the irritation. He stubbed out the cigarette. "Tomorrow's gonna be a bitch. We'll go on a walk or a picnic or something then we can disappear for awhile. Everyone's think we're up here screwing."

"Where will we be really?"

"Back in Eden. I need to find out how to open that safe."

Molly shook her head. She only went into town when there was a compelling reason to do so. She figured this didn't qualify.

"I'll stay here."

"No."

She stared at him. "You want it to look like we're in our room, right? So if anybody comes to the door, I'll call out something like 'we don't want to be disturbed.'"

He looked as if he wanted to argue. He also looked exhausted.

"We'll discuss that tomorrow. We'll take a walk in the morning right on the grounds then go over to the Blackbird spinney for the picnic."

The Blackbird spinney. Pain sliced through Molly. Had he chosen the spot just to punish her? Was he deliberately taking her back to the one and only place they'd made love?

"No," he said, reading her thoughts as usual. "It's the only picnic area around. There'll probably be others there, too."

So he'd chosen it for safety.

He didn't want to risk another impromptu make out session. Molly gazed at the scowl on his face. Not much chance of that. Cam was all business.

"Once we grab the laptop, your husband will have to take the next steps."

She didn't bother to correct him this time.

"I hear he's moving back to Maine."

She nodded. She wished she could tell Cam that Daniel had never taken his place in her heart. That he'd never even tried to. That nobody ever could.

Cam eyed her. "I suppose you know he's planning to live in the studio at the *Garden of Eden*," he said.

She hadn't know that.

"What are you talking about?"

He raised his dark brows. "Is there a communication problem between the lovebirds? Grey Wolf plans to write a book about the history of western Maine and Sharon is lining up folks from Eden and Bangor for him to interview."

Molly knew suddenly, this had nothing to do with Daniel. Cam had deliberately introduced Sharon Johnson's name to remind both of them that he belonged to another woman. She lifted her chin.

"You don't mind another man living with your fiancée?"

"She's not my fiancée."

The response was bullet-quick and he looked as if he regretted it the moment the words were out of his mouth.

"In any case, I trust her."

Another dagger in the heart. This time he'd chosen a woman he could trust. She thought, again, of all he'd been through since they'd been together. Of all both of them had been through.

"Let's not fight," she said.

But he wasn't finished with the subject.

"Kinda strange Grey Wolf moving to Eden," Cam said. "I thought you people always stuck to the rez."

She knew he wasn't really talking about Daniel or any other Penobscot. He was talking about her. Her fear of leaving the comfort of the rez. He believed her decision all those years ago had been based solely on that fear. She longed to tell him there was more to it. She longed to beg him to understand that she owed the people of Blackbird and that she still felt that debt. She longed to tell him that, all of that notwithstanding, she had loved him then.

And she loved him now.

She thought about the baby she'd lost. The old ache throbbed and a deep sense of loss wrapped around her heart. Old grief mixed with new weariness. It splashed up on Molly like angry waves over the side of a canoe. She just wanted to go to sleep. As always, he seemed to read her mind.

"I'm sleeping on the couch. You take the bed." He snagged a blanket from the bedroom closet and, ignoring her protests, he strode into the bathroom. Moments later he emerged, walked through the bedroom and closed the door so that she was left with the bathroom, the bed and privacy. She stood very still for a moment.

"Goodnight," she murmured, finally, although she knew he couldn't hear her.

****

Cam checked the luminous dial on the watch buried in the dark hair covering his wrist. Five a.m. He shifted again in yet another futile attempt to fit his tall frame on the awkwardly curved divan.

Molly's scent haunted him but he knew he was imagining it. A sturdy wooden door separated them. He couldn't smell her. Not really. But her fragrance was in his head, like a siren's song.

Damn. Over the years he'd forgotten how perfectly they'd fit together. She hadn't been his first girlfriend but she'd been his first love. He'd mourned her loss with real grief and he'd never felt the same depth of emotion with anyone else. He'd told himself he didn't want that kind of vulnerability again and it was true.

But he wanted Tiger Lily. Just as he had all those

years ago.

He shifted again, trying, in vain to get comfortable. He had to remember that it hadn't been a shared passion. She'd dumped him without so much as a Dear John letter. Nothing. The only thing that had greeted him that December when he'd arrived home from school had been her absence and the information that she'd married Daniel Grey Wolf.

Information that had torn out his heart.

Forget it. He forced himself to focus on the situation at Blackbird. The Indian casino business was notoriously under-regulated and under-policed. Its cash-and-carry nature appealed to shysters. He'd known that, but it had seemed to him, to others in Eden and to the Tribal Council that it was the best way to increase revenue for the rez. When he'd started work on the project, he'd paid close attention to the financial details. Then his partner, contractor Joe Packer of Packer, Inc., had been murdered and he, Cam, had had to finish the project alone. During the course of that investigation, Cam had come into contact with Molly Whitecloud and they'd talked for the first time since their break up. She'd confirmed his persistent belief that she'd broken up with him because she'd been unable to leave the rez after all.

The experience of reliving and rehashing the painful past had prompted him to stay as far away as he could from the reservation. He'd seen the project through to completion mostly with surrogates and, as a result, there were problems.

He'd been negligent, no question about it. His pathetic efforts to protect his own heart had led to disaster at the casino and spa and now the tribe was paying the price.

He stared up at the white ceiling. It was time to suck it up and take care of business here. He'd get this mess cleaned up. He and Molly would do it together.

And then they'd go their separate ways for good.

Cam flung his legs over the side of the divan and got to his feet without making a conscious decision of where he was going. He crossed the vanilla carpet and put his hand on the knob to the bedroom door. He expected it to be locked. He hoped it was locked.

It turned easily under his hand.

He pulled the door open and stepped into the shadows.

Her even breathing told him she was asleep. With the curtains open the moon shone through the latticework on the window tracing a crosshatch design on her petal-smooth complexion. She looked like a Native American Sleeping Beauty. Cam knew Molly was a mixed breed, a woman with a white mother and a father from a small Mohawk tribe in Ohio. He knew she'd been orphaned and, through a national Native American adoption organization, brought to Blackbird and the Whitecloud family.

For the first time he wondered about her childhood. His own mother had left him and his baby sister Lucy with their father while she'd moved across the country with his elder brother, Baz. Cam knew that experience had crippled him, embittered him. Had it been the same with Molly? She, too, had been abandoned by her mother and ultimately her father.

Cam thought about Daisy. Would she suffer permanently from the loss of a mother she'd barely known? He hoped not. If things had gone right, she'd have been Molly's daughter. His heart twisted. She would have made a wonderful mother. Why hadn't she gone that route? Why had her marriage with Grey Wolf ended? The man obviously cared about her.

He couldn't stand to think about Molly's husband. Ex-husband. Hell, he should be thinking about his own future wife.

He stared at her face. The dark lashes lay against high cheekbones. She looked soft and sweet and vulnerable. His heart was full. He wanted to crawl into the bed with her, to feel her heart beating against his chest, to feel her warm breath sigh out against his neck. He fisted his fingers to keep from touching the soft cheek as he stood and stared at her.

Time went by. Cam didn't know how long he stood in her room staring at her, feeling her in his bones and skin. He didn't know at what point need overcame reason and he touched her soft cheek, a contact that warmed his soul. He didn't know when he gave in to the overwhelming need to lie next to her. He only knew that when he woke up he was stretched out on the heart-shaped bed, Molly's cheek was pressed against his chest and his arms were around her.

Chapter Four

Molly awoke to find a yellow Post-It affixed to her forehead. Cam's bold printing informed her he'd gone to the kitchen to collect their picnic. She smiled at the note. He was so responsible. Always had been. Naturally he'd let her know where he'd gone. In writing.

She'd bet his late wife had loved his consideration. Cam's manners were impeccable but the underlying kindness he hid behind his gruff manner was what touched her. Soon they would touch Sharon Johnson, too. Molly's heart thumped hard but she shrugged away the pain. She was at the resort to do a job. Cameron Outlaw's habits, considerate or otherwise, were not her business.

She dressed in the black cocktail dress. She thrust her black stockings into her purse and hurried to the room she'd been assigned by Dwight Winston. After a quick shower, she re-braided her hair and slipped into a short, buttercup-colored sundress, strapped on a pair of sandals and grabbed a sweater. It had been warm for late September but this was Maine. Harsh winter, the Moon of Freezing Rivers, was never far off.

She glanced at herself in the mirror. Her cheeks glowed and her dark eyes sparkled. The moments behind the sofa had been surreal but they'd supplied her with a new memory. Long ago she'd decided not to fight her feelings for Cam. She knew she'd never forget the pleasure of his weight against her or the sound of his roughened breathing. She'd never forget his uniquely masculine scent or the heat of that kiss. She wrapped her arms around herself. The memory of this adventure would haunt her for a long time. It would be painful, of course, but it would also be sweet.

As she locked her door and started down the hall, another memory came to her.

She'd recognized the voice of Dwight Winston's companion and wished she hadn't. Davey Tall Tree, the tribe's sagama, had brought her back from a trip to another reservation in Canada. Sandra Tall Tree was half his age, slim and pretty and her nose rode high in the air. None of the women on the rez liked her much and Molly was guiltily aware that she hadn't spent any time welcoming the newcomer. Was that why she'd taken up with Dwight Winston? Molly considered that. Sandra dressed well and liked pretty things like the shiny sports car Davey had bought for her. Life with the staid, former tribal cop, must be dull but it seemed more likely that Sandra had gotten involved with Winston for mercenary reasons.

Molly sighed. She feared Sandra might be involved as an accessory in illegal activities. But whether that was true, Davey would be devastated when this came out. If it came out. It wouldn't do the tribe any good, either.

In any case, the habit of protecting the rez and those who lived there, held strong. Molly decided to keep her mouth shut and her eyes open. At least for now. If necessary, she'd talk to Sandra herself.

She took the elevator to the ground floor and found

her fake lover in the breakfast bar. He wore a denim shirt and khakis and looked more appetizing than anything on the menu. Tall, dark and dangerous with those snapping blue eyes. This morning he looked like a poised, mature, successful financier on vacation with his girlfriend.

Most of that description was true.

A memory of the butterscotch sofa rippled through her. He hadn't been poised last night. She shivered with desire.

He frowned at her. "You okay?"

She summoned a smile.

"Fine."

"Got a sweater?" His tone was curt, impersonal, but the question touched her just the same.

"Yes," she said, showing him.

They stopped in the kitchen to pick up a picnic basket prepared by the staff. Molly admired his organizational skills. Cam had always been good on anticipating needs and follow through.

Except once.

He caught her hand in his for the benefit of any curious bystanders, he explained, and they strolled out the back, across the sparsely populated golf course and through the woods that separated the entertainment complex from Blackbird Reservation. They did not exchange a word as he led her to the spinney by Blackbird Pond and Molly soaked in the morning sun and inhaled the familiar woodsy smell and shamelessly pretended that it was thirteen years earlier when she'd had a right to Cam's company.

He stopped at the familiar spot and Molly's heart turned over. He spread a red-and-white tablecloth on the ground, a grim look on his hard mouth. It wasn't thirteen years ago. He was all business.

He knelt down to unpack the picnic and the sun on his shiny, dark hair revealed something new.

"Oh my gosh," she said, involuntarily, "you're going gray."

He turned to look at her, an unreadable expression in the morning-glory colored eyes.

"Time passes."

They'd wasted so much of it. More than a decade. Sorrow and regret hit her like a hail of bullets. She could barely speak. He reached a hand and pulled her down to the grass and she could read his thoughts.

I know you're sad but we have today. Let's enjoy it.

She sat and took in a deep breath while he set out the lunch.

"How's your dad?"

He looked at her oddly. "He's all right. Retired to a little town in Arizona last year after a heart attack. Didn't you know that?"

She nodded. She had known it, of course. Hallie kept her up to date with the latest happenings in the Outlaw family. He waited but she didn't explain why she'd asked the question. His eyes probed her face.

"Did you ever meet dad?"

"Once."

"I don't remember that."

"At the graduation picnic. You were playing softball, I think." She didn't think. She knew.

Something about her tone must have made him suspicious.

"What happened, Lily. What did he say to you?"

The old nickname caught at her emotions. She

shrugged and looked away. It was all ancient history now.

"He congratulated me."

"That all?"

"He asked me about my plans. You know, whether I was going to college."

"And he pointed out my bright future."

She looked at him, quickly. He understood.

Cam sighed. "Dad had met John and Susan Larkin at a party in Boston. They became friends. All three of them thought it would be a great idea to set me up with Elise once we got to college."

She nodded. She knew all about that. She knew, too, that Elise had been the one to answer the phone the night Molly had finally gotten up the courage to call Cam, to tell him about the pregnancy. The other woman had been friendly enough but clear. She was Cam's girlfriend now. He wouldn't be returning the phone call.

When Molly learned, several years later, that Cam had married Elise Larkin, she hadn't been surprised. Jesse Outlaw, she thought, had gotten his wish.

She thought suddenly of the grief Cam had been through.

"It must have been hard to lose her."

He stared out at the lake. His lack of comment didn't surprise her. His wife's death still hurt. Why would he want to share it with Molly, a woman who'd betrayed him? She felt anxious to change the subject.

"Do you remember your mother?"

Cam's lips twisted.

"Sure. She left when I was ten. She took my brother with her and left Lucy and me with Dad. She died a few years ago. Why?"

"No reason. I always picture you as a little boy playing in the backyard amongst sheets billowing on a clothesline." She grimaced. "I guess that sounds pretty silly."

"Not so silly. I must have told you about that. Baz and I liked to play tag in between the sheets. Asia would scold us when we got them dirty because she'd have to wash them over again, but she never reported us to Dad so I guess she didn't really mind." He grinned at the memory. "What about you? What did you like to do as a kid?"

Molly appreciated his interest but she didn't really want to tell him about her unemployed, alcoholic father or the mother she barely remembered.

Laundry hadn't been a priority in her chaotic youth.

"We never had a really settled home," she said. "And I didn't have any siblings. When my dad died I came here. By then I was a little old for tag."

Cam's gaze lingered on her. She felt him waiting for details. Was he still looking for answers? Did he still wonder why she'd married Daniel? Probably not. It was all so long ago.

The resort's chef had provided slices of broiled chicken, cups of potato salad and bite-sized pieces of melon and papaya. Molly ate little but she felt a welcome sense of peace. This place was home to her. More than that, it was sacred ground. She'd come here many times by herself over the years. She liked to feel the presence of earlier generations, in particular, the other Mollies.

And, sometimes, she'd just sit here and recall every detail she could remember about the afternoon she and

Cam had made love.

"Thinking about the past?"

She looked at him. "Can you read everybody's mind the way you read mine?"

He shrugged. "It's just this place. Lots of memories."

She nodded, not wanting to destroy their détente by introducing old hurts.

"I love it here," she said, softly. "I feel a connection with nature. A link to the past. I mean the distant past. You know, history."

Cam nodded as if he understood. Then he surprised her.

"What makes you happy these days, Lily?"

The friendliness in his tone warmed her heart and made her throat ache. She tried to answer honestly. "Sitting in my garden. Seeing folks from the rez get jobs or healthcare or a new double-wide. Watching new parents after a safe delivery." She realized she was approaching dangerous ground so she paused.

"After you've delivered a child you mean."

She nodded and opened her mouth to change the subject but she wasn't fast enough.

"You haven't wanted a child of your own, I gather."

Molly had been asked the question before. She'd developed a stock answer but she found it difficult to lie to Cam. The irony of that struck her. She'd lied easily to him twice before—by omission.

"I've found fulfillment in my work. The women on the rez have no health insurance. They can't afford doctors and hospitals. I'm all they have."

"That doesn't answer my question."

She gave him a quick, vague answer.

"Some day, maybe."

He let it go. Probably he didn't really care.

They spoke about his years of college and graduate school, his stint in London and his job at the bank in Boston. He'd traveled extensively at the time. Molly was glad. He'd always wanted to travel.

"I left the fast lane when I returned to Eden."

"Do you miss it?"

His clear blue gaze clouded.

"Daisy needed more than an absentee dad. I came back to Eden to provide her with a family."

Molly had always known he'd make a great father. It didn't surprise her that he'd sacrificed the corporate ladder for his small daughter. She knew he would have sacrificed his future for her child if he'd known. A knife twisted inside her. Cam Outlaw was a good man. He'd been a good man at eighteen. He deserved the honesty he wasn't getting from her.

"Daisy likes you," Cam said.

Molly's heart jerked.

"I like her, too. She's a beautiful child."

"She looks like her mother."

Molly felt certain the hard expression on his face reflected his grief. She touched the back of his hand. To her surprise he didn't jerk away. He turned her hand over and threaded his fingers through hers.

"Sharon will make a good stepmother," she said, wanting to comfort him.

She felt the muscles tighten in Cam's hand.

"I'm not getting married again just to get Daisy a stepmother."

"I know." Sharon Johnson was a good and loyal

woman. The redhead was beautiful, too. He was marrying her because he wanted to build a life with her.

Because he trusted her.

Because he loved her.

And Molly knew that, perhaps even more than Elise, Sharon deserved him.

His face darkened and he scowled. At the same time Molly noticed the sky had clouded over. Thunderheads gathered on the distant horizon. There would be a storm tonight.

"We'd better get back," she said, as she rose to collect the picnic things. His fierce grip on her wrist shocked her but not as much as the raw intensity in his voice.

"Why did you marry Grey Wolf?"

Molly's heart slammed against her ribs like a tiger desperate to break out of a cage. She wondered if the frantic organ would batter itself until it burst.

She knew she should have been prepared for it.

She wasn't.

She wondered why he wanted to know? Did he still care about her? Was this an effort to find some kind of closure? Or was it simply a function of being back in the spinney—together.

Molly realized she'd been silent too long. She blurted out a random answer, which turned out to be partly the truth. Of course, Cam already knew it.

"I needed to belong to the tribe."

He glared at her. "You belonged to the tribe. Muriel and James had already adopted you."

She read the lack of comprehension behind his words. And the hurt.

"I know. They did share their lives and their

heritage and their name, but it was new. I didn't feel secure. Not then."

"And now?"

She nodded. "Now I belong," she said. "I've earned my way into the tribe. I have a home."

His voice came out in a low growl. "You could have had a home with me."

The words sliced her in two. Over the years she'd told herself she'd done the right thing for Cam. She'd told herself over and over it couldn't have worked. They were too young. They were from different worlds. It would have held him back. She'd come to believe she'd married Daniel for Cam's sake. His words made her face her own insecurity, her cowardice. She needed approval. She couldn't have handled his father's disapproval. She couldn't have left the safety of Muriel and James. She couldn't have disappointed the generous couple that had taken her in.

And she would have disappointed them and humiliated them with an unwed pregnancy.

She could explain none of it so she remained silent but she felt his anger in the pressure of his fingers on her wrist.

"You aren't married anymore."

"No."

"How come? Did you betray him, too?"

Her eyelids flickered. She hadn't betrayed Daniel but she'd accepted his protection and, for a long while, he hadn't been free to find a woman of his own.

"No."

"So why the divorce?"

"It was the right thing to do."

"The right thing?" He spat the words. "What do

you know about the right thing, Molly Whitecloud?"

"Cam." She had to stop him. She couldn't afford to get embroiled in an emotional fight that might end with her giving up precious secrets.

"It would never have worked for us. We were too young."

The blue eyes became azure slits. "How do you know? You didn't try."

She shrugged her shoulders and spread her hands to the sides, palms up.

If she told him about the baby they'd lost he might forgive her but it would break his heart. And, anyway, she couldn't afford to get onto the subject of babies. Not with Cam.

"I'm sorry," she said.

They walked back to the resort in silence.

There was nothing left to say.

****

Molly's heartbeat accelerated later that afternoon as she hurried through the hallways of the big hotel in defiance of Cam's orders. He'd told her to stick to the honeymoon suite while he drove into Eden but she had no intention of doing that. This was a perfect opportunity for her to do a little sleuthing on her own. She'd been "hired" as Cam's escort for another twenty-four hours so if she ran into Winston or Fat Eddie she'd have an excuse for not working. She wouldn't, however, have an excuse for roaming around the spa.

As it was, the place was a wasteland. She ran into nobody until she reached the laundry room in the basement where she found Lynn Brown Bear, a middle-aged Penobscot whose teen-age children and invalid husband depended on her paycheck. Lynn was loading white sheets into a dryer while piles of dirty linens sat on a nearby table. She looked up when Molly came in. Long gray hair escaped from what Molly knew had started out that day as a neat braid. Lynn's round face shone with sweat.

"Molly," she said. "What are you doing here? Is someone having a baby?"

"No. I'm moonlighting. I want to make some renovations to my cottage so I've taken a part-time job here. As a masseuse."

Lynn eyed her doubtfully. "Seems like you're busy enough."

Molly's face burned and she knew it wasn't from the heat of the steamy room. She didn't like lying to anyone, much less someone from the rez. She abandoned the pretense.

"You're right. I'm here to get some information. There's a rumor that some of the employees have been taken advantage of by guests and I want to find out whether it's true."

Lynn's brown eyes grew sad. "You're talking about Lenaya Dove, right?"

Molly nodded, as always, impressed with the reservation grapevine. "What can you tell me, Lynn? Are the girls being used as escorts?"

The laundress looked troubled. "I need this job, Molly."

"I'll protect your confidentiality."

"It's not just that. I don't want to start a scandal. I just can't afford to have the resort shut down."

Molly felt a surge of anger. Not at Lynn Brown Bear but at those who were treating the casino and resort as some sort of money-making playground. This venture was supposed to have provided a better future for the residents of Blackbird Reservation. She knew, too, that Lynn was right. An investigation into illegal activity would result in a scandal and a shutdown and more unemployment for the Indians.

Molly made a mental note to check on Lynn's family no matter what happened to the casino. She'd make sure they had food and clothing for the coming winter.

"I understand," she told the older woman, "but Lenaya's only sixteen."

Lynn brushed a strand of hair off her face and sighed. Molly saw the conflict in her eyes and she breathed a sigh of relief as loyalty to the tribe trumped personal concerns.

"Every afternoon there are parties."

"Parties?"

The older woman nodded. "Mr. Winston takes the girls to his rooms."

Adrenalin shot through Molly's veins. Private parties. Orgies? Muriel's information had been good.

"Where is Mr. Winston's suite, Lynn?"

"On the very top floor. The ninth." She looked immeasurably sad. "He likes the young girls the best, Molly. But there won't be any up there now. They come to work after school and on weekends."

Anger knotted inside Molly and something else. Anticipation. She couldn't wait to nail this jerk.

The laundress pointed out a service elevator that made Molly smile. If she and Cam had known about the service elevator last night her feet might not hurt so much today. As it was, aching feet were a small price to pay for rescuing the teenagers and other women who worked here. She thanked Lynn and punched the button for the ninth floor.

When she stepped off the elevator she found there was only one suite. Molly stared at the gold lion's dolphin that served as a knocker. She felt like Dorothy seeking entrance to the Emerald City.

The middle-aged man who responded to her knock was tall and beefy. A pair of Bermuda-length swim trunks presented his pale pink stomach like a cone holding a giant scoop of strawberry ice cream. A former jock, Molly thought, one who'd exchanged the locker room for a recliner and ESPN.

A tall, willowy brunette slid a slim hand through his thick arm and stared at Molly. Molly stared back at the *sagama*'s wife.

"Is someone having a baby?"

"No. I'm here because," it occurred to Molly midway into the sentence that she hadn't figured out a cover story. She decided to go on the offensive.

"What are you doing here?" *And what were you doing in Big Eddie's office last night?*

"I'm Dwight Winston's secretary," Sandra said. "I work here."

"I work here, too," Molly suddenly remembered. "I'm the new part-time masseuse."

"I feel my body tightening up as we speak," Mr. Ice Cream Cone said. He winked at Molly. "How 'bout a little rubdown?"

Sandra's brow furrowed and her voice was anything but gracious.

"I guess you can come in."

Molly looked past the other woman to an oversized hot tub filled with frolicking guests, most of them nude.

She gulped. *What had she gotten herself into?*
****

Cam made a quick trip to Eden. He checked on his daughter then stopped by his office where he made a call to Boston. He'd met Sam Salinger, a defense attorney, through Elise's father. Salinger had made an extensive study of breaking and entering techniques in the course of defending clients and he told Cam what he knew about combination locks. Even better, he faxed him a drill-point diagram of a typical lock. Sam told him the drill-hole would most likely be close to the axis of the dial but possibly in the sides or back of the safe.

"There are only two real problems with this kind of entry," Sam explained. "Firstly, you have to have a drill." He went on to explain where Cam could get the tool on short notice.

"Okay," Cam said, jotting down notes. "What's the other drawback?"

"You could run into hard plate steel or composite hard plate beneath the surface which would shatter the cutting tips of a drill bit. In that case you'd need a tungsten-carbide drill bit and even then the process can be time-consuming."

Sam paused as Cam muttered a curse.

"Or there could be a glass re-locker. It would be mounted between the safe door and the combination lock. It has wires that lead to randomly located, spring-loaded bolts, which will be released upon contact with the drill. One other possibility is a thermal re-locker that could be used in conjunction with a glass-based re-locker. It's usually a fusible link that is part of the relocker cabling. It would rebuff the efforts of your drill."

Cam gritted his teeth. "In other words the drill-hole approach will only work on simple, old-fashioned combination locks."

"Basically."

Cam thought about the operation at the casino. He figured his odds were about fifty-fifty. DiMarco and the others had put money into the furnishings and décor but, he suspected, they'd have skimped on the stuff that didn't show. Maybe.

"Thanks," he said. And because he knew Sam was a man with a connoisseur's interest in locks he added, "I'll let you know what happens."

"I'd appreciate it."

Cam considered making a quick stop at *The Garden of Eden*. He knew Sharon wouldn't condemn him for the evening—and night—he'd spent with Molly. It was just business. A charade. But he felt guilty. Not about the instinctive response of his body on the dance-floor and in Big Eddie's office but about the way he'd stood by the bed and watched her sleep. He didn't want to feel anything for Molly but he did and, while he'd never again trust her, he'd begun to question whether he could build a life with another woman until those feelings were resolved.

Sharon deserved someone heart-whole.

Cam gripped the steering wheel of the Mercedes and drove past the inn without stopping. There would be time enough to examine his relationship with the beautiful redhead when this godforsaken assignment was over and Molly Whitecloud was back in the past where she belonged.

He wondered what she was up to now. He wondered if there was any chance she'd obeyed his order to stay in the honeymoon suite.

He stepped on the gas.

When he returned to the empty Sugar Cube room in mid-afternoon he found a Post-It note on the white marble coffee table.

"Gone fishing. See you for dinner."

Cold fingers gripped his heart. The gray skies of morning had finally produced a steady downpour. Cam thrust his fingers through his thick hair as he scowled at nobody in particular. The damn woman had decided to snoop on her own.

Chapter Five

Daniel Grey Wolf worked slowly, methodically unpacking and arranging his few belongings in the studio apartment. He thought about Molly up at the resort. She hadn't called yet but he wasn't worried. He knew Cameron Outlaw would protect her. He shook his head. She was probably ready to turn Daniel into bone meal. She wouldn't thank him for calling in that particular cavalry. But Daniel had thought long and hard about Molly and he'd concluded that she would never find happiness until she'd faced her demons.

And that meant Cam.

Daniel's thoughts switched to his own future. He'd known for some time he was finished with Washington, D.C. and the endless and hopeless task of monitoring the growing number of Indian casinos. He was ready to return to Maine. He was ready to recapture his soul. He planned to start by writing about what he knew, the Abenaki tribes that had originated in New England and Canada. He wanted to bring an understanding both to his own people and to everyone else that the Native Americans were more than a conquered nation.

Daniel had made another important decision, too. He wouldn't move back to the rez. Molly had occupied his cottage for twelve years and it was now her home. Besides, he wanted something different. He was restless, unsettled and not in harmony. He did not want to go backwards and he did not want to stay where he was. There was something out there waiting for him and he knew he couldn't find it on the rez.

This outbuilding, originally a music studio when the Garden of Eden, then a private home, had been built a hundred years earlier, was the perfect place for solitude and reflection.

But Daniel had found something even more valuable than peace; he'd found a friend.

Sharon Johnson, tall, beautiful and oddly shy, had made him welcome here. More than that, she'd made him feel valued, not fin his customary role of protector, but for himself.

Daniel ran his long fingers along the worn surface of the sturdy oak desk that dominated the studio's main room. A sense of well-being descended on him like a warm cloak. He felt sure this move had been the right one in spite of a most surprising complication.

At the age of forty-eight Daniel Grey Wolf had fallen in love for the first time in his life. It was a love without expectation. Sharon was nearly engaged to Cameron Outlaw and, besides, she and Daniel were just friends, the same way Molly and he had been just friends. On paper, the two relationships were the same but they were different in his heart. He loved Molly as one loved a favorite sister or a niece. He loved Sharon as a man loved a woman. His love would remain unspoken. Even if Sharon's heart had been free, Daniel was not the right man for her. But she was the right woman for him and, for the most part, he was thankful to have found her.

And there was something between them. A kind of quiet understanding. The innkeeper seemed to enjoy his company. She had stopped by several times yesterday while he'd moved into the studio. He wondered what she'd say if she knew those visits were the brightest spots in his day.

Daniel gazed around the studio. Yeah. This place felt more like home than anywhere he'd been in a long, long time.

A knock on the door interrupted his thoughts.

Sharon stood outside holding a tureen of hot soup between two bright blue oven mitts. She had a fragrant loaf of fresh bread under one arm and a bunch of fall wildflowers clasped between her teeth.

"Just a little housewarming," she said, after he relieved her of her burdens.

He gave her his rare, quiet smile.

"You didn't have to do this."

She shrugged her shoulders. As always, she looked sophisticated and elegant. Her thick auburn hair had been pulled into a severe twist that emphasized her large hazel eyes. She wore a tailored suit the color of wild honey.

"Well, I figured you hadn't had time to go to the market." She was silent a moment as if carefully considering her next remark.

"Mr. Grey Wolf, I realize the kitchen accommodations here are skimpy." She indicated his small refrigerator and hot plate. "You are more than welcome to eat in the dining room. Or, if you'd prefer, you could eat with me. I usually have my meals sent to my suite." Her pale cheeks turned faintly pink.

Daniel was completely charmed. And he saw past her kind offer of hospitality to the real motivation. She was lonely, too. Just as he was. The exquisite, elegant, almost-engaged innkeeper needed a friend.

And if there was a place where Daniel excelled it was friendship.

"I'll accept your offer if we can move to a first-name basis."

He wasn't prepared for her blinding smile or the effect it had on his heart. He felt a sudden, burning desire to study the galaxy of freckles sprinkled across her nose at close range. He longed to touch her full lips with his fingertips. He banished the improper thoughts and grinned at her.

"What?" Sharon sounded self-conscious.

"How did those flowers taste?"

She laughed. "Not bad. Luckily we don't use pesticides in the garden here."

"Good thing." He drank in the scent of her expensive perfume. It seemed to close around him like a comforting cocoon.

"Do you have time to share the soup?" He heard himself with surprise.

She hesitated.

"Please don't feel you have to stay," he hastened to add.

"It's not that. I just don't want to take up your time. I know you took the studio to get some privacy."

She didn't understand. Daniel intended to make sure she never understood.

"There's always time to eat," he said, easily.

While he ladled the soup into native-made earthenware bowls Sharon moved about the small room inspecting his sparse decorating efforts. She commented on the turquoise pottery and the hand-loomed rug. He was aware of her interest in the unframed pen-and-ink drawings he'd left on a countertop.

"Forgive my nosiness," she finally said, "but these are wonderful. Did you do them yourself, Daniel?"

The compliment was nice but the real pleasure he got was from hearing his name on her tongue.

"Yes."

She picked up one drawing and studied it for a long time.

"This is Molly Whitecloud."

Daniel knew which sketch she'd found. It was one of Molly seated in the garden wearing a long gingham dress. Her raven-colored hair had been cut short emphasizing the unusual indigo eyes and high cheekbones.

"She's breathtaking," Sharon said. "But she looks so sad."

She had been sad. She'd just lost her baby. And the man she loved. The man Sharon was about to marry. Daniel said nothing.

"The two of you must be very close."

Naturally Sharon knew nothing of his long-ago marriage. She was a relative newcomer to Eden.

"Why do you say that?"

"I don't imagine she lets too many people see this vulnerability."

The woman had insight. Molly hadn't let him sketch her. He'd done it from memory. Her grief had been like a living thing and very private. Normally he'd have shared none of it but he found he wanted to tell the innkeeper the truth. At least some of it.

"Molly and I were married briefly many years ago."

The look on Sharon's face perplexed him. She seemed almost dismayed.

"Oh."

Daniel felt compelled to reveal more.

"It was necessary for legal purposes," he said, vaguely, "not intended as a real marriage."

She looks at the sketch again.

"But you loved her."

Daniel set the bowls of soup on the table.

"I did love her."

He noted a slight droop in Sharon's shoulders and realized the attraction was mutual. It would be safer for both of them if she did not completely understand his relationship with Molly.

"You've never remarried," Sharon said. "Didn't you want children?" Almost immediately color burned her pale cheeks and her eyes dilated. "Oh, I'm sorry! That was too personal."

He smiled and pulled out a chair for her at his small table.

"It's a natural question. I've never really thought about children," he said, deliberately giving her a false impression, "and, of course, now it's too late."

"Surely not."

Sharon's hazel eyes held his. No, they did more. They drew him in, embraced him. She made him at home.

"I'm almost fifty, Sharon."

"You'd make a good father," she said.

Because he had a strong sense of responsibility, a natural protectiveness. He refused to feel disappointment that she saw him the same way others always had.

"I've always wanted to be a mother," she admitted.

Daniel caught the wistfulness in her voice. He knew about maternal longing. He'd seen it on a daily basis with Molly. Cam Outlaw had a small daughter. Had he and Sharon come together over a shared interest in parenting? No. He rejected the idea immediately. Cam and Sharon were young, single, and attractive. The attraction between them had been natural.

"I don't believe it's in the cards."

Her forthrightness startled him into a question. "Why?"

She shrugged.

"I really don't know why I'm telling you all this, you'll think me very indiscreet." He wanted to tell her to stop, that he didn't want to hear about her dreams and disappointments. Except she obviously needed to talk and he wanted to hear whatever she had to say.

"Cam Outlaw and I have been seeing each other. He's indicated that one child is enough for him. And, apparently, there's a fertility issue." She blushed again.

Of course. Outlaw's fertility issue explained why he and his late wife had used the sperm-bank clinic. Daniel wished he didn't know about Molly's insemination. He wished he didn't know that Molly might be carrying Cameron Outlaw's child. The project, which had always seemed like a mistake, now loomed as a betrayal of the lovely woman across the table.

Daniel reminded himself that, in this matter, neither Molly nor Sharon was his business. For a moment he pitied Cameron Outlaw.

****

Cam fought to hold onto his temper. It had taken

him half an hour of interviewing maids to find out about Dwight Winston's Suite of Sin. He'd bet everything he owned that Molly Whitecloud had found her way there in half the time.

The glass elevator climbed slowly to the ninth floor. Cam tried to pass the time by planning how he would punish the little witch but the rain-dark sky on the other side of the glass wall and the ominous rumbling of thunder exacerbated his anxiety. He'd *told* her to stay put. If either Winston or Big Eddie suspected why she was at the casino, she'd be in real danger.

Worry morphed into anger.

She'd always been interested in the rez first and foremost but in the years since they'd been together, she'd become a damn saint. Apparently she was willing to sacrifice anything for the good of the rez.

Damn the woman!

He pounded his fist against the suite's door. It opened almost immediately and Cam found himself staring at Dwight Winston's rubbery lips and gummy smile.

"I wondered when you'd show up."

Cam started to ask what the hell he was talking about until he remembered, belatedly, that he had "hired" Molly Whitecloud as his escort. He bared his teeth in a possessive snarl as his eyes raked the room.

"Yes. I believe you have something that belongs to me."

Winston's chuckle managed to be both lascivious and oily.

"The management takes no responsibility for personal belongings left unattended."

Cam eyed the lounge "loveseats" set at odd angles around the large room. Several of them were occupied by couples in various stages of undress. Some were partially obscured by potted palm trees but there was an air of hedonism, possibly the scent of whisky and gin or the pounding thrum of the base in the music that filled the room. Several closed doors indicated there might be other more private spaces for a couple to engage in a tete-a-tete.

The focal point of the room was a huge hot-tub from which steam rose. Cam spotted one couple standing waist-deep in the water, the woman's long legs wrapped around the thick waist of a man whose lobster-red face and glazed eyes implied an intimate joining beneath the surface.

Cam's fists clenched and only relaxed when he realized the woman's black hair ended just below her ears. His eyes skimmed the other couples until he found what he was looking for. Every muscle in his body tensed as he watched her leaning, provocatively against the side of the pool while, above her, a bald middle-aged man with a kangaroo's pouch, sat on the side, his feet dangling in the water.

Molly threw back her head, her long, black hair sleek and wet against her bare back and laughed at something the man said and he grinned, obviously pleased with himself. She hauled herself up onto the deck and looked up at Cam as if she'd sensed his presence.

He gaped at her, his first fear, that she was wearing nothing at all, was unfounded. She was wearing something, all right. A Spandex body suit. With a tail. His lips thinned.

Tiger Lily had turned into a mermaid.

He closed the space between them.

"Cam," she said.

"Hold that thought," her companion said, with a heavy grin, "we were about to adjourn this meeting to somewhere a little more private."

Cam ignored him as his eyes quartered Molly's face and dropped to the nearly transparent fabric of her clothing.

"Let's go," he said.

"Well," she said, a rueful smile on her lips, "I can't really stand up. No legs."

He wondered if she had any idea of what she was doing to him. The combination of irritation that she hadn't followed instructions, fear for her safety and frustration that he still wanted the faithless woman from his childhood, pushed him over some indefinable edge. He let out a harsh growl as he bent down and scooped her into his arms. Her body was sleek and compact. And wet. The moisture had no discernible impact on his now fully aroused body.

Molly's companion protested. "There're lotsa fish in the sea. I caught this one."

"Forget it, pal," Cam shot back. "This one's too small to keep. Anyway, she's mine."

Molly's arms came around his neck and she grinned at him. He wished, for a moment, they were just a man and a woman embarking on an affair. As they reached the door it was opened by Dwight Winston. He leered at Molly.

She tightened her hold on Cam's neck but managed a smile.

"Got caught by the old ball and chain," she said.

Winston's lip curled.

"Just until tomorrow. Then it's my turn."

Cam felt the shudder that ran through her.

"Hang on," he said, for Winston's benefit, "I'll get you warmed up soon enough."

A long minute later they were in the elevator.

"You can let me down now."

"And you'll what? Strip off your tail?"

She swallowed convulsively and didn't answer.

The elevator ride seemed to take forever, as did the walk down the corridor to the honeymoon suite. Just before he reached the door he stumbled.

"I'm sorry," she murmured. "I'm too heavy for you."

He didn't argue. Better to let her think he was struggling to carry a hundred pounds than to admit she'd made him so hard he could barely walk.

"My room key's in my right pants pocket."

She eyed him, doubtfully, but retrieved the plastic key card and inserted it into the lock.

He strode through the suite to the bedroom and dumped her, unceremoniously, on the heart-shaped bed. Then he turned to the door.

"When you're dressed, we'll talk."

"Uh, Cam?"

"What is it?"

"I don't have any clothes here."

Goddmmitall to hell.

"I'll get them from your room."

"Thanks."

He'd reached the door and had his hand on the knob.

"There's one more thing."

He gritted his teeth. "What?"

"The zipper to this get-up is in the back. I can't reach it."

He turned to stare at her.

"You want me to take off your clothes?"

One dark eyebrow lifted in apology.

"I need your help."

"For Chrissakes, Molly! For two cents I'd just leave you here and go back to Eden." *And for less than that I'd strip off that bodysuit and prove to you just how badly I want you.* "You don't listen to instructions, you can't take care of yourself, you're a damn millstone around my neck!"

He crossed the room and started to work on her zipper, waiting to hear her outrage and accusations but she hadn't spoken by the time his fingers touched the soft flesh of her back. He heard her sharp intake of breath and felt his own body tighten like a coiled spring.

Molly.

Unthinkingly he began to peel the wet latex off her slim, shapely body. She hadn't changed in all these years except that the baby fat had disappeared and her curves were more womanly. He wanted her so badly he couldn't speak.

For a minute she leaned against him and he knew she wanted him, too. Cam lowered his head, their lips separated by less than an inch. Suddenly, he remembered who he was about to kiss and he pulled away from her. She sat very still for a moment. When he returned from the bathroom with a towel, she'd pulled herself together.

"It's exactly like we thought," she said, her voice

only slightly breathy. "Dwight Winston holds what amounts to an orgy every afternoon. The girls aren't forced to attend and they aren't all Indians, but there's plenty of free food and they get generous tips. They aren't forced to sleep with these guys, either, but again, they make some money."

He said nothing, just turned back toward the door but he couldn't make himself leave.

"You're angry, aren't you?" She sounded apologetic. "I didn't wait for you because I knew I could investigate this sex part better on my own. I'm sorry if you were worried. But it's all good. I'm going to call Lena Tallchief. She's a Penobscot attorney in Augusta and she'll know whether we can take any legal action against Winston and the resort." She paused. "Did you get what you needed to break into the safe?"

He stared at the indigo eyes and wanted to tell her how worried he'd been when he couldn't find her, how jealous he'd been when he'd seen her with the guy in the pool, how much he'd missed her in the past thirteen years. He couldn't tell her any of that. He was nearly engaged and, besides, she was part of the past.

"Yeah," he said. "I got it."

****

Molly leaned against the tiled wall. The shower spray did nothing to cool her down. She'd thought he was going to kiss her the way he had last night. It would have been a mistake on so many levels. It had been right for him to pull back. But the sense of loss was almost as devastating as it had been the first time.

She'd wanted that kiss.

She supposed she was lucky Cam was both smarter and more disciplined than she. He'd wanted the contact, too. And it wasn't like last night when circumstances had thrown them into an unwanted intimacy. She could tell the difference. This time, he'd wanted her.

It was mildly gratifying to know the chemistry between them had survived the years but they couldn't afford to indulge it. There were too many others to consider, too many lives that could be destroyed. She reminded herself that she didn't deserve even an interlude with Cam, not now.

But it had felt so sweet to be in his arms even with the tail. He'd smelled the same as she remembered, soap-fresh, male, Cam.

Tears pricked the backs of her eyes. If only Daniel hadn't sent him to help with the investigation. She could've handled the exploitation of the girls but Molly was honest enough with herself to know she'd never have figured out how to get into Big Eddie's safe.

She'd needed somebody. She just wished it had been somebody else.

When her skin turned pruny she finally got out of the shower and stepped into the bedroom. He wasn't there, naturally, but he'd brought all her luggage.

She moved slowly, taking her time to put her hair into a braid and pin it up onto her head before slipping into a floor-length silver dress that fit like a second skin.

First the sexy cocktail dress, then the mermaid suit and now this. It was quite a change from her usual overalls, denim skirts and work shirts. She turned sideways in the mirror. The sophisticated creature that looked back at her looked confident and secure. She wouldn't have raided a sperm bank. She'd have moved on with her life.

Unfortunately, she didn't really exist.

Molly slipped on the three-inch spiked heels and applied some lipstick. She hoped the evening would go smoothly, that Cam would be able to open the safe without incident, that they'd grab the laptop and get out of the casino without having to get near the butterscotch sofa.

A wry smile twisted on her lips and she made a little sound of disgust. The plain truth was that neither Molly nor her sophisticated doppelganger really hoped that. They both wanted to be with Cam Outlaw one more time.

And they both knew it couldn't happen.

He arrived to pick her up, elegant in a white dinner jacket and tie. She started to ask him where he'd changed his clothes but she changed her mind when she read the fatigue on his dark face. In all the years he'd figured in her dreams, he'd looked confident and happy. He'd never looked like a man at the end of his rope.

Molly's heart squeezed. It was up to her to make this situation something he could live with, something he could walk away from with his head held high. She grinned.

"Tonight," she said, brightly, "We'll be Nick and Nora Charles."

His long lashes flickered but he answered in a teasing tone.

"How about Ike and Tina Turner. Then I could beat you."

The chuckle they shared warmed Molly's insides. She slid her hand through his arm. "Come on soldier. We've got a job to do."

Over scallops as light as cream puffs they

discussed logistics. Cam outlined all the possible scenarios they could face.

"You'd have made a great general," she said, when he finished. "Lots of attention to detail."

His eyes darkened.

"I considered enlisting at one time."

Molly grimaced as she caught the implication. He meant after she'd married Daniel. She wished she could explain. Since she couldn't, she'd have to be careful not to refer to the past, in the future.

Except there wouldn't be any future. They'd finish up tonight and go their separate ways, meeting, only very occasionally in Eden. He'd be with Sharon and Daisy and probably a couple of new red-headed children. She'd be with...her stomach twisted. What would he think when he saw her dark-haired son or daughter?

Nothing. He, like everyone else, would think she'd been indiscreet with somebody on the rez. Unless the baby had those morning-glory eyes. Her heart turned over. Would she really keep his child from him? Could she do anything else?

His lean, brown hand covered hers.

"Don't worry so much," he said, in a quiet tone. "This will all work out."

Except it wouldn't.

"Are we following the same schedule tonight," she asked, finally, for something to say.

"This time we've added some insurance," he said. "We'll hit the office during the half hour Dwight Winston's supposed to be on the floor and I've taken care of Fat Eddie."

"How?"

"I got some professional entertainment for him."

Her jaw dropped. "You hired a hooker?" She felt a flash of wholly unreasonable irritation. "How'd you know where to find her?"

He grinned at her.

"The Yellow Pages."

Chapter Six

"Poor thing."

He let out a sound somewhere between derision and amusement. "Maybe you can control things on your reservation but you can't protect the whole world, Lily. People choose things for all kinds of reasons. You should know that. People make their own choices."

The man knew how to stick in the shiv. He'd made her feel foolish for worrying about a prostitute while reminding her that she alone was to blame for her lonely life.

Not that he'd meant to do that. But the whole evening was a symphony in torture.

It was worse tonight because they'd spent twenty-four hours together. The explosive chemistry between them had become almost a physical ache for Molly but worse, much worse was the hollowness she felt. She'd known, at the tender age of seventeen, that Cam Outlaw was the man for her and she'd been right. She loved everything about him from his occasional taciturnity to his dry sense of humor to his intelligent leadership to the way he became irritated when she failed to follow him.

Everything.

He was like catnip and she was the cat. He stared into her eyes and brushed his callused fingers down her spine as they crossed the casino floor. He bent down, repeatedly, to peck her on the head or the mouth when they stood at the craps table or the roulette wheel. He slid his long, lean fingers up the back of her neck in a possessive gesture that sent shivers through her as they headed to the bar. She finally turned on him.

"Do you have to touch me so much?"

"People are watching."

She had to admit he was right. "Why, do you think? What's the big deal about us?"

The dark brows lifted.

"We're beautiful, Molly. Didn't you know?"

He was beautiful. She knew that. She eyed him, doubtfully.

"We look good together," he explained, "Young and exotic with our dark hair and blue eyes."

She looked around at the other couples on the dance floor and in the casino. Most were overweight and middle-aged. She shrugged.

"I guess."

While they waited for their drinks he stepped behind her and skimmed his palms lightly down her waist to her hips. She felt him against her back as if they were joined together, spoon fashioned, and Molly's entire body tightened with need. She melted like a stick of butter in the hot sun.

She wondered if someone would just scoop her up and smear her on a piece of toast. She wondered if he were doing it to her on purpose, torturing her in retaliation for her long ago rejection. And then he pressed against her to make room for someone else and she felt the hard proof that he was as turned on as she and she chuckled.

"What's funny?"

His words were spoken in a low, husky voice. She turned in the cage of his arms and started to play with the stud in the center of his snow-white tuxedo shirt. Cam stiffened and tried to draw back.

"What're you doing?"

"Acting," she murmured. She let her fingers drift down his torso until they came to his cummerbund. She slid a finger into it. His eyes snapped. "I'm supposed to be your hired plaything, remember?"

He grabbed her hand and dragged her across the room to a scarlet loveseat located in one corner.

"Stop it," he commanded.

"Sure." She held a glass of wine in one hand. The other she laid on his thigh.

"Molly!"

It was too loud. Too irritated. A man nearby turned to see if there was a problem.

Molly grinned at the other man.

"I startled him," she explained.

"Well, you can startle me any time you want, Sugar."

Cam grabbed both their glasses and set them on a table then he took her hands in his and turned away from the small audience. His eyes shuttered and his lean cheeks were flushed.

"Enough," he said. "This is a disaster. As soon as I get myself together we're going up to the room."

Molly's heart thumped hard.

"Upstairs?"

"To get your things. We'll come down the backstairs and you'll take your car and leave."

"What about the computer?"

"Dwight's assigned to start on the floor in half an

hour. I've got the drill and instructions. It'll only take a minute to get the safe open. I'll be out of here an hour behind you."

She stared into his brilliant blue eyes.

"Two things," she said. "There's a service elevator that goes to the laundry room. That's better than using the stairs."

"Fine. What's number two?"

"I'm not leaving. This is my investigation. Our investigation," she amended. "You might need my help."

"You gonna tackle anybody who gets in the way? You're a peanut—a hundred pounds soaking wet."

She pursed her lips and narrowed her eyes.

"Unless you can give me a damn good reason, I'm not leaving, Cam, not just because you asked."

A shuttered look came over his face and the blue eyes turned hard.

"No, of course not. You never have done anything just because I asked."

Another reference to the bitter past. Suddenly the melting stopped and the yearning and Molly was all business.

****

He was furious with her. The woman did not know how to follow an order.

The anger, however, was not intense enough to take the edge off the need. Half an hour to go, he told himself. Maybe less.

God, he wanted her.

All he had to do was inhale her scent of wildflowers or look at the curve of her cheek and beads of sweat popped out on his forehead. He hadn't been this aroused since...this afternoon after he'd retrieved her from the pool.

Shit.

His physical discomfort was so great he couldn't even get really heated about the past. The remark intended to remind her of her perfidy was nothing more than a throwaway. He was no longer just afraid he'd compromise his relationship with Sharon. In fact it had become abundantly clear to him that he could not propose to Sharon Johnson or anyone else. Not when he was in this fever about Molly. Neither was he worrying about his long-held, firm conviction that he would never again have anything to do with the woman who'd betrayed him.

His main concern was that, any minute now, he'd abandon everything, throw down and take her right here on the casino floor. He loosened his bow tie, sucked in a deep breath and tried to fight the hunger.

"Looks like Fat Eddie's taking a break," Molly murmured. Cam looked up to see the casino manager bearing down on them.

Eddie DiMarco was shaped like Humpty-Dumpty with an enormous waist and no neck at all. Like his deputy, Dwight Winston, he had an insincere, flashy smile but whereas Winston was just oily and irritating, DiMarco gave off a dangerous vibe.

And that made sense if, as Daniel Grey Wolf believed, he was all mobbed up.

Cam, watching him out of the corner of his eye, knew the minute he'd zeroed in on Molly. While the fat man waddled across the garish casino carpet, Cam bent over the woman next to him, the woman who had his drill inside her slightly oversized evening bag.

He cupped the back of her head and brought her lips to his in a light kiss that was intended to discourage DiMarco, but which, unfortunately, triggered flames in his own lower body.

Well, damn.

"Dodged the bullet," Molly answered. Cam controlled his breathing with an effort and looked toward the glass elevator where Eddie now stood, his ham-like arm around the waist of a shapely blonde.

"Maybe she was late," Molly said. An instant later he felt her cool palm against his forehead. She frowned. "Are you all right?"

Cam thought about the collapse of the relationship he'd built with Sharon and the fate that awaited the casino and spa he'd spent two years working on. He thought about Daisy, who was at home waiting for a new mom and the fact that, because of this woman, she wouldn't get one anytime soon. Fury balled up in his gut. He grabbed her hand and plastered it against his crotch.

"Does this feel like I'm all right?"

Her small hand curled around him. It felt so damn good.

"It feels like you're perfect," she said.

His groan was deep and sincere and mostly silent. He looked into the wide indigo eyes.

"I can't fight it anymore. I want you."

"I want you, too."

He could take her up to the honeymoon suite and do what they both wanted. He could haul her out to his car, in spite of the rain he heard dancing on the casino's roof. He could pull her into a restroom. While he was hesitating she was thinking.

"Cam," she said, "what about Sharon?"

Guilt and resentment took the edge off the need. "That's over. It's got to be over."

She grimaced. "You should reconsider. It's not too late. You haven't been unfaithful yet and we have a job to do tonight."

What was this, a power play? He had to remember this was the woman who'd betrayed him once already. The woman who had broken his heart. He steeled himself against her.

"You're right. It's time to get back to work." He paused to gather himself. "I want your promise that you'll leave as soon as we find the laptop."

He anticipated an argument but she didn't give him one.

"What about you?"

"I'll go back to the rooms, gather up our things and head for town. You can hand the evidence over to Grey Wolf."

She looked at him. "Agreed."

He had a feeling he'd just missed the second chance of a lifetime but accompanying the regret was an unmistakable feeling of relief. He hadn't been able to trust Tiger Lily all those years ago. Who was to say he could trust her now? He would break up with Sharon though. She deserved someone better. Daisy would just have to wait a little longer for a mom.

They stood and headed, in a meandering fashion, across the room and down the back hall. Cam made short work of the lock on DiMarco's office door and then they were inside where the dragonfly lamp, large and squat much like its owner, bathed the room in a low, warm light.

Cam moved the dogs-playing-poker picture and studied the mechanism on the combination lock. He was aware of his partner moving around the office when she opened and shut a couple of drawers.

Damn. Sam had told him the drill-hole would only work on a simple lock. This one looked state-of-the-art. The terms "composite hard plate" and "glass re-locker" floated through his head. There was no choice. He was going to have to come back tomorrow night and cut this thing open. But he was coming back alone. He turned to deliver the bad news.

"Listen, Molly," he started to say.

She glanced up from the open desk drawer. "Problem?"

He scowled. "I need a different tool."

"What kind of tool?"

He thrust his fingers through his hair. This whole thing was turning into a colossal disaster.

"Just something else. A hack saw, probably."

"Maybe there's something in here that would help."

He glared at her. "In DiMarco's desk drawer? Like what? An address book?"

Her eyes were clear and mischievous. "Like a combination. There's one here. Taped on the side of the drawer."

Moments later the safe was open and they both gaped at the thin laptop lying on its floor surrounded by stacks of money.

"Well, hell," Cam breathed.

"It was just luck," she said, obviously afraid his male ego was damaged because she'd found the way to open the safe.

"No, it was smart. We should have looked for a combination in the beginning." Her grateful smile sent a shaft of warmth through him but this time it wasn't sexual.

He took off his dinner jacket.

"We'll slide it into the waistband of my pants," he said.

"Isn't that going to be uncomfortable?"

"It's not for long."

They stood facing one another, each of them reluctant to take the next steps that would carry them out of the casino and back into the world where they would resume their parallel lives. He sensed that she was as reluctant as he. He told himself to let this go, to let her go but he couldn't seem to move. He gazed a last time into the depthless indigo eyes and memorized the contours of her lovely face.

"Molly," he said just as they heard voices outside the door. "Christ!"

"Oh my God," she whispered. "Déjà vu."

Cam tried to force his brain to work. That better not be the fat man. He'd paid the hooker well to keep him upstairs for an hour. And it shouldn't be Dwight. They'd seen him on the floor before they came in.

But it was somebody. The voices got louder and a key scraped in the lock.

"Cam?"

"Lie on the sofa," he told her, as he ripped off his cummerbund and tore his shirt out of his pants. For once she did what he said. He slid the laptop under the piece of furniture and came down on top of her at the same time. He shoved up her skirt and unzipped his pants.

"Cam!"

"It's called hiding in plain sight," he hissed. The knob jiggled again and he thrust into her and stifled her shocked cry with his mouth.

When the door opened, seconds later, the intruders gasped in shock, stared and apologized profusely.

****

At first, Molly was too shocked to think at all. When reason kicked in, she felt like a porn star. Despite her performance at the hot tub, she'd never even thought of making love with an audience.

Not that this was making love. This was just sex and bad sex at that. She'd been dry, unprepared and he'd hurt her. She didn't care. She put her arms around him and pulled him down against her, reveling in feel of his full weight and the familiar scent, the knowledge that they were finally together in bed.

Well, on sofa.

The door opened and she heard a harsh gasp.

"Oh my God, Arty," said a female. "There's already someone doing it in here."

If she'd had any command at all over her facial muscles, Molly would have smiled. The other couple had been looking for a quiet corner.

"Sure is." Arty sounded tanked. "Hey, man," he called out. "What's goin' on? This is s'posed to be reserved." He hiccupped in the middle of the two syllable word.

"Buzz off," Cam muttered, without turning toward the man, without allowing him to see any of Molly except her feet. "We're a little busy here."

"Uh, yeah, uh, okay. I'm sorry, man. I didn't…"

Molly stared at Cam's dark eyes. She'd only seen

him from this position once in her life out in the spinney thirteen years ago. It was a magical view.

"Get out," Cam barked. He kept his eyes on Molly's face. His voice was hoarse.

"Uh, okay. Sure, uh…"

"And lock the damn door."

"Right. Right."

Molly heard the drunken voice trail off. She heard the door click shut. She held very still and prayed that Cam wouldn't suddenly come to his senses and end the whole thing.

Just this one more time. Please.

"What's the matter," he asked.

She choked out the words.

"I don't want you to stop."

He made a sound in his chest that was half laugh, half groan.

"Honey, I couldn't stop if a dozen mobsters with machine guns came through that door."

"Oh." She tightened her grip on him and felt his erection expand inside her. It was too tight and too sore and too exciting for words.

"Come to me," she whispered.

He dropped his head and spoke into her mouth.

"Lily."

An instant later he began to move. She felt the restraint he tried to impose on his body and she rejected it. She arched up and thrust her tongue into his mouth.

"Come to me," she repeated. "Now."

Cam launched himself like a heat-seeking missile, his breathing rasped in her ear, his body drove hers deeper and deeper into the faux leather, his need was her need and she felt tears on her cheeks. His climax exploded, rocketing them both into another dimension. She gathered him against her and stroked his back while he struggled for breath. Then she just held him tightly, thankful for this unexpected gift fate had brought her when she'd thought it was too late and especially when she no longer deserved it.

Too soon he lifted off her.

"It was too fast," he said. "I'm sorry." She shook her head.

"There was no time to get you ready. I don't know what happened. You were just so tight."

"It's okay."

"It seemed like a good way to hide."

"It was."

"But I got carried away. I didn't mean to do it like that."

She wished he'd stop reviewing his technical performance and talk about love. She wished he'd stroke her face and tell her he still cared, that he'd always cared.

But those things didn't happen because they hadn't made love. They'd had emergency sex. Sex as a diversion. A quickie designed to conceal their real purpose for being in Big Eddie's office.

"I really am sorry," Cam said, again. She summoned a weak smile.

"I know. I'm sorry, too." She pushed him, gently, and he moved away from her. "It's time to go," she murmured.

Almost immediately he looked as cool as usual while she felt sticky and her dress was crumpled beyond repair. It took two full minutes to find and get into her shoes.

"Your hair's a mess," he said, dispassionately, fingering one of the long strands that had worked its way out of her updo.

"It doesn't matter. I'm heading out to the parking lot."

"Right."

They decided he should go first with the laptop. She'd follow a few minutes later. He had his hand on the doorknob when he turned. She felt her heart thump. *Say it. Just once. Tell me you still love me.*

He frowned at her.

"We didn't use any protection but it's all right. I'm healthy. And I'm sterile."

Molly went very still.

Sterile? Was he kidding?

"You have a daughter."

The words were faint but he heard them.

"Yeah, well, that's a story for another time. I just wanted you to know there won't be any unpleasant repercussions."

Molly watched the door close behind him. *No unpleasant repercussions.* What irony there was in those words. She thought about the baby she'd mourned and about the baby she'd broken all the rules to try to get. *I'm sterile.*

But it wasn't true. He had fathered two children already and nine months from now, during the Sowing Moon, he might have another son or a daughter.

Of course he wouldn't know it.

She'd just had a chance to reconnect with Cam Outlaw, something she'd wanted for thirteen years and she'd never felt worse in her life.

The old saying was true. You had to be careful

what you wished for because you just might get it.

****

Regret hit him like a tidal wave. He couldn't believe what he'd done. It wasn't so much that he'd slept with the enemy, although they were certainly not friends. It was the way he did it. The terms, ham-handed, ox-like and Neanderthal came to mind.

He'd dreamt, over the years, of tying up the loose ends, a prospect that usually ended in bed with a bitter sweet connection.

Instead, he'd lost control and plowed her like a pig in rut. Damn. He hadn't meant to treat her like that. Tiger Lily deserved better. And there was nothing he could say or do at this point. It was just a huge mistake. Remorse for his behavior was mixed with a helpless sense of a missed chance. Cam sought a word for the unpleasant sensations roiling inside him and found it.

Anguish.

He wanted a do-over.

He wanted another chance.

There wouldn't be one. Not unless he was willing to forgive the past, to seek a future with a woman who'd proven she couldn't be trusted.

Cam realized, suddenly, that he'd accepted Grey Wolf's summons because, buried under the layers of time, was a hope that he could let go of the pain he'd carried in his heart all these years. On some level he'd *wanted* to see Molly again, see her, make love to her, and walk away.

The seconds on Big Eddie's faux leather butterscotch sofa had not fulfilled that wish.

Pride had kept him from approaching her last night when they'd shared a room, anger had prevented anything from happening after he'd found her at the hot tub and, tonight, he'd been scuttled by lust.

Three strikes. He was out. Tiger Lily was, once more, in the past and this time he had to let her go.

He entered the casino intending to make his way through it then step into the adjoining lobby of the Blackbird Spa. He'd go up in the glass elevator, gather their belongings from the honeymoon suite, then return to the ground floor in the service elevator. Then he'd exit the building from the back and circle around to the front parking lot where he'd left the Mercedes.

His heavy heart and preoccupation allowed him to get halfway across the casino floor without noticing that something was missing. It was the noise. There was no click of the wheels or calling out of numbers. There was no hum of conversation punctuated with bursts of laughter.

The game room was virtually silent.

Something was very wrong.

A large group of people were huddled near the Black Jack table, all of them facing the same direction like a field of flowers turned to the sun. A terrified wail drifted up through the crowd like a thin column of smoke from a chimney.

Everyone on the floor was distracted, the circumstances perfect for a slick getaway but Cam found he couldn't ignore the stricken cry. He moved toward the group.

"What's going on here?"

The onlookers, probably responding to the authoritative note he'd deliberately adopted in his voice, started to chatter. He held up a hand.

"One at a time," he said, wondering how this clutch

of adults could be so shocked they couldn't figure that out themselves.

"We need a doctor," a woman explained. "There's a young woman giving birth and no one knows what to do."

"We're on an Indian Reservation," a man said. "They don't have a hospital and probably don't have any medical care."

"There's Molly," said a young woman, who was plainly a croupier. Cam noticed she was Penobscot. "Molly Whitecloud. She's the midwife. She'll come."

Christ.

The thin wail turned into a bovine groan and Cam looked past the forest of people. A young woman, her thin, tent-like dress twisted around her distended belly, lay on the dirty carpet of the casino, her head cradled by a youth whose bare arms were covered with tattoos and whose chubby cheeks had suffered a recent outbreak of acne. Neither of the two principles could have been much older than eighteen. Babies having a baby and in a very unsanitary place. Cam bit back a curse. He'd have to involve Molly. She'd certainly hear about it if anything went wrong and she'd never forgive him.

He hunkered before the youngsters for a moment.

"How close are the contractions?"

"Real close," the boy whispered, his face sweaty, his eyes glazed.

"All right. Hang tight. Help's on the way."

Cam caught her in the parking lot about to step into her Jeep. Within minutes she'd taken charge. She instructed Cam to phone for an ambulance, and the croupier to find clean sheets, a blanket, hot water and scissors. She told one gawker to find some ice chips for the sufferer and another to herd the crowd out of the casino.

Cam admired her efficiency but one part of his mind recalled the night Daisy had been born. The child's appearance had brought a sudden shaft of light into the barren midnight of his marriage.

It hadn't lasted.

"Cam?"

He shook off the memories.

"Can you change places with Bobby so she can see his face?"

He didn't argue. A minute later he found himself curled around the straining and surprisingly strong body of Patty Sue Stottlemyer as she pushed and panted and tried to expel her baby.

Patty Sue stopped groaning as she focused on Molly's face and her quiet commands. Cam found himself listening, too. It was the first time he'd seen Molly in her professional capacity and, because he'd been through a birthing scene, he knew just how good she was. No one had been able to comfort Elise or to help her work through the experience and she'd been medicated.

The pains came faster and faster, tumbling over one another with no let up in between. Cam needed most of his strength to hold Patty Sue at a slight angle so that she could push against his chest. Cam felt the sweat gather in his armpits and run down the inside of his shirt. Fortunately, he'd left the purloined laptop in Molly's car. As labor intensified Molly kept up a stream of instructions, which included telling Patty Sue what was happening and what was going to happen and, at the same time managed to sterilize a pair of scissors and to instruct the young female croupier to rip up the clean sheet.

Cam watched her run the operation like a drill sergeant, albeit in a silver dress hiked up so she could rest on her knees. Her hair had escaped it's pins and the black silk streamed down her back. The indigo eyes lit with a fierce concentration. Cam never doubted that Patty Sue was getting the best possible care for herself and her baby.

And then he heard Molly's excited words.

"Look, Bobby! There's the baby's head."

The teenager's face was the color of moldy cheese.

"Ma'am," he said, "When's it gonna be over?"

"Really soon," Molly told him. "Just hold her hand now. It won't be much longer. I know this is hard on you."

"Hard on him?" The words spewed out of Patty Sue's mouth. "You better remember this Bobby Ray Stottlemyer, cause it sure as shootin' isn't gonna happen again."

Cam choked back a laugh.

"Okay, Patty Sue," Molly said, cheerfully, "one last push. Two at the most. Give it everything you've got, girl."

With a trumpeting sound like that of an enraged moose, Patty Sue followed the instructions.

Chapter Seven

Molly was aware of Cam the entire time she was working with Patty Sue. His quiet strength and gentle manner provided comfort and support for the frightened girl. Her pride in Cam mingled with a familiar sense of loss.

She knew he was a fine father to Daisy and now she knew he'd been a good husband to Elise. The knowledge twisted her soul.

She massaged the softened, stretched perineum to try to keep it from tearing.

"Push, Patty Sue," she crooned. "Down deep in your bottom. That's it. That's right. Take a breath and push again with the next contraction. You're doing a great job. You must have been practicing."

"No," Patty Sue puffed, "not practicing. Wanted drugs."

Molly smiled at that even as she thought about how drugs were not possible on the rez. It took a medical doctor, an anesthesiologist to administer an epidural. Even with a clinic the reservation women would have to give birth naturally.

The birth was smooth enough until the little head popped out and a subsequent push failed to release the shoulders. Molly maneuvered the baby as best she could. When Patty Sue cried at the additional pain, Molly sought Cam's eyes. His steady gaze calmed her down and within less than a minute she'd caught the baby.

She cleaned up the newborn, instructed Bobby on how to cut the cord and handed the child into his mother's arms. And then she shook with relief. And fatigue. Cam's voice brought tears to her eyes.

"Great job, Tiger Lily."

An approaching siren brought an additional sense of relief. Molly checked her watch. The delivery had taken less than half an hour, which meant that Chester Appleton, not his wife was behind the wheel of the vehicle. Edna Mae drove with the speed of sap leaking out of a maple tree.

And then they were all outside in the parking lot and the rain had stopped. Chester, with Molly's help, got mother and child settled into the ambulance. When she glanced out the back at the people milling around, she caught sight of Dwight Winston standing ominously close to Cam. His right hand was jammed into the pocket of his trench coat as if he were covering Cam with a gun.

Good heavens! Had Winston and Big Ed discovered the laptop missing? Already? If so, they must have been suspicious all along. Molly's heart jack-hammered in her chest. She had to save Cam, but how? There was no time to think. She called to the young croupier who had helped her inside.

"I need Mr. Outlaw—that gentleman there—to sign the birth certificate before we go to the hospital," she explained. "Could you go get him and bring him over here? And Candy, don't explain that to him—just bring him with you."

In Molly's experience, people didn't question a

firm command during a crisis and this was no exception but her heart was in her throat until Candy showed up with Cam in tow. Winston, unfortunately, was only a few feet behind them.

Chester started to close the back of the ambulance when Molly stopped him.

"We've got a problem here," Molly said, in a low voice. She prayed the ambulance driver, who tended to be argumentative, wouldn't balk but he must have heard the tension under her words. "I need you to get behind the wheel. Give me ten seconds to close the doors then take off, okay? And use the siren!"

She must have communicated her fear because the old man studied her briefly then agreed. "Whatever you say, Miss Molly."

Even with the plan in place, Molly was nervous.

"Cam," she called out, her voice a little shaky, "Patty Sue wants to speak with you just for a second. Could you come up here?"

"Of course." He glanced back at Winston, as if to say he'd be right back, stepped into the vehicle and shut one of the doors as Molly shut the other. It was as if they'd rehearsed the move a hundred times.

Instantly the ambulance jolted into gear and started to pull away, the siren blazing. Through the back window, Molly stared into a pair of very angry eyes.

"Did he have a gun?"

"Yes. I don't think he was planning to shoot me. He just wanted the laptop back."

"Oh, damn! The laptop is still in my Jeep!"

Cam grinned at her and produced the computer from where he'd stashed it in the waistband of his pants.

"I picked it up. Your suitcase, however, is still in the car."

Relief washed through Molly and she grinned at him.

"Good thing it's Chester behind the wheel," she said as the vehicle took the corner from the casino's driveway onto the road.

"Yeah." He returned her grin. "If it had been Edna Mae, Winston could have followed us on foot."

Molly looked out the window. Would Dwight Winston follow them to the hospital? Would he shoot out the ambulance's tires? She shivered.

"I hope Daniel gets this place shut down quickly."

Cam's face took on a remote look.

"Thanks for saving my hide."

She looked at him a long moment. Despite the danger of the past moments and the bleakness of the future she was glad to be with him.

"Thanks for your help with Patty Sue."

Molly helped Bobby fill out forms at Eden Memorial while the resident on call examined mother and baby. She waited with the young couple until their parents arrived. By the time she was ready to go it was four a.m., she was almost asleep on her feet and she realized her Jeep was still at the casino. She headed for the lobby to call Daniel but found him already there and in what looked like an intense consultation with Cameron Outlaw. Cam's hair was disheveled and lines creased his forehead and bewhiskered cheeks. His evenings clothes were stained with blood and dirt.

Molly's heart jerked. She felt an almost irresistible urge to walk into his arms and stay there forever. Instead, she spoke without thinking.

"You didn't have to stay."

Cam's blue eyes were hooded, whether from fatigue or anger she couldn't tell. He didn't answer and Molly knew that he hadn't wanted to stay. She tried not to feel hurt.

"Outlaw gave me the laptop," Daniel said, his dark eyes were kind. Although her ex-husband was nearly a generation older he and Cam were built along the same lines and each gave off that aura of confidence. A woman could feel safe with Daniel. With Cam, too, she thought. At least until he touched her.

"Come on," Daniel said, slipping his hand through her arm, "I'll give you both a ride back to the casino."

Molly gasped and stared at him. "What?"

"To pick up your cars. Don't worry. By now the cops have come in to shut the place down."

Molly's last thought, before she fell asleep in the backseat of Daniel's old sedan, was for Lynn Brown Bear and all the others who would lose their jobs.

****

The flashing lights woke Molly. Cam could tell because she made a small rustling sound as she sat up. He'd hoped she wouldn't wake up, hoped she was a heavy sleeper. It irritated him that he didn't know. He turned to see her fumbling with the door handle.

"Stay in the car," he said.

"What?" She sounded half-dazed.

"You'll just get in the way of the cops."

"Why are you mad?"

He couldn't explain that he was trying to protect her. In addition to the black-and-whites, there was a medical examiner's wagon on the scene.

"Let her go in," Grey Wolf said, quietly.

"Whatever it is she'll find out soon enough. And she can handle it. I promise you."

"Handle what?" She sounded fully alert.

"Apparently someone's died," Grey Wolf explained.

Molly said nothing. She just scrambled out of the car. Cam swore and opened his own door only to feel Grey Wolf's hand on his shoulder.

"You can't protect her from everything," Grey Wolfe said to Cam. "She's a grown woman. She's taken care of herself for a long time now."

Nevertheless, Cam noticed, Grey Wolf was right behind him as he strode into the casino after Molly.

It was so quiet in the casino it reminded Cam of a trip to Coney Island in January. Spooky.

He found Molly talking with Rusty Walks Tall, who had been hired to help chief Davey Tall Tree after the later was elected tribal chief. Walks Tall was big, a college baseball player who'd decided to return to the reservation after graduation. His open, friendly face looked worried.

"I don't know, Molly. I'm not supposed to let anybody back there," he said. "I'll check with the sheriff." He nodded at Cam and Grey Wolf then ducked down the corridor that led to Big Eddie's office. Molly turned to look at Cam, her eyes huge.

Cam figured that handling any kind of a major crime at the casino would be complicated. While it wasn't located on the reservation it was owned by the tribe, which had its own, separate police force. When Jake Langley, Eden County's sheriff, appeared behind Walks Tall, it was clear that the jurisdictions were working together.

"Hey Cam, Molly, Daniel."

Like the others, Cam shook hands with the tall, broad-shouldered sheriff, until recently a single dad. Now, thanks to his marriage to Cam's sister, Lucy, Jake was Cam's brother-in-law. He grinned at Molly.

"I heard about the delivery. Nice going."

She smiled, absently.

"What's happened here," Cam asked, abruptly.

Jake looked more closely at Cam and his eyes widened. What was he seeing? Fatigue? Dishevelment? Frustration? Probably all three. He was also, undoubtedly, wondering why Cam was with Molly and Grey Wolf. It was time to explain.

"I should tell you that I was here earlier and, in fact, I broke into Eddie DiMarco's office from which I stole a laptop."

Jake's green eyes slitted.

"I helped him steal it," Molly volunteered.

Cam's jaw tightened. He'd wanted to keep her out of this. Foolish idea.

"Daniel? Have you got anything to confess?"

"I'm just the chauffeur," he said. "Unless you're talking about the stolen laptop. I've got custody of that."

Jake sighed. "You'd all better come with me."

"I'd like to speak with Davey," Grey Wolf said. Across the room the rez's chief and former tribal cop lifted his hand to wave at Molly who waved back. "I'll be out here if you want to talk to me, Jake."

"Suit yourself."

In spite of the grim circumstances, Cam thought, it was amazing how much it lightened his mood to see Grey Wolf abandon Molly.

They followed Jake down the corridor and into the room. It looked the same as they had left it, with the dragonfly lamp still burning. Except for the body on the butterscotch sofa. Eddie DiMarco's stomach, straining to pop the buttons of his tuxedo shirt, was not a smooth pumpkin; instead it rippled downwards, a triumph of terraced flesh. His short, fat legs sprawled to each side and his arms rested at his sides. But what made Molly clutch her neck with both hands was that the casino manager appeared to have no head—just a white, blood-stained towel wrapped around whatever was now atop his sloping shoulders.

Cam took Molly's shoulders and turned her away from the macabre sight.

"She just delivered a baby, Cam." Jake's voice was mildly amused. "I think she can handle the sight of blood."

It wasn't the blood that worried him. Eddie had been killed shortly after he and Molly had burgled the office. Molly would be afraid they'd caused the man's death. Cam, on the other hand, was afraid someone was after Molly.

And then there was the sofa where they'd…he forced himself to forget about that. It was over and done. The murder made their amateur undercover attempt look foolish.

"I'll want to talk with you both about the robbery," Jake said, casually. "In the meantime go on home. You look like you could use some sleep." He nodded at the body. "This looks like a professional job. One shot to the brain. Right on target. DiMarco died instantly."

"An execution," Molly whispered.

"Probably. The safe's been emptied." He gave

them each another hard look.

"There were stacks of money in it," Molly said, faintly, "along with the laptop. We were trying to find proof of fraud."

"Dwight Winston held a gun on Cam last night right after the birth incident," Molly said. "He must have figured out that we'd stolen the laptop."

"Winston's disappeared as far as anyone knows," Jake said. "We've got an APB out on him."

"Who found the body," Cam asked.

"A croupier…kid named Candy Red Fox."

Molly nodded. "She's sharp." Her frown bothered Cam.

"What?"

Her eyes were weary but full of concern.

"This isn't going to do your family or your business any good if it gets out, Cam. You were doing it for the rez. You shouldn't have to pay a price."

Whatever else it cost him, he'd already paid a helluva price for spending two days with Molly Whitecloud but he didn't tell her that.

"I can handle it."

"I think," Jake said, "we'd better talk about this a bit now. Want some coffee?"

They rejoined Grey Wolf and between them they filled the sheriff in on the alleged fraud and the exploitation of local girls. Jake listened, intently.

"I assume," he said to Cam in a casual voice, "I don't have to tell you how foolish it was to try to handle this alone or to put Molly in danger."

"It was my choice," Molly said. "Daniel asked Cam to come out here to protect me. The whole thing," she indicated the slumped body and her voice caught on a little sob, "the whole thing is my fault."

Cam felt a rush of emotion. Without considering his audience, he circled her with one arm and pulled her against him. When he looked up he found Jake's curious green eyes on him.

""Connect the dots for me," he said.

"We believe the laptop contains the casino's real financial records, including the percentage of the profits siphoned off to the Jersey mob. Grey Wolf needs the records to shut the place down so Molly took it upon herself to get those records. She came to work here as a masseuse which is code for hooker. I came up here to 'hire' her and help search for the evidence."

Jake's eyes shifted from Cam to the top of Molly's head where it was buried in Cam's chest, and back again.

"Is there any point in my asking why you got involved?"

Cam liked and respected his new brother-in-law but there was no way he was going to talk about his past with Tiger Lily. He shrugged.

"I got the resort funded and built. I felt responsible."

"Hm."

"I feel so responsible," Molly said, on a sob. "If I hadn't tried this undercover stunt, maybe Dwight wouldn't have killed Eddie."

"It was a professional hit," Jake said. "Whoever killed Eddie intended to kill him. I doubt it had anything to do with either of you."

Unless Dwight Winston was a professional hitman. Cam left the thought unspoken.

Jake looked at Cam.

"So where's the computer now?"

"In Daniel's car," Molly said. "I was just resting my head on it."

"I'll need to take it in as evidence," Jake said.

Cam nodded. Grey Wolf and the Indian Gaming Commission would have to wait to look at the data. There was no hurry now. It was unlikely there'd be any more crimes committed at the now-closed Blackbird Casino and Spa.

"I wonder if the casino will reopen," Molly said. "A lot of people depend on these jobs, you know. And the rez needs the income."

Cam felt a shaft of anger. As usual, she was concerned about the rez—first, last and always.

"Time will tell," Jake said. He leveled his gaze, once again, at Cam. "Take her home."

Cam shepherded her out to the cars.

"What if they test the butterscotch sofa," she said, in a low voice. "They might find, er, evidence, that we'd been there."

That had occurred to him, too.

"They might. Nothing we can do about it now."

She groaned. "I'm so sorry."

"For what?"

"For this weekend. And for everything."

He nodded, too tired to maintain his usual defenses. "There's nothing we can do about anything right now. Tomorrow I'll tell Jake about the other couples who visited this place. Maybe he can start there. C'mon. I'll take you home."

But he didn't. In the end, he suggested that Grey Wolf take her home. Cam had no business at her cottage and he figured he'd already done enough damage to her reputation and his own for one evening.

But it was hard to see her climb into Grey Wolf's sedan and even harder to watch the taillights disappear. Cam knew, without Grey Wolf saying a word, that he'd spend the night with Tiger Lily.

And that was hardest of all.

The darkness had thinned and the birds were greeting the morning when Cam finally pulled into his garage at the Victorian home he'd bought for Daisy and himself and Asia, his family's housekeeper. He figured he'd grab an hour or two of sleep then he'd clean up, spend some time with Daisy, check in with Jake then go into the office. He'd neglected it enough during the past few days. Wearily he unlocked the back door then he walked through the darkened kitchen, the butler's pantry and on through the old-fashioned dining room with its high ceilings and on to the foyer and the glass doors that separated the staircase from the front parlor. Someone had left on a light. He stepped through the glass door to turn it off and discovered there was a woman asleep on the Victorian sofa. She was beautiful and sexy, her auburn hair mussed, her long lashes resting on her peach-colored cheeks, her long, tapered fingers holding a homemade, blue-and-white striped afghan around her shoulders.

Shit.

Cam's heart curled as he sat down next to Sharon. The jostling woke her and she sat up and rubbed the sleep from her lovely, hazel eyes

"Hi," she said, with a sleepy, but warm smile.

He was struck again by her natural beauty and her innate kindness. She looked just as good all tousled and sexy as she did in her tailored business suits. Her pale skin glowed in the low-wattage light and her half-lidded eyes were trusting. *Damn.*

Cam genuinely liked Sharon. She'd been his friend before they'd started to date. He'd chosen her deliberately because she was a friend. Like Elise. He grimaced. *Like Elise.* He should have known this was doomed. He rubbed the back of his neck with his palm. Damn, he was beat. He needed to tell her they had no future together but not now. He was too tired for tact.

"You look strung out," she said, in a sympathetic voice.

Cam knew the depression he felt was less due to fatigue than the gut-twisting experience of watching Tiger Lily ride off with another man. No, not *another* man. Her ex-husband. He tried to infuse some life into his smile.

"What are you doing here?" The question sounded too stark. He tried to soften it by picking up her hand and holding it a moment. Guilt cascaded through him.

"You don't mind my being here do you?" He heard the anxiety in her voice. When he'd met her, Sharon had seemed confident and complete but his lukewarm courtship seemed to have undermined all that. "Asia called me. Her niece's husband broke his leg and they needed her to go over to Andover for at least the night. She would have called Hallie but it was late and the children were already in bed."

"So you got to sacrifice a night of sleep, eh?"

Sharon was like Molly in that way. Generous. Elise had never given up anything without getting something in return. But then, Sharon had every reason to expect something from Cam: An engagement ring and the promise of happily ever after.

Sharon glanced out the window and blinked.

"Oh my gosh! Morning already?"

"Just about."

"Is it true you've been sleuthing out at the casino?"

He frowned. "Where'd you hear that?"

"Oh, I'm sorry." She sounded genuinely distressed. "Daniel Grey Wolf is my tenant. I got the idea from something he'd said."

"Damn. It was an undercover operation. What the hell was he doing talking about it?"

"He wasn't. Not really. Don't blame him, Cam. I could tell he was anxious about something. Someone. I thought it might be Molly Whitecloud so I asked him. He admitted she was digging for information but assured me that someone was keeping an eye out for her. You were gone," she said, simply, "and I put two and two together."

She sounded so anxious. God, he was acting like a jerk.

"I helped put together financing for the casino. If there's something wrong out there, it's my fault."

Shit. He sounded defensive and hostile. He searched his conscience and figured it out. It wasn't yet morning and Daisy wouldn't be awake for a few more hours. Would Sharon expect him to take her to bed?

"Is there something wrong?"

He jumped. "What?"

"Out at the rez."

"Oh." He leaned his head against the back of the sofa and closed his eyes. There'd be no way to keep DiMarco's death a secret.

"Yeah." He told her about the murder.

"I'm sorry." He felt her fingers on his arm. "What

119

does it mean?"

"It means the casino and resort will close down for the present. It means there's probably a contract killer on the loose. Beyond that, I don't know."

"But Molly's all right?"

Cam didn't want to think about Molly. "Yeah. She's fine."

Sharon was quiet a moment. Cam held his breath waiting for her next words. He didn't want to have to break up with her. Not now.

"I'm going to go," she said. "I need to get back to the inn before breakfast."

He looked into the beautiful, sad hazel eyes and was aware that she knew. She wouldn't say anything now. Sharon Johnson was discreet and proper. She would probably never say anything but, after all, it should be up to him. He felt a tidal wave of guilt.

"Let me run you home."

Crinkles appeared next to her toast-colored eyes when she smiled at him. They were attractive but they reminded him that she was several years older than he. She'd waited a long time for marriage. He cursed himself. She'd have to wait awhile longer.

"I know you're exhausted. Listen, I actually got a decent amount of sleep and anyway, I've got my car. Talk to you later?"

He nodded. Her words were fading in and out. He wasn't sure he'd make it upstairs.

"I'll call you tomorrow, I mean later today," he managed to say. She leaned in and gave him a brief kiss on the cheek. He inhaled her fresh scent and felt a small pang of regret. She'd have been perfect as a mother for Daisy and a wife for him.

If there hadn't been Tiger Lily.

****

Molly sat at her kitchen table with her head in her hands. Until a few months ago she'd been a law-abiding midwife, a respectable resident of the rez, a pillar of the community. She'd worked with the lawmakers in Augusta to get permission to build the casino. She'd even started to work with the businesspeople of Eden to build a community crafts cooperative where all the locals, Penobscots included, could sell their wares.

But her bona fides meant nothing in the face of what she'd done to Cameron Outlaw. She wished—oh, how she wished—she'd never heard of the Spotswood Fertility Clinic and its sperm bank.

And last night she'd compounded that mistake by sleeping with Cam Outlaw thereby destroying the dreams of a fine man and a fine woman. Cam had said he wouldn't marry Sharon Johnson now and she knew he'd be as good as his word.

She knew he was a man with high ethical standards now. Had he always been? When he'd told her he'd come back the year she was seventeen, would he have done it? Yes. He *had* come back but too late. She'd made the decision to handle the situation her own way. She thought about what would have happened if she'd gotten ahold of Cam, if he'd come home and married her and then she'd lost the baby anyway. He'd have been a teenage husband with no education and no future and he'd have ended up hating her.

At the moment, Molly did not like herself much at all.

Daniel put a cup of chamomile tea and a slice of Murial's homemade twelve-grain toast in front of her but she wasn't hungry. How could she be hungry when she was full of self-loathing and regret? She wished he'd just go away.

"You didn't have to stay," she muttered, ungraciously.

He was nice enough not to point out that the cottage belonged to him.

"Drink your tea."

"Sure. Why not? Tea can solve any problem, can't it?"

"It will taste good. And it will settle you down."

Molly lifted the cup and inhaled the steam. She was so ashamed of herself. And now she was taking her misery out on Daniel.

"I suppose you want to know what happened in DiMarco's office."

"Eat your breakfast first. Small bites."

Small bites. Molly shivered. The words evoked a memory of Cameron Outlaw sprawled on top of her, crushing her body into the butterscotch sofa, taking little nips out of her neck and shoulders.

"I can't eat."

"Look," he said, with a gentle sigh. "I get it. You had sex with Outlaw. There never was any choice, you know, not once you launched that undercover business and shared a room. The two of you are like magnets. There's no point beating yourself up about it."

She wondered how he knew. Was it because he was a shaman and, as such, filled with extraordinary insight? Or because he knew her so well?

"We didn't have sex in the room."

Daniel's dark eyes bored into hers. He didn't even have to ask the question.

"In DiMarco's office," she admitted. "Just before I delivered Patty Sue Stottlemyer's baby. On that sofa."

Daniel let out a long hiss. "You like to live dangerously."

"It wasn't on purpose, really. We were looking for the safe and another couple came to the door. The position on the couch was just a pose."

"And then it wasn't."

She nodded, miserably. "And then it wasn't."

In typical Daniel fashion he didn't scold her. She knew he was on her side even when she was wrong.

"What now? Are you going to tell him about the baby?"

"We don't know yet if there is a baby." She flashed on Cam's words about infertility. What on Earth had he been talking about? And then she realized he wasn't talking about the hypothetical baby but about the real one that she'd lost all those years ago.

"I don't see how that would be helpful."

"He deserves to know."

She sighed.

"I haven't told him anything. If no baby results from the insemination, I probably never will tell him. Why complicate his life?"

He looked out the window. She knew he could see her morning glories, which had burst into beautiful, full trumpets in the morning light.

"Because it's the right thing to do."

Of course he was right.

Tears pricked the backs of her eyelids. Her arms and legs felt as heavy as her heart. She wished she could click her heels three times and disappear.

Daniel got to his feet.

"Where're you going?"

"I'm gonna track down the sheriff. See if he'll let me take a look at that laptop computer. Whether he does or not I've got to formally shut down the casino and get a report in to the bureau. Then I need to get home to shower and clean up."

Molly thought about Lynn Brown Bear and the others who depended upon the entertainment complex to put food on their tables and she felt sick. Then the man's last words pierced her consciousness.

"Do you think of the *Garden of Eden* as your home now, Daniel?"

"I'm starting to. It's the right place for right now."

She nodded. "Does that mean you want to sell the cottage?"

"The cottage doesn't belong to me, anymore, *nizwia*. The deed is in your name."

She gaped at him. "Since when?"

"Since the day the divorce was final. You need this place more than I, Molly. It's your home."

Hot tears welled up in her eyes and streamed down her cheeks. How like Daniel. He'd spent two years comforting her, trying to soothe her broken heart. He'd gotten nothing at all out of their hastily arranged marriage but he'd still given her everything he had to give, including the house.

"I love you, Molly. I want you to be happy."

"I want you to be happy, too, Daniel."

Chapter Eight

Molly stepped out her back door and wandered around her garden. The hollyhocks and roses and the lilies and iris and peonies were all in full bloom and the air was fresh and fragrant in pale light of morning. The Abenakis were known as "people of the dawn," and Molly had always felt a special affinity for first light. The garden never failed to soothe her ruffled spirits but today might be an exception. She walked to the swing Daniel had built near the fence covered with honeysuckle and she sat down. Insects buzzed nearby, including honeybees and early cicadas. Song birds filled the air.

Molly tried to center herself by focusing on the beautiful sights, sounds and smells but her mind was troubled. And not just about Cameron Outlaw. She was concerned about the woman whose voice she'd recognized, Dwight Winston's companion and the woman she'd encountered at the hot tub party.

Sandra Tall Tree.

Molly knew she should talk to Jake about Sandra but she couldn't bring herself to turn in Davey's wife, both for his sake and that of the tribe. And she felt a certain kinship with the half-Indian woman who, like Molly, had been left without any people or a clear identity.

Molly had been lucky. James and Muriel

Whitecloud had made her feel more than welcome at Blackbird. Sandra's fate had been different. She'd met a man at a pow-wow near Rankin in Quebec and married him immediately. Davey was nearly twenty years her senior and, while well-liked, he was the frequent butt of jokes. Sandra must have believed Davey had money or possibly she'd heard about the casino, which, by rights, should be enriching the coffers of the Blackbird Penobscots.

Whether it was boredom or the quest for independent means, Sandra had taken the job as Dwight Winston's assistant but that didn't necessarily mean she was guilty of anything except poor judgment. After all, there was no proof that Winston was guilty of fraud or murder and only anecdotal evidence that he was supplying spa guests with female companionship.

Molly sighed. She was making excuses for Sandra and she knew it. She had to tell Jake the sagama's wife had been with Dwight Winston in Eddie DiMarco's office and she would. But not yet.

First, she'd talk to Sandra herself.

****

The autumn day was unseasonably mild but Daniel barely noticed as he drove back to Eden. He feared for Molly but knew he couldn't help her this time. Cameron Outlaw, both the man and the illusion had become an obsession with her and only she could find her way through the tangled maze of years and emotions.

Daniel had some sympathy with the guy. Oh, Cam should have considered the possibility that Molly was pregnant all those years ago, but he'd been young and heedless and Molly's sperm-bank heist could not be laid at Cam's door.

But while Cam and Molly were flitting in and out of each others' lives, they were hurting an innocent party. Sharon Johnson was all but engaged to Cam and, it was as plain as a full moon in a cloudless sky that Cam still had feelings for Molly.

Daniel did not want to see Sharon hurt and the strength of his reactions made him realize he'd allowed himself to feel too much for the innkeeper. The unsought, unexpected emotion had set him back on his heels. He needed to seriously consider whether he should forget his plans to stay in Eden, whether he should return to Washington, D.C.

After a stop at the sheriff's office to reclaim the Blackbird Casino's laptop, Daniel turned down Walnut Street. As always, his pulse raced when the yellow clapboard inn came into view and he felt a surge of excitement when he spotted the tall, slim figure raking leaves out of a garden bed. She wore a red flannel shirt that clashed with her hair, a pair of designer blue jeans and a white baseball cap. Her auburn ponytail was drawn through the hole in the back and it gleamed in the morning sun.

Daniel parked and walked toward her, a slow smile on his face. She smiled back at him and blushed when he tugged the end of her ponytail, her hazel eyes wide above high cheekbones.

"How many are there," he asked.

"How many what?" She sounded breathless.

"Freckles." He studied her nose. "I count thirteen."

"Thirteen. That's right. I tell myself there used to be more it's a lie. There used to be nine."

He laughed.

"Have time for a cup of tea?"

She sounded hesitant as if she feared encroaching on his time. He knew he should decline. He needed to start searching the computer. He needed to protect his vulnerable heart. He smiled at her again.

"Sure."

Minutes later they sat at Sharon's kitchen bar. The brown marble surface felt cool under Daniel's hands. Old-fashioned Priscilla curtains framed her sunny kitchen window and small pots of flowers marched along the sill. It was a serene room despite the color of the walls.

"I like the pink walls," he said, surprising himself.

"The paint's called Eros Blush."

Eros? *Eros?*

"It seems less erotic than cheery," he said, to defuse the gathering sexual tension. "Like a sunrise."

She nodded, her eyes lidded and unreadable.

"I'm gathering a few leads on folks around town you can interview for your book. I'll be able to give you some names and numbers in the next few days."

"Thanks." He was happy to change the subject. "There's no hurry. I'm tying up some loose ends for the bureau at the moment."

"Anything to do with what happened out at the casino last night?" He didn't answer immediately and she sounded defensive. "I heard the manager was found dead. Everybody heard that."

"It's no problem only that I can't talk about it yet."

"But you'll tell me when you can?"

"You'll be the first to know."

"He was murdered, wasn't he?"

There had been no question about that. No doubt

everyone in Eden already knew it.

"Yes. The question is, why."

"For money I'd imagine," she said. "Doesn't sound like Big Eddie was a candidate for a crime of passion."

Daniel thought of the egg-shaped casino manager.

"I agree."

"I know Cam was there. And Molly Whitecloud."

Daniel frowned. "He told you?"

She shook her head. "I was babysitting at his house when he got home in the wee hours of the morning."

Of course. She was his almost fiancée. Daniel struggled not to let the jealousy and dismay show on his face.

"I imagine the casino will close down for awhile." He nodded. "That'll be hard on the tribe. I know Molly is counting on profits to pay for a clinic." He nodded again. She tilted her head to one side.

"You didn't come home last night."

"No. I stayed out at the rez."

"With Molly?"

His dark eyes met her light ones. What was she asking? And why?

"I stayed at the cottage. She was exhausted and upset."

A wounded look flashed on her face and he felt oddly guilty. He wanted to point out that he'd done her a favor. If he hadn't stayed with Molly, Cam would have.

"You obviously care about her and vice versa."

"We go back a long way."

"And neither of you has remarried."

Daniel was silent, unsure of how much he should share with her about Molly.

"Our marriage," he said, carefully, "was a long time ago. Molly and I are just friends."

Sharon looked as if she didn't quite believe him. Her next question caught him even more off guard.

"Is that why you didn't move back to the rez?"

He thought she'd be embarrassed if she realized how personal her questions were but he didn't mind telling her.

"Not really. I've lived in D.C. for years and I wanted to live in town. The rez is a little remote for me these days."

"And Molly?"

"It suits her," he said, aware that he was not telling the whole truth.

Something flickered in her golden eyes. Daniel thought he recognized it. He knew a lot about loneliness.

He drained the last of his tea. "C'mon," he said, "Let's finish raking the leaves."

****

Molly spent the next days and nights virtually sleepless as a full harvest moon sent three new moms into labor. During her travel time between Millie Sharp's trailer, Joan Wolf's bungalow and Letha Blackmon's mother's home, Molly admired the unfurled glory of autumn.

She'd always loved the Moon of Ripening Berries when nature flaunted its beauty and its bounty just as she loved the sense of wonder and satisfaction she felt upon placing a tiny infant into a mother's arms.

The brilliant red and yellow leaves of the maples and oaks warmed her heart even as the piercing blue of the sun-filled sky tore at it.

She could not put Cam Outlaw or the sperm heist out of her mind. She wanted to apologize to him, to explain. She wanted to see him again but there was no excuse, nothing she could say and, on top of that, there was no time to say it.

Finally all the babies were safely delivered. Molly celebrated by visiting her parents for supper. Muriel laid out a feast of late tomatoes and cucumbers, pumpkin and squash and late summer corn. After countless snacks consisting of a piece of fruit or sandwiches-on-the-run, Molly ate so much of the wholesome food she nearly burst at the seams like the milkweed pods by Blackbird Pond.

She drove home bolstered by her parents' love and more at peace than she had been in days.

If the insemination worked, she'd get the baby she'd always wanted. True, it would complicate her life and Cam's but the deed was done. There was no going back. Molly knew it would be better for everyone if she were not pregnant but she refused to pray for that outcome.

She still wanted Cam's baby and if the fates gave her the chance, she'd raise him or her with all the love in her heart.

It was just past dusk as Molly made her way back to the cottage. As she passed the circular road that ringed the rez she remembered something that had been shoved to a back burner for the past few days. She had not yet talked to Sandra Tall Tree.

In spite of her weariness, Molly made a U-turn on the main rez road and turned west on the circular road.

The Tall Trees lived in a tumbled down farmhouse on Small Bear Drive off the circular road. The warmth of the wide, welcoming front porch was offset by the rooftop gutters that hung at odd angles like disapproving eyebrows. Molly grinned at the rakish image. Davey's father had been handy with a hammer and nails but he'd died nearly five years earlier. The vibrant vegetable garden maintained by Davey's mother had gone to see since her death two years earlier.

It looked like Sandra had about as much interest in pulling weeds as Davey had in home repair.

Molly drove up the dirt driveway that circled in front of the house. Window shades were pulled against the slanted evening sunlight. Molly felt a stab of guilt. She should have made more of an effort to welcome the new bride to the rez. It couldn't have been easy for a young woman with aspirations to sophistication, to be stuck out here in this isolated house.

Davey wore a peach-colored terrycloth bathrobe with matching bedroom slippers when he answered Molly's knock. His pudgy face flashed its usual friendly smile but, for once, it didn't reach his eyes. Molly's heart ached for him as he led her into the shadowed parlor. There was only one lamp burning— an old-fashioned globe that she remembered from visiting his mother years ago. The furniture was still the same, too, dingy and shabby.

Molly thought, suddenly, of the Tall Trees' fancy new sports car and wondered where he'd found the money to pay for that. At his invitation she sat on a faded chintz sofa. She crossed her jeans-clad legs and tried not to cross her arms. Her long-sleeved canary colored tee shirt had been warm enough in Muriel's cozy trailer but it wasn't enough in Davey's gloomy house. His gloomy, empty house. She knew Sharon was not home.

"What can I do you for," the *sagama* asked.

His smile was strained. He had to sense, on some level, that his new domestic arrangement was faltering badly. She wished he'd never have to know what his wife had been up to with Dwight Winston. It was a wish that could not possibly come true.

She launched into the cover story she'd prepared.

"I came to talk to Sandra about the crafts cooperative, the *Maine Attraction*." She tried to keep her voice light and cheerful. "As you know we'll be selling items from crafters all over western Maine, including those on the rez and we could use some help with the marketing plan. I know Sandra's had some experience with business and thought she might be interested in helping out."

Davey brightened a little. "She worked in a department store in Canada. She liked retail a lot. I'm sure she'd be glad to be included," he said. "She'll have some free time now since the casino's closed. She was working up there, you know, as an assistant to Mr. Winston. " He shook his head. "You know, Molly, she's scared. I almost think she knows something about this business that got Mr. DiMarco killed. She wanted to get away so I sent her up north to her people for a few days."

"Oh yes," Molly looked deliberately vague. "She's from a reservation near Rankin, isn't she?"

"There's nothing like family to hold you up during hard times."

Molly was certain Sandra had no 'people' up North or anywhere else. She was a stray, just like Molly. The woman had obviously bolted, most likely with Winston.

The move practically proved she was guilty of something even if it was just avoiding her husband's company.

Molly looked at Davey sitting in his old recliner wearing the pastel bathrobe and she felt a wave of sadness.

"I let her take the Porsche," he said. Molly wanted to ask how on earth he'd been able to afford the luxury vehicle but such a question would be unpardonably rude.

"It's a beautiful car," she said.

"I had some money from mother," he said, as if aware of her question, "and Sandra made a good salary at the casino. And, of course, the car isn't new." His eyes looked troubled. "She really wanted it, Molly. She hasn't had much in her life."

Molly nodded. She didn't doubt that at all. Davey hadn't had much either but she didn't point that out. She got up.

"Could you let me know when she gets back?"

"Sure." Davey lumbered to his feet. He glanced at a photograph on a side table and fingered it. Davey, dressed in a suit and tie, beamed at the tall, dark-haired woman beside him. Sandra's wedding dress was simple, elegant and expensive and her sharp features were softened by a smile. She looked almost happy.

"My wife's a beautiful woman."

Her heart ached for him. "Yes," she said. "I know she is."

Molly found herself wanting to reassure him.

"You know she and I are a lot alike. I was lucky to find Muriel and James. And everybody on the rez. Sandra was lucky to find you, Davey."

The *sagama* smiled his sweet smile. "I'll tell her you stopped by."

As Molly stepped out into the crisp, fall night, a deep sadness tugged at her heart. She'd spent the last dozen years trying to nurture and protect the people of Blackbird Reservation but she couldn't help Sandra and she couldn't help Davey anymore than she could provide Lynn Brown Bear with a decent living. At least they'd put a stop to the exploitation of the girls up at the casino. She thought of the sixteen-year-old pregnant with some unknown man's child and her lips compressed into a straight line.

Sometimes life could be very cruel.

Her phone jangled. It was Nancy Dove concerned about her daughter who appeared to be in some pain. Molly grimaced before she acknowledged to herself that Lenaya would be better off without the unborn baby.

"I'll be right over," she promised. She stopped at her cottage to pick up a toothbrush and a change of clothing in preparation for a long siege but the pains lessened and stopped and by the time the gray dawn had chased away the midnight sky, Molly was back in her own bed.

****

Cam pulled into his accustomed spot in front of the *Garden of Eden.* He'd had to postpone the dinner he'd promised Sharon when he got the call from Grey Wolf.

First there was the business up at the casino and then he'd responded to a summons from his former in-laws to appear at a family function. And then he'd needed to spend time with Daisy.

Excuses, he thought, irritated with himself. He

dreaded telling Sharon Johnson, one of the nicest women he'd met, that they couldn't see each other anymore, particularly since they worked together on Eden County's Economic Development team and she was friends with all the other women in his life, including Molly Whitecloud!

Damn.

Not that this was about Molly. Cam had refused to let his mind dwell on her during the days that had passed since their time together at the casino. He hadn't, however, been able to control his dreams and he'd awakened nearly every night with a terrible sense of emptiness—and a painful arousal.

Damn. Damn. Damn. Damn.

He'd thought he was over her. He'd wanted to be over her. He had to get over her.

But he couldn't marry Sharon Johnson. The woman deserved more than a fool who was still in love with the high school sweetheart who'd dumped him more than a decade earlier.

Cam sucked in a breath. He not only had to break up with Sharon, he had to do it with a lie. He had to do it without compromising either Molly's reputation or his own.

He got out of the Mercedes and strode up the short walkway to the inn's front door. At least he'd send her off with a good meal. He'd made reservations at *Minotaur's* in Bangor.

The late summer night felt more like early fall and the fire crackling on the hearth in the inn's cozy lobby was welcoming. Libby Campbell, a junior at Eden Consolidated High, was doing desk duty. She smiled at him.

"Hey, Mr. Outlaw," she said. "Nice flowers."

He'd brought a bouquet of white orchids. He'd been unsure of floral protocol for a break up.

"Ms. Johnson's in her suite."

Cam nodded. He knocked on the door but didn't wait for a response.

Sharon was standing by an arched window. She wore an amber-colored silk dress that came to her knees and revealed her long, well-shaped legs. Her hair was pulled into a sleek knot. The man next to her stood close enough to put his arm around her although the two were not touching. The shaman's shoulder length hair was thick and mostly gray. It was held in place by a leather strip. The severe hairstyle accentuated the man's high cheekbones and noble profile.

Cam frowned at Grey Wolf. What the devil was *he* doing here? He growled the other man's name.

"Outlaw," said Daniel. He remained by the window as Sharon hurried toward Cam.

"Hey," she said, softly. "What lovely flowers. I hope I have a vase that'll do them justice." She sounded oddly nervous as she plucked the flowers out of his hand. He said nothing. He couldn't seem to look away from her companion, the man Molly had chosen over him.

Sharon, a perceptive woman, couldn't miss the tension.

"Daniel's writing a history of western Maine," she said.

"On Friday night?"

The redhead's laugh was nervous. "I'm helping him set up interviews with a few of the old-timers in town," she explained.

He scarcely listened. He'd assumed Grey Wolf was out on the rez with Molly. The man adored the Penobscot midwife, always had. So what was he doing in this intimate setting with Sharon Johnson? Cam scowled at him, unsure whether he was angry at Grey Wolf for hanging around Sharon or for failing to be with Molly.

Or, perhaps it was for marrying Molly all those years ago.

"I'll get out of your way," Grey Wolf said. His dark eyes met Cam's but his words were for Sharon. "Thanks for the names and numbers. I'll give these folks a call right away." He started to stride past Cam.

"Wait," Cam said, stopping him. "Anything new out at the rez?" He cursed himself, silently. He'd successfully stayed away from Molly all week. He didn't need or want to know what was going on with her. "Never mind," he said. "Forget it."

Grey Wolf 's dark eyes held his as if he knew exactly what the other man wanted to hear.

"The state crime lab reviewed the information on the laptop. It looks as if the fraud and embezzlement charges will hold long enough for an indictment of Dwight Winston and Eddie DiMarco. Obviously, only Winston will be charged."

Cam nodded. He already knew that. And Grey Wolf knew that he knew. "That it?"

Sharon had disappeared into her small kitchen. Daniel fixed him with a long look.

"Are you asking about Molly?"

"No."

Grey Wolf glanced toward the kitchen then back at Cam. His dark eyes were steady.

"Decide which one you want," he said, in a low voice. "And do it quickly."

Cam seethed internally as Grey Wolf nodded and left the room. How dare the man give him an order? Did he think it was that easy? That a man could just choose a woman and everything would fall into place? How could he explain that he'd chosen the wrong woman and she'd rejected him but his heart refused to let her go? Hell, he shouldn't have to explain. Grey Wolf should understand better than anyone.

Sharon returned a moment later.

"I thought we'd go to Bangor," he said. She held very still for a moment. "What?"

"Would you mind very much, I mean, I'd rather not go all that way."

He searched the hazel eyes. The woman was no fool. She knew things had changed between them. Perhaps even on her side.

"I understand. How do you feel about the pork chop special at *Little Joe's*?"

She didn't indicate by even the flicker of an eyelash that she was surprised by his quick capitulation. She just smiled and took his arm.

"Pork chop night is my favorite," she said. "Joe does some kind of brining thing with them. They're wonderful."

Cam patted her arm. He envied the man who finally got this warmhearted, classy woman. One thing was certain. Despite the oddly intimate tete-a-tete he'd interrupted, he knew it wouldn't be Grey Wolf. When all was said and done the Penobscots stuck to their own.

Sharon chatted all through dinner. She spoke of her plans for expanding the inn and of the progress on the cooperative. She told him that the inn's cellar was filled with furniture and books and other antique paraphernalia and that, after she'd weeded through it, she thought she might launch an historical society.

He made her laugh with impersonations of some of the characters at his in-laws dinner and she made him laugh with an anecdote about shopping with Hallie and Daisy and Robert. And, finally, she told him how much his friendship meant to her.

"I feel the same," he said, taking her hand and silently blessing her for making his miserable job so easy. Her smile was tinged with sadness, though.

"You're one in a million," he said, meaning it. "I wish I could explain."

Her oval nails brushed his hand. "There's no need. I learned a long time ago that there's no logic to emotion." She smiled, sadly. "Love is inexplicable. I guess that's why we're all so obsessed with it. I know you must miss Daisy's mother."

She'd misunderstood. He conquered the sudden urge to tell her the truth. Hell, he didn't even really know the truth.

"If it makes you feel any better," she said, with a slight blush, "I've had second thoughts, too. Just because something's great on paper doesn't necessarily mean it's right."

He searched her face, hoping she was telling the truth.

"I'm perfectly sincere," she assured him, "but I do have a favor to ask."

"Anything."

"This is a bit awkward. I can't explain why but I'd really appreciate it if we could just sort of let our relationship fade."

"You mean you don't want me to post a giant 'We Broke Up" poster on the gazebo?"

"Exactly. I'd like to avoid the endless offers of sympathy and all that well-meaning curiosity you get in a small town. I mean, we're both trying to run businesses here."

If he'd consulted his own interests he'd rather have made a clean break. Until the news made its way back to Molly, she'd feel guilty for betraying Sharon. But Cam owed the redhead much more than a favor and she'd asked for silence.

"Whatever you want."

"I don't feel like a dumpee you know," she said, suddenly.

His heart lifted. "You don't?"

"Not really. I'm ready for marriage and a family but I've known for awhile now that it wouldn't be with you. You've just never looked at me with that hungry gleam in your eye."

His lips twitched.

"You mean we haven't had sex."

"Yep. That's what I mean."

He picked up her long slim white fingers and kissed them.

"That was an oversight, my dear."

"That," she replied, "was probably the only thing we did right!"

Chapter Nine

Three days later Daniel was in his studio apartment. He'd opened a file of notes from his recent interview with Ebenezer Whitfield, the nonagenarian who was Eden's oldest living inhabitant. Whitfield had been able to give him a lot of background on the woolen mill that had shut down some two decades earlier. He'd talked about the old days of milk delivery and ice boxes and the Indians who'd come from the reservation to sell their homemade baskets. He'd known one of the early Molly's, Molly Spotted Elk, the one who had become a famous dancer in New York City.

Daniel stared at the font on the screen. He hadn't spent any time with Sharon since she'd returned from her dinner date with Outlaw. He'd expected to hear either through the grapevine or osmosis or from her that the relationship was over but he'd heard nothing but crickets. Folks in town still anticipated an engagement announcement and everyone was pleased at the eminently suitable match between the lovely, maternal innkeeper and Eden's golden boy, the wealthy, handsome single father. Daniel was puzzled by the inaction. He believed Outlaw to be a fundamentally decent man. Did this mean he'd chosen Sharon and put aside his feelings for Molly? Daniel told himself it wasn't his business, that there was nothing he could do to make things right for either woman.

But he couldn't stop wondering.

A tentative knock made the hand holding a mug of tea shake violently enough for the liquid to spill on the floor. Daniel pushed himself to his feet, walked to the door and let her in.

"Hi." Sharon sounded so tentative. "I hope I'm not interrupting."

He tensed. Was she here to tell him about her engagement? He forced his fingers to unclench. With long practice of hiding his feelings Daniel maintained a pleasantly neutral expression on his face.

"Not at all."

She'd obviously been working in the yard again. The bill of her baseball cap was tugged low, nearly covering her soft eyes. The stained jeans hugged her curves and Daniel felt his whole body react. The brown-checked flannel work shirt accentuated the rosy hue in her cheeks. A smudge of dirt marred one lightly freckled cheek.

He envied the damn dirt.

"You look sort of funny, Daniel. A little dazed."

He schooled his features into a brotherly smile. "You haven't been around for awhile. It's good to see you. Will you come in for tea?"

She nodded. Daniel turned toward his kitchenette as she came closer knowing it would be suicide to be within touching distance. He was so wrapped up in his good intentions he didn't realize she'd followed him until he felt a slight pressure on his forearm. Her finger tips. He sucked in a breath.

"What can I do to help?" She didn't remove her hand. Her scent, a light cologne mixed with fresh air, a hint of pine and the smoke that is part of autumn in western Maine, invaded his senses. He heard a low sound but didn't realize it had come from him until she snatched her hand back.

"Sorry," she said.

He wasn't offended. He couldn't let her think he was. He turned to her and cupped her face with his hands. "You just startled me. That's all. I missed you, Sharon."

Black eyes met pale brown ones and neither blinked.

With an effort, Daniel let his hands drop away. He turned to the sink and began to fill a kettle with tap water. "I meant, I missed seeing you. Talking. What're you up to today?"

A ridiculous question considering she'd just come in from yard work but if she noticed she didn't say anything.

"I'm planning to sort through the stuff down in the cellar," she explained. "I've put it off since I bought this place two years ago. It's time to get serious."

It was an implicit invitation. Daniel thought about being alone with Sharon in a cellar. It would be dim-lit and quiet. It would be dirty and her face would get smudged and he'd want to clean it off with his fingers...or his tongue. He had no business going to this party. He opened his mouth to utter and excuse.

"Need some help?"

She grinned at him. "I'd love it."

He thrust his hands in his pockets to keep them honest.

"Maybe we'll find a local legend or two."

Her laughter enveloped him like morning sunshine and he felt a happiness that bordered on pain.

Why her? He'd asked himself the question many times over the past weeks and he'd never found an answer but he'd known the why didn't really matter. This was his woman. After all this time, all these years, he'd found her. But he couldn't have her. He had to remember that.

By the end of the afternoon, they'd talked and laughed, emptied boxes and drawers and piled dilapidated furniture—several large armoires, a handful of chairs, mirrors and antique clocks into a pile earmarked for repair and refinishing. Another larger pile was labeled "recycle," and a third pile was destined for the dump. Daniel had salvaged a dog-eared copy of a farmer's report that was nearly one hundred years old as well as a set of novels written fifty years earlier by a long-dead Maine author.

He viewed the organized room with satisfaction and, unthinking, he placed his hands on the small of his back and stretched out his throbbing muscles.

She walked toward him and he watched her, his eyelids hooded. He wanted to yell stop. He needed to turn and run. He did neither of those things, just stood there while her hands replaced his. He closed his eyes.

"Does it hurt here?"

"You don't have to do that."

She continued to rub her thumbs into his tight muscles, massaging them until they relaxed, transferring the tension to other even more sensitive parts of his anatomy.

"You got stiff cleaning my cellar."

Stiff. It took him long seconds to realize she was responding to his earlier comment. He'd gotten stiff all right. Painfully stiff.

She spread her fingers so they covered more territory and he felt them on his ribs. Sweat broke out between his shoulder blades and he knew he was reaching the point of no return. He turned, causing her hands to drop, and he caught them in his.

"This isn't right, Sharon."

She held his gaze.

"It feels right, Daniel. I want you."

"We're friends. That's all."

"I think we can be more. I believe you're attracted to me."

He had to give her credit for extraordinary courage. She had to know he'd reject her. She had to know he *had* to reject her.

"I'm not with Cam anymore," she went on. "We decided not to make a big deal of the break up but I'm a free woman. I can choose who I want to be with and I choose you."

He shook his head, anguished for her and himself. She needed someone younger, someone with her own background even for just an affair.

"I know what you're thinking," she said, but her voice wobbled. "I know you think you're too old and whatever but you're wrong."

"I'm almost fifty years old."

"A man in his prime."

"I can't give you what you want."

"I want a good man, a decent man, a man I love who will love me back."

"And children."

She nodded, too fundamentally honest to do other than admit to the truth.

"And children, God willing."

"I'm sorry," he said. Her lovely face twisted but there were no tears. Daniel could not remember a worse moment in his whole long life but he was careful not to let his regret show on his face. He was older than she. He knew such a union wouldn't work. A ringing cell phone, for once, was a welcome sound. Daniel jammed his hand into his pocket, retrieved the phone and flipped it open.

"Grey Wolf."

"Daniel?"

"What's up?"

"I need to talk to you about the casino. About the murder. I think I've got an idea about who did it."

"Can it wait?"

"Oh, of course. I'm sorry I bothered you."

Guilt crashed in on him. It was one thing to encourage Molly to find her own way. It was quite another to turn his back on her for a relationship that was all wrong. And this was important.

"You didn't bother me, *Nizwia.*"

"Nevertheless, this can keep. In fact, I want to think about it a bit more. Sleep tight, Daniel. I'll see you in a few days."

When he hung up Sharon was standing in the same spot a few feet away from him but she might have well have been on the moon. He felt the change. Whatever they'd had between them was well and truly broken. He knew it was because she believed he still loved Molly. He did not correct the mistake.

It was better this way.

****

After her call to Daniel, Molly dropped in at Cully's Market to pick up a few groceries. She drifted

147

over to the pharmacy aisle and eyed the pregnancy tests. She knew she could buy one here without risking any gossip. After all, she was the tribe's midwife. She reached for the lone box on the shelf but changed her mind.

It was still too early to tell and, besides, she didn't really want to know. She paid for her toothpaste and bread then drove to a narrow, aluminum trailer to check on one of her new mothers. The family invited her to stay for a meal. Most of her patients had little cash but they were proud and insisted upon paying with hospitality and Molly always accepted.

Tonight, though, despite the delicious venison stew, she ate little. Her theory about the murder depressed her. She had heard nothing of a break up between Cam and Sharon Johnson, which meant he had cheated with Molly on his wife-to-be. And, perversely, she felt depressed because she hadn't seen or heard from Cam. She told herself she hadn't expected anything from him but her feelings were hurt.

Her heart was hurt.

Apparently that slam-bam-thank-you-ma'am stuff on the butterscotch sofa had been just a passing ship to him.

She felt so low on the way home she decided to stop at the home of her foster parents. It always cheered her to see Muriel and James. Her father teased her a bit then busied himself with chores while she sat in the bright yellow kitchen with her mother.

"Something's bothering you," Muriel said. "Is it the you-know-what?"

Molly knew her mother meant the insemination attempt but she didn't want to talk about that now. She needed to focus on the murder. She shook her head.

"Then what, *nizwia*?"

"What do you know about Sandra Tall Tree?"

"Probably no more than you know. She thinks she's too good for Blackbird Reservation. Davey's a fool."

"Have you seen her around lately?"

"No. But then no one sees her except for in that red sports car she drives. What makes you ask about her?"

"Just a feeling. If you hear anything about her, can you let me know?"

"Anything like what?"

"I don't know. Davey said she'd gone back to Canada for awhile. I'd like to talk to her if anyone sees her around."

Muriel nodded and asked no more questions. She could be discreet when necessary. It was one of her best qualities, Molly thought.

"And what about the other?"

"I don't know yet."

"If it didn't work, if you're not, will you try again?"

"No." *No.* She still wanted Cam's baby but she was finished with her own selfish games. She would not betray him again. Whatever else happened, she would let go of her obsession. She'd devote herself to the People and she'd be happy.

"I heard he was with you at the casino."

Muriel's blunt statement startled Molly. Of course her mother would have heard about Cam's presence at the casino. The grapevine never failed.

"Yes."

"So did you go to bed?"

"Mother!"

"It's a good question. I know you love him."

There was no judgment behind the statement. They both knew it was true.

"He's marrying someone else, *n'onon*. He loves someone else."

"Are you so sure?"

Molly thought about Cam's hands on her, his urgent breath against her neck, the deep groan of relief when he'd found his satisfaction with her. She nodded. "He has a woman he can trust. I'm happy for him."

Muriel murmured a soothing, clucking sound and took Molly's hand in hers. "It will all work out, *nizwia*. You'll see."

Molly hugged the woman who was her family. "I love you, Mother."

"Your father and I thank the Creator every day for sending you to us."

****

Shadows stretched across the fields as late afternoon hurried off the stage to make room for early evening. Dusk was arriving earlier and earlier these days. Winter was not far off. The Moon of Freezing Rivers. She breathed in the scent of Fall for a moment before she went inside. This was the time of year the Penobscots had traditionally returned home after a nomadic summer of camping and socializing. It was the time to prepare for the long winter months ahead.

Wearily she pushed open her front door and turned on the recessed lights. She'd decorated her great room to look like the outdoors with unvarnished wooden floor and the sky blue walls and subtle, low-wattage lamps. She flicked them on and they blended with the magical twilight outside the large window that was a door to her garden. Usually she felt warm and calm when she returned home, but not tonight. Tonight her heart was troubled. The message light on her phone blinked at Molly. She punched the button hoping no one was in labor. She felt tired to the bone.

Hallie Scott Outlaw's cheery voice greeted her. Molly smiled at the extended message.

"Hey, Mol, you can start bringing crafts to the co-op anytime. We've got everything set up now. Let me know if you need help transporting them. Robert's been fussy today and Daisy was over for awhile. She may have been poking him. That reminds me, Daisy says 'hi' and she told me to make sure you join us for the Harvest Festival. There's gonna be tons of food and fun and you've got to be there. Oh, and Daniel should come, too. Take care now."

Nothing new there. Molly listened to the next message.

The voice was low and mysterious and Molly couldn't identify it. She couldn't even tell whether the caller was male or female, but the husky voice sent shivers dancing down her spine. The message itself was eerie, too. The caller told Molly to look on her bed.

Molly's heart jerked. Someone had been in her home? Someone had invaded the sanctity of her bedroom? What would she find in there? A coiled snake? A horse's head? A pink-and-white early pregnancy test kit? She paced across the heart-of-pine floor in her living room. Her imagination was out of control. She just needed to calm down and refuse to be intimidated by the androgynous caller's message. She sucked in a breath, marched into her room, snapped on the light and darted a glance at the half-made bed. She felt an incongruous stab of self-consciousness. The intruder knew her guilty secret. Well, he knew one of her guilty secrets. She almost never made her bed. She inched toward the piece of furniture, her arms around her waist, her heart slamming against her chest. What was it? What was there?

Molly's heartbeat didn't calm when she saw it was a slip of paper. She used only the tip of her forefinger and her thumb to lift it high enough for her to read the message written there.

"M.Y.O.B." *Mind your own business?*

Molly's fear morphed into excitement. Had her visit to Davey prompted this? Was this from Sandra? Had she returned from her bogus trip to Canada and heard Molly had been snooping around? Did this mean she was on the right track?

What should she do next? Call the sheriff? Daniel? Cam? Molly glanced at the cheery teddy bear in the center of her wristwatch. His right paw pointed to the "nine" his left paw to "twelve." It was too late to call anybody. A wave of exhaustion hit her hard. What she needed, more than anything, was a good night's sleep. The note was merely a warning. Whoever wrote it expected her to back off the investigation and it would look as if she had and, anyway, she didn't feel threatened. The style of the note told her the unhappy truth. It was sophomoric, the product of a teenager or someone who thought like one.

Tomorrow, she thought, I'll tell Jake what I know about Sandra Tall Tree.

Despite her fatigue Molly didn't fall asleep immediately. She couldn't banish the contrast of

Davey's hopeful face and her certainty that his marriage was doomed. In her tired mind, the disappointments of Davey and the tribe fused with her own blighted hopes from years ago. The images mixed and mingled like the shifting bits of glass in a kaleidoscope and when the sunlight poured across her face announcing the dawn of a new day she barely felt rested. She felt something else though. Her stomach lurched and she flew into the bathroom.

Was it morning sickness or the summer flu? Molly bent over the bowl again. Time to figure it out after she'd emptied her stomach.

But there wasn't time. She'd barely finished when Lenaya's mother called with another report of cramps.

Molly wolfed down some soda crackers as she threw on her clothes. This was the second alarm. It seemed as if the teenager's body was doing everything it could to expel the fetus. Molly knew that one in four pregnancies aborted naturally but she always intervened if she could in case there was a way to save the baby. The statistics didn't mitigate the sadness at losing even the prospect of another precious life.

Half an hour later Lenaya's bleeding appeared to have stopped. Molly knew the respite might be temporary and she conveyed her thoughts to Lenaya's mom, Nancy. A miscarriage was still a distinct possibility and she could tell from the flash in Nancy's dark eyes that she, too, would have mixed emotions about such an outcome.

Molly left the Dove's trailer with a fresh loaf of poppy seed bread under her arm. She made the rounds of her postpartum patients to check on their health, state of mind and whether they had any questions about breastfeeding. By the time she returned to her cottage, twilight had arrived. She felt a jolt of apprehension and was surprised at herself. She'd never before been reluctant to enter her darkened house. Maybe the M.Y.O.B. note had upset her more than she'd realized. Her home was isolated on its small back road that led to nowhere and there was no moon. She had to squint to see the front stoop. She didn't see the obstacle until she stubbed her toes against it.

Molly's heart caught in her throat and she reached for the object with shaking hands. A sigh of relief escaped her when she realized it was just a box. A shoebox. She smiled. Someone, probably her mother, had sent over some baked goods.

Inside, Molly snapped on the lights. The stylized writing on the box surprised her. She knew something about shoes and she knew there was no one on the rez, least of all her mother, who would have shoes that cost hundreds of dollars. She stared at the logo.

Papagallo

Suddenly Molly went very still. She was wrong. There *was* a woman who might wear the expensive footwear, a woman whose Jimmy Chus had set off a crown fire of gossip several months earlier.

Molly's hands shook as she set the box down on the gray Formica top of her kitchen table.

She punched in her mother's number just to be sure.

"You didn't leave me a Papagallo shoebox, did you?"

"A papa-what?"

"That's what I thought."

"What is happening?"

"Someone left me a shoebox, that's all."

"Cookies?"

"I don't think so. I'll call you back after I open it."

Muriel must have sensed some tension in her words.

"Open it now, baby. While I'm on the line."

Molly knew she'd made a mistake. She shouldn't have involved Muriel in this but it was too late now. She lifted the lid and peeked inside. She had no time to control her reaction. No chance to stifle her shriek at sight of the feathered carcass.

"What is it? What's wrong, *nizwia*?"

Molly pulled herself together for her mother's sake. "It's just a joke," she faltered. "A silly joke. Looks like the work of Bobby Black Bear and Len Whitetail. Those kids just don't have enough to do."

"What's the joke?"

"Let me call you later, Ma. I need to take care of this."

She disconnected her phone and gazed at the shiny black feathers. She understood nature and the food chain and, generally speaking, she wasn't squeamish but death always saddened her. She wondered where the crow had been obtained and hoped it had died of natural causes. Molly examined the narrow head and the long, heavy black beak. This crow seemed larger than the ones she saw habitually around the rez and there was something weird about its tail. It was unusually long with very distinct graduations. The feathers around the bird's throat were shaggy, too. She went very still as she realized what she was looking at. This was not a crow's carcass but that of a raven.

Chills skittered up and down Molly's spine sending

shafts of real fear through her body. The sender of the M.Y.O.B. message had just upped the ante. Made it more personal.

Someone had taken the trouble to search Molly's background, to discover that in a previous lifetime she had been the child of John Wind, a Wisconsin Mohawk who'd spent his last months in prison after accidentally killing his non-native lover.

Snapshots of the past clicked through her mind like the reel on an old-fashioned projector. Her father, proud and tall, reduced to a mind-numbing loneliness after the death of Molly's mother. His love of liquor that turned a quiet, gentle man into a brawling, boozing, ultimately violent, womanizer. His ravaged face during their last father-daughter visit in prison when he'd told her he was sorry. Her fresh start at the Blackbird Reservation when she'd changed her name to Molly Whitecloud, erasing, forever, her former identity.

Raven Wind.

Was the sender threatening to expose her background if she didn't stop investigating the murder? But how would that hurt her? Not many on the rez knew the details of her background but they were a forgiving people. Was this meant to discourage her relationship with Cam Outlaw? People in Eden might be less accepting of a half-Indian woman whose father had been a felon. But there was no question of a relationship between her and Cam.

What did the raven mean?

She felt certain she knew who had left the dead bird. She'd made it clear that she wanted to talk with Sandra Tall Tree. The official word was that Sandra was still away but she could have returned and hidden out in Davey's farmhouse, which, like Molly's house, was isolated. Molly shook her head. Didn't the foolish woman realize that these amateurish attempts to frighten Molly away just pointed more and more to her guilt? If only she'd come forward to speak with Jake Langley on her own. Sandra was young and had been influenced by the obvious arch villain of this case, Dwight Winston.

Molly stared at the shiny feathers. She knew she'd waited too long to tell what she knew. She should pick up the phone, this minute, and call Jake Langley but she hesitated, still reluctant to bring shame upon the tribe.

She put on a pair of the gloves she carried in her backpack then slid her hands underneath the carcass. Afterwards she didn't know whether she'd done so because she was stalling or because she'd felt some sixth sense that there was more to the message. There was more. Underneath the dead raven, tucked into a nest of tissue paper, was a pile of petals and a stamen.

A mutilated flower. A Daisy.

Molly's blood turned to ice.

The raven was just to get her attention. The real threat was to Daisy Outlaw.

Fear, intense and blinding, exploded inside Molly. Her fingers shook so badly she could barely grab the phone. It took three tries but finally she was able to punch in the phone number for Cam's sister-in-law, Hallie Scott Outlaw.

"Where," she said, in a voice pitched so she could hear it over the thundering of her heart, "is Daisy?"

****

They'd run into each other at a chamber of commerce meeting and, along with others, had stopped by *Little Joe's* for a beer. Afterwards Sharon asked Cam to stop by the inn.

He didn't ask her why. She was, after all, a friend and, until recently, a close friend. He followed her into the pleasant sitting room that served as her suite.

"Wait here," she said. She disappeared down the short hallway then reappeared a moment later carrying a stuffed Piglet and a copy of *The House at Pooh Corner*.

"What's all this?"

"I found these online and couldn't resist. I thought they might help Daisy adjust to the Robert-invasion." She grinned.

"You didn't have to do this."

He knew, instantly, it was the wrong thing to say. The gifts were no doubt intended to help his daughter but they were also a peace offering. She didn't want their failure to affect any of the other relationships between herself and the Outlaws who had become like family just as they had to Hallie before her.

"Daisy will love this," he said, with a grin. "I only hope the pig doesn't upset Wilbur."

"Oh, I think he'll be okay as long as Piglet doesn't commandeer any of his food."

Cam laughed. "Thanks." He lifted the pig. "Looks like you understand both animals and the hearts of jealous little girls. You'll make a great mother someday."

He'd meant the words as a compliment but he could have ripped his tongue out when he saw Sharon's peachy complexion pale. Dammit. He hadn't meant to hurt her again. He reminded himself that she'd easily agreed to their break up. This was about her desire for a family, not about him. He pondered the strength of the maternal instinct and, because his thoughts always roamed toward Molly, he wondered that he hadn't observed it in her.

Why not? Had her tumultuous childhood turned her against parenthood? If she'd wanted a child she wouldn't have divorced Grey Wolf.

"My late wife was desperate to have a child," he said, quietly. There was no reason to keep the details from Sharon. They might help her come to grips with her own childless state. They might also reassure her that she was well rid of him. He wasn't exactly a fertility god. "I think I mentioned that we had problems conceiving. Apparently I'm one of those low-motility guys. Lazy sperm." He grinned so she'd know he wasn't self-conscious about the affliction. "Elise arranged to mix my, admittedly sluggish sample with more vigorous swimmers. That way the resulting child—Daisy—might or might not belong to me biologically."

Her eyes widened. "So Daisy might not be your biological daughter?"

He shrugged. It was the first time he'd talked about this with anybody. He found it surprisingly easy with Sharon.

"It turns out Daisy is my daughter. We had her DNA tested to provide more information for her down the road, not because it mattered to me whether or not we shared the same blood. In any case, she is likely to be the only child I will have and that's never bothered me."

"It may bother you when you meet the right woman."

The words shocked him not least of all because he recognized the truth in them. He had entertained fantasies of another child—with Tiger Lily.

"I'm sorry," Sharon said, her eyes stricken. "I didn't mean to imply that your wife wasn't the right woman. I meant a second time."

Cam knew he couldn't tell her about Elise. He couldn't tell anyone. He had a duty to protect the memory of Daisy's mother.

"No harm done. I'd better be going. Thanks again for these." He lifted the book and stuffed animal and headed for the door. His ringing cell phone stopped him and he answered it automatically.

"Yes?"

"Cam?"

It was only one syllable but it was enough to spike his temperature. The room that had, seconds before seemed chilly, blazed and Cam felt butterflies explode in his lower body. She spoke again but a haze of desire blocked his comprehension and he thought he'd misunderstood her.

"What?"

"I said, where's Daisy?"

"At home. With Asia. Why?"

"Not with you?"

"No. I'm at the *Garden of Eden.*"

There was a brief pause. If it had been anyone else he'd have attributed it to taking a breath. Since it was Molly, he knew it was pain. He hardened his heart and resisted the impulse to explain.

Chapter Ten

He was at the *Garden of Eden*. With Sharon. Molly's imagination immediately conjured up a cozy scene that involved a couple of brandy snifters, a blazing fire and a sofa.

Or maybe a bed.

She stood very still and stared at the living room wall she'd painted the color of Cam Outlaw's eyes. She'd give herself a second.

"Molly?"

She struggled for words. "I'm here."

He paused and Molly felt the dense fog of despair gathering around her heart. He hadn't ended his relationship with Sharon. Maybe he'd never intended to break it off. She had to remind herself it wasn't her business.

"You okay?"

The question sounded reluctant. Like he was forcing himself to check up on a rodent he'd hit with his car. She had to suck it up. She couldn't bear to let him see how much he could hurt her.

"I'm fine. Listen, I've got to talk to you."

"Shoot."

She considered her options. She'd prefer not to talk about this on the phone but, on the other hand, she didn't really want him in her house and, anyway, he wasn't offering to come to the rez. She glanced at her watch and realized it really was late. *And he was at the inn.* She closed her eyes, briefly. She reminded herself this wasn't about her or Cam or even Sharon.

It was about Daisy.

"I've received a couple of threats that I'm pretty sure are related to the murder."

She told him about the M.Y.O.B. note on her bed but before she could continue, he exploded.

"What the hell?"

His voice zinged through the phone line like a rifle shot. Molly had to hold the little receiver away from her ear.

"Hang on, Cam. I haven't even told you the important part yet. Today, just now, I found a shoebox on my front step."

"Wait a minute. Get back to the note."

She could feel him sliding into his knight-in-shining armor mode just as he had at the resort and casino. Her heart twisted. She loved that about him but this time it would only get in the way.

"Listen to me," she infused her voice with a sense of urgency. "The threat isn't to me."

"I'm waiting."

"There was a dead raven in the shoebox," she told him. "The bird was lying on top of a mangled flower."

"The raven's a Native American symbol of death."

She was surprised that he knew. In the old days Penobscot customs were of less interest to him than the standing of the Eden Consolidated High's chess club.

"The flower, Cam. The flower was a daisy. That's the threat."

"Daisy?" there was a world of danger in the way he said the word. Molly felt a twinge of jealousy. Cam

Outlaw would kill anyone who touched a hair on his daughter's head. She tried to imagine being loved like that.

"Hang on," he said, in a calmer voice. "You've got to be mistaken about the meaning of the flower. I'm not even involved with the murder investigation. Not really."

"But I'm involved. Don't you see? Someone has taken the trouble to look into the past. Our past."

"Shit."

Finally he was starting to get it.

"I think it may be Sandra Tall Tree. She was the woman with Dwight Winston that night in Eddie DiMarco's office. I think she's involved in the murder unless Winston has put her up to this."

"You recognized her voice that night."

She heard the mounting anger.

"But you didn't tell me. More importantly, you didn't tell Jake. You were trying to protect the tribe, weren't you?"

His voice was hard and accusatory and she didn't bother to answer. She didn't need to.

"Never mind all that. You just need to make sure Daisy's okay."

"Listen, Molly. Nobody knows better than I how much you're willing to sacrifice for the tribe. *Who* you're willing to sacrifice. But if anything happens to my daughter I will make sure you spend the rest of your life paying for it."

"I want her to be safe, too, Cam. Please let me know that she's all right."

"Kind of you to be concerned with my child especially since she doesn't live on the rez. Just figure no news is good news."

The words felt like a sucker punch and Molly had to remind herself, again, that nothing had changed between them. They had never had a future together, not since the November thirteen years ago when she'd quietly married Daniel.

She paced the wooden floor of her small kitchen and prayed that Cam's daughter was safe. Twenty minutes later her phone rang and she snatched it up.

"Daisy's fine. She's here at home in bed."

Relief surged through her weary body. "Thank you."

The news steadied her. Daisy was safe for now and it was up to Molly to make sure she stayed safe by getting this business resolved. She stepped into her bedroom and changed into black jeans, a turtleneck sweater and a gray slicker that Daniel had left in her closet. She scooped up a heavy-duty flashlight and headed for the Jeep.

The pitch black of the evening had lightened slightly to charcoal due to a low cloud cover and a persistent drizzle. The drops were cold and, in spite of her clothing, Molly shivered as she drove to the *sagama*'s house. If Sandra had left her the note and/or the shoebox, it meant she was back on the rez, and if she was back on the rez she had to be holed up at Davey's.

She wondered if Winston had sent Sandra back specifically to check up on the investigation. She wondered how much Davey knew or suspected.

Molly's heart ached for the chief. He'd hate to lie to everyone about his wife's presence but he'd do it for her. Davey was besotted for the first time in his life.

She drove past the lone house on the dirt road. At first it appeared as a ghostly outline just slightly darker than the night sky. Molly drove a hundred yards then turned the Jeep and cruised past the house again. This time she drove more slowly and was able to glimpse a faint light burning behind the curtains in the living room window. She also noticed a vehicle in Davey's graveled driveway. It wasn't the sagama's old pickup truck and it wasn't the Porsche. She peered through the raindrops on her windshield. It looked big, like a boat. A Cadillac? A Lincoln? Whatever it was, it did not belong to the rez.

Thankful that she'd had a new muffler installed by Ray Gray Squirrel just last winter, she parked along the shoulder under a stand of trees that hadn't yet lost their leaves. It was a good hiding place.

She turned off the engine and slipped the keys into her pocket. She had come to the Tall Trees with no clear plan but she didn't question the instincts that led her to use stealth. She could always change her tactics if called for. She grabbed the flashlight, got out of the car, shutting the door quietly behind her, and started toward the house.

Molly stopped dead as a tiny orange light flared. A cigarette.

There was someone standing on Davey's front stoop.

Molly's heart thumped against her ribs as she made her way through the long wet grass. Her sneakers were soaked but the rain hid any noise she might have made so she didn't mind the trade off. She strained her eyes trying to make out the identity of whoever had just lit up. As far as she knew, neither Davey nor Sandra was a smoker.

Davey's front yard consisted of coarse grass, bald spots and a few overgrown bushes. The bushes provided islands of cover as she moved closer to the house. Halfway up the long yard, maybe twenty-five feet from the house, she heard a rumbling voice.

The smoker was not alone.

And then she was close enough to see that there were two people on the stoop. Sandra wore a jacket with a hood and Winston wore a long, dark trench coat with an old-fashioned fedora. They reminded Molly of Boris and Natasha.

As she watched, Winston moved closer to Sandra and she drew back as if in fright. What was happening? Was he threatening her? Would he hit his lover?

Hysteria nearly choked Molly. *Good grief!* Of course he'd hit her. He'd killed Big Eddie and Sandra knew it. He was probably planning to kill her, too.

Molly had to stop him. She wished she'd called Jake or, failing that, that she'd told Cam she was coming out here. Davey had a gun, of course. Many folks on the rez had hunting weapons but until recently, Davey had been police chief. She wondered, suddenly, where he was. Had Sandra and her lover already bumped him off?

Winston grabbed Sandra's lapel and she let out a small cry. Suddenly Molly had no time left. She bolted toward the house, but the long, wet grass wrapped around her ankles slowing her down and the cold rain numbed her hands. She had to concentrate to maintain her grip on the flashlight. She felt helpless as she grew near enough to hear them but not close enough to prevent Winston from hurting her. She knew she was about to witness a terrible crime and she knew she couldn't do anything to stop it. The odd thing was that the pair on the front stoop were so focused on one another neither heard her approach.

"You're hurting me, Dwight," Sandra whimpered.

"I'm asking you for the last time," he half-whispered in a furious tone. "What the hell did you do with it?"

"I already told you." Molly noticed Sandra sounded more irritated than frightened. "I stored it in my makeup case."

"Don't lie to me you redskin bitch. The case is empty. What did you do with the money?"

"How many times do I have to tell you? I don't know!"

In the fury of the moment they'd forgotten to whisper. The words were intelligible now and there was no mistaking the desperation in Dwight's voice.

"I want that money and I want it now." He grabbed her lapels and shook her. Molly, still wading through the sea of grass, expected to hear a shriek. Instead, Sandra laughed.

A very cool cucumber, Molly thought, even as she tried to figure out how to save the woman. She was about ten feet away but the big car was between her and the couple. If she threw her flashlight it would hit the car. The distraction would probably save Sandra for another minute or two but not for long and then Molly, too, would be a target.

The real question was, did Dwight Winston have a gun? And the answer seemed obvious when she remembered the gigantic body on the butterscotch sofa with the bullet in his head. Her heart jack-hammered.

"You've got it, haven't you, bitch? You and that buffoon you married. You saw what happened to Eddie and if you think I'm gonna go easy on you because of the blowjobs, you're nuts. I'm getting the hell out of here tonight and I'm taking the damn money with me."

"You're outta your tree, Dwight. Davey knows nothing about any of this and you and me are partners. If you go, I go with you."

He jammed a pistol at her midsection. Molly gasped and lifted her flashlight to fling it at the big car. A hand gripped her wrist and a quiet voice exploded in her ear.

"Don't."

Molly froze.

"Did it ever occur to you," Cam hissed, "to just call the damn police?"

Molly thought she'd never been so glad to see anyone in her life. Even though she couldn't actually see him and even though Sandra Tall Tree was still in danger.

Cam was here.

"I'm afraid he's got a gun," she whispered.

She could feel his tension in the way his fingers tightened around her wrist. He didn't even have to say what he was undoubtedly thinking. *If Winston's got a gun he could have killed you, too.*

"We've got to save Sandra."

"I know," Cam whispered. His hands released her and she felt bereft. "You stay here."

"Do you have a weapon?"

He didn't answer her. Instead he moved soundlessly, easily toward the car and positioned himself only a few feet from the man in the fedora.

Molly wanted to scream in frustration. He'd come to rescue her and now he was directly in the line of fire. She had to do something and there was only one thing she could do.

It was critical that the timing be perfect.

As Cam crouched behind the back end of the vehicle, Winston grabbed Sandra Tall Tree's arm and wrenched it behind her back.

"Get in the house, bitch and get me that money."

"I told you, Dwight. I don't have the money." Understandably she was starting to sound a little more uneasy.

"You goddam double-crosser, I want the money and I'll give you three seconds to get it for me. One," he counted off, like an irate preschool teacher, "two…"

Molly saw Cam start forward, saw Winston notice him and jerk around, still holding onto Sandra and she screamed at the top of her lungs. Her ears were still ringing when she heard the pop of a pistol and saw the threesome, now a jumble of arms and legs, drop to the stoop and roll onto the wet grass. Sandra's scream rivaled hers.

Molly rushed forward. If Winston had shot Cam, she would personally pummel him to death with her flashlight. But when she reached the pile of humans, they'd separated and Cam was on his feet, his arm around a sobbing Sandra Tall Tree. The body of Dwight Winston lay on the ground as still as death.

"Call the sheriff, Molly," Cam said, only slightly out of breath.

"Is he dead?"

"Call the sheriff."

"But he had the gun."

"Listen to me, Tiger Lily. Call. The. Sheriff."

"Omigod," Sandra moaned. "Omigod. You killed him, you son of a bitch."

Molly looked into Cam's closed face. She hadn't thought he had a gun.

"He must have shot himself," she murmured to the hysterical woman.

Sandra shrieked and cried. A moment later Davey Tall Tree, disheveled in his terrycloth bathrobe, stepped out onto the stoop. He blinked like a sleepy owl.

"Sandra, sweetheart," he said, in his mild way, "are you all right?"

She collapsed in a heap on the wet grass and Davey, good husband that he was, knelt down next to her and gathered her into his arms.

"Molly," Cam said, "I'll call Jake. Take Davey and his wife inside."

"Come on," she said to the sagama. "I'll make us all some hot chocolate."

It took a couple of hours of explanations and arguments but Jake decided not to bring charges against anyone. At least not then. The pistol belonged to Dwight Winston and there were only his finger prints on it. It seemed likely that he'd lost control of it when Cam jumped him and Molly had screamed. Sandra swore Dwight wouldn't have shot her or anyone else but since he was the number one suspect in Big Eddie's murder, no one really believed that.

Jake agreed to Davey's plea that he leave Sandra at home with her husband on the understanding that the chief would bring her down to the station in the morning for questioning.

Molly and Cam walked out to their cars a short

time later.

"I hope Jake's not making a mistake not to arrest Sandra," she said.

"He hasn't got anything on her. No stolen money, no eyewitness account that she shot her boyfriend. He didn't have much choice."

Molly felt sick. "If Dwight Winston did lose control of the weapon, it was probably because of either you or me."

"Yeah."

"Doesn't that make you feel guilty?"

"It makes me feel like Winston was an idiot. If you're gonna threaten someone with a gun you'd better know how to use it and how to prevent it being used against you."

"But he knew a lot about guns," Molly protested. "He killed Big Eddie with one shot to the head."

"We don't know for sure that he did it. It could have been Sandra. Or someone else."

Molly thought back to the scene she'd just witnessed, Davey with his arm around a dazed Sandra.

"She didn't do anything," he said, over and over to Jake. "She's not like that, is she Molly? She's a good woman."

She sighed. Poor Davey.

"Connie Black Squirrel wanted to marry him, you know. She's a widow and close to his age but not bad looking. Got kind of a sharp tongue."

Cam sent her an unreadable look.

"Too bad he went off the reservation."

Molly's heart twisted. His point was that she'd played it safe all those years ago. She'd avoided bullets, battles and babies. Suddenly she wanted him to know.

It would make no difference now and it would make him angry and probably sad but she wanted to tell him anyway. She wanted to be finished with one of her terrible secrets.

"Come on." Cam gripped her upper arm. "We're going home."

"Home?"

His eyes looked steely in the artificial light. "Back to your place."

She started to protest but the words died in her throat. She wanted him to go home with her. She needed him. And she needed a chance to tell him her secret. And then she remembered. "What about Sharon?"

"I'm not engaged, Lily," he said, quietly. "In fact, we've broken up. It was a mutual decision but Sharon wanted to keep it on the down low for awhile."

Her heart expanded.

"All right," she said. "Come home with me."

He followed her down the dirt road and the strong headlights of the Mercedes filled her with a sense of wellbeing. She'd have this one night with him, one night to salve old wounds and to forge a memory to live on for the rest of her life. It was an unbelievable gift.

Molly turned down the dirt road to her cottage and thrust the thought out of her mind. Just one night with Cam. She might not deserve it but she intended to take it.

He took the key from her and opened the door. Then he stood back and let her enter. Only a low light illuminated the cozy living area. She stood just inside the doorway and looked up at him.

New, harsh lines bracketed Cam's mouth. His sky

blue eyes filled with storms. The soaking rain of earlier had turned into a steady downpour. The night was cold, dark and wet and dangerous. So was the man. He cupped her face.

"I want you," he growled. "Now."

Molly's heart went crazy. She slid her fingers through his thick, wet hair. Cam's mouth met hers. Molly expected the kiss to be hard and fast, a quick prelude of the passion to come. Instead it was slow, thorough, and eminently rewarding, like one of Cam's slow smiles. He tasted her as if savoring a fine wine. He stroked area behind her teeth and he sipped at her warmth.

Long before he'd finished her knees had buckled. He supported her with his strong arms.

Finally he broke contact.

His breath was a little uneven but he seemed sturdy enough on his feet.

"How do you do that?" Her voice was little more than a gasp.

"Do what?"

"I've dissolved into a mass of quivering jelly but you're still calm, cool and collected."

"It's an act. I'm as hot as hell."

"Huh."

"Don't believe me?"

He pulled her to him, his hand pressing her against the hard, pulsing length of his erection.

"Wow."

Her awed response made him groan. He scooped her up in his arms and headed for the bedroom.

Suddenly Molly remembered he'd never been in there before.

"Don't turn on the lights."

The warning was too late. In the soft glow of the bedside lamps she knew what he saw. There was a native throw across the blue bedspread. A dream catcher hung above the pillows and one wall was full of framed photographs consisting of the Whitecloud family, the four Mollies, and the families of the babies she'd delivered.

He looked at her silently.

"I know what you're thinking. You were right about me. I never have had the courage to leave the rez."

His expression didn't change.

"You're wrong." His blue eyes twinkled. "I was thinking about what a slob you are. Don't you ever make your bed?"

"Never." She put her arms around his neck and brushed her lips against his hard jaw.

"I want you, Cam."

His eyes glittered. "Soon," he said. "First, a hot shower."

A hot shower? What was she, six? Before she could protest though, he'd stripped off his clothing. The sight of his lean, muscular frame and his obvious desire kept her distracted until he'd removed her clothing and positioned them both in her small shower. The hot spray felt good on her head and back but not nearly as good as the imprint of his need pressed against her stomach. Molly's blood raced and, once again, her knees felt weak. She compensated by twining her arms around his strong neck while he shampooed her hair.

Cam patted her dry then wrapped a towel around his waist.

"You aren't gonna need that," she said.

His grin was slow and full of anticipation. He found her robe on the back of the door and held it for her to step into. She sent him an uncertain look.

"We have plenty of time, Lily, and this time we're going to do it right starting with making sure you don't catch pneumonia."

He sat her down on the closed toilet seat then he used the blow dryer on the long, dark strands. When it was nearly dry he began to brush it. She watched in the mirror as he applied himself to the task, frowning, occasionally, when he found a potential tangle. She smiled. That was the Cam she remembered. Attentive to every detail. The warmth of the room, the physical contact and the pure luxury of having someone tending to her hair lulled Molly into a state of relaxation so complete that her eyes closed. She heard the dryer shut off and felt his hands in her now-dry hair.

"Sleepy?"

"Mmm."

He lifted her in his arms and carried her toward her bed. Molly buried her face in his neck. The tight rein she'd had on her emotions for so long broke free. He froze.

"Lily?"

She couldn't get out any words.

"Honey? Are you crying?"

It wasn't what they'd planned. Wasn't what she wanted. She was both mortified and disappointed but both emotions were quickly drowned in a flood of tears.

Chapter Eleven

Molly sobbed until her eyes were puffy and her throat was hoarse. She cried until she hiccupped and then she cried some more.

For a long time Cam sat on the side of the bed, his arms around her, and let her tears run down his neck and onto his shirt. Finally he drew her down next to him. His deep feeling of sadness was overlaid with a sense of peace and contentment. He didn't ask her any questions. He didn't even think of any questions. He just stroked her back and waited for the storm to pass.

When she cried herself to sleep he held very still but allowed his eyes to survey the room. The first thing he noticed was a rocking chair, a wooden one with a long back and cushions. It reminded him of the chair he had bought for Daisy's nursery. He'd spent plenty of hours rocking the baby to sleep before Elise's death and after it. He wondered why Molly had chosen a chair like that, one that took up so much room, for a such a small bedroom. Maybe she just liked to rock.

Or, maybe, she had bought it hoping that someday she'd have a baby of her own.

He permitted himself a brief fantasy of Molly in that chair rocking a baby with dark hair and blue eyes. His baby. A pipedream, of course. It always had been. Daisy had been a lucky hit. Even if he and Molly had a future, which they didn't, it was unlikely he could make her pregnant.

He listened to Molly's light, even breathing. Why was it that this one woman could turn him inside out? When she'd called him earlier tonight he'd gone home to check on Daisy but it hadn't taken him long to get back in the car and drive out to the rez. The dead raven was a threat against her. He knew she'd investigate on her own and he had no intention of letting her get hurt.

She'd been hurt plenty, he thought, as he gazed at her tear-stained cheek. All those tears. What had they been about? He knew she wasn't indifferent to him. Was it possible she regretted her decision all those years ago?

Cam didn't know. He didn't know how he felt about the future, whether he could learn to trust Tiger Lily again, whether he even wanted to do so. He only knew that she felt right in his arms and that, even though she was in a dead sleep, the feel of her soft curves against his body was making him hard.

And then her hand moved on his chest and he saw that her lashes, still stuck together from the earlier tears, were open.

"Cam," she whispered, "do you still want to make love with me?"

I'll always want to make love with you.

He smoothed a long, silky strand of black hair away from her face.

"Yes."

The hand on his chest began to work one of the buttons on his shirt.

"In that case," she said, "you have on way too many clothes."

The words sent a bolt of desire through his body

but he didn't make a move. Last time he'd taken her in a firestorm. This time he was determined to go slowly, to let her set the pace.

"Help me take them off."

She chuckled and continued to unbutton his shirt. Each time she freed a button she nuzzled his chest, her nose burrowing in the curly dark hair, her mouth sending electric shocks through his skin. She blazed a trail of fire down the center of his chest and, when she reached his belt, she stopped to unbuckle it. A moment later she'd found her way inside his zipper and the pressure of her warm mouth on his erection made him cry out.

"Cam?"

"Sorry." He fought to control his response. "I didn't mean to scare you."

"But you liked it?"

Didn't she know? Was it possible she'd never done this with Grey Wolf of anyone else?

"Yeah. I liked it a lot. Too much. That kind of contact drives a man to finish too quickly and I want to go slowly with you this time."

She rolled so that she was facing him, her indigo eyes clear and wide.

"I haven't done any of this in a long time," she said. "Tell me what you want me to do."

"Lie back," he whispered, "let me know what feels good." He slid his hand into the opening of her robe and cupped one small, resilient breast.

"Your body is perfect," he murmured, as he gently rubbed the taut nipple with his thumb, "small and perfectly proportioned. Sleek. Your body has always driven me crazy, Lily."

Her lashes fluttered and her breathing roughened as he continued to fondle one breast with his hand and used his tongue on the other one. He felt her fingers in his hair and he took one breast into his mouth and sucked, gently. A low moan came up out of her throat.

"Like that?"

"I-I didn't realize they were so sensitive."

He grinned at her. "Nature's put nerve endings in all sorts of interesting places to make sure the species will endure."

"Hmm," she said. Her eyes were closed and he knew she was barely listening. He kissed her neck and the hollow of her throat and behind her ears, then let his mouth, once again, drift down to her breasts. At the same time he slid his fingers between her legs, caressing the soft flesh on the insides of her thighs and easily finding the most sensitive flesh of all. He touched her there and she jerked.

"Oh my God, Cam."

He reveled in her responsiveness but wondered, again, why this all seemed like such a surprise. She'd been married for over a year and she was a beautiful woman. She must have had sexual experiences after her divorce from Grey Wolf. Her head thrashed back and forth as his fingers, practiced in the art, exerted just the right amount of pressure to bring a woman to the edge.

"Cam, Cam," she cried out, her eyes popping open. "I don't know what's happening to me. I need…something."

"It's okay," he soothed, coming up over her and continuing to work her with both his fingers and his mouth. She was wet but not wet enough. "I know what you need. I'm just making sure you're ready for it."

"I am ready for it. I want it now."

He started to chuckle at her demanding tone but her fingers, small and strong, curled around him. She squeezed and the sound in his throat turned into a groan.

"Dammit," he hissed. "I'm not going to be able to wait. I'm sorry, honey."

He slid into her with another harsh groan and she tightened her legs around him.

"Slow is overrated," she murmured. "I want you, now, Cam."

He began to move inside her. He closed his eyes and focused on exercising as much control as he could summon. He wanted to give her time to adjust to him, time to enjoy this, time to find her own pleasure but she arched up and rubbed against him and desire swamped him. When her nails bit into his shoulders and he heard her breath hitch, need plowed into him and he thrust into her, hard and fast and with a desperation he could not control.

"Come for me," he pleaded, barely able to say the words. "Come for me, Lily."

He knew it would be a near thing. He was too close. He felt her thighs tighten as her body gathered. He heard her breathy cries in his ear. He squeezed his eyes shut and tried to hold onto the rhythm he'd established, the one that would bring her satisfaction.

"Cam," she shrieked, as she peaked. He heard her call his name but an instant later his own climax hit. It was like being in the middle of a sky full of fireworks, like a rocket launch to the moon. It was the moment of unalloyed happiness he'd waited for all his life.

When he finally stopped shaking he gathered her

against him until her own tremors stopped. She fit perfectly but then he'd always known she would.

"Wow," she said, drowsily. "Wow."

He smiled against the top of her head.

"I couldn't have said it better myself."

****

Fingers of sunshine slipped through the blinds on Molly's east window. They gently touched Molly's face and she lifted her eyelids, which felt unaccountably heavy until she recalled the bout of crying the night before. She should probably apologize to Cam for that but, at the moment, she was just enjoying the warmth and comfort in the cozy bed.

The comfortable sense of wellbeing ended seconds later, destroyed by a sudden attack of nausea.

"Oh, no." She struggled to her feet, staggered toward the bathroom, flung open the door and launched at the toilet bowl. She discovered that space was occupied when she got herself tangled in a pair of bare, hairy legs.

"What the hell?"

There was no time to apologize or explain.

"Move," she yelped.

Cam had good instincts. Or maybe it was his previous experience with a pregnant wife. He got out of the way in record time and the contents of Molly's stomach swished into the bowl.

Two points.

She didn't have time to savor her accuracy. The next wave hit immediately. As she retched and hurled she felt him lift the hair out of her face and off her sweat-soaked neck. Long minutes later she felt settled enough to get off her aching knees and rest her back

181

against the cool tiles of the wall. She closed her eyes, hoping that, against all odds, when she opened them again that both the nausea and the man would be gone. She was not up to any explanations at the moment.

There was no miracle. She opened her eyes to find him leaning against the wall, his arms crossed, staring at her with those sky blue eyes. She closed her own eyes again. This was no more than she deserved. Her sins were finally coming home to roost.

And then she felt the butterfly light touch of his fingertips on her cheek. She moaned, fully aware that she didn't deserve his concern.

"Again?"

She didn't know. She wished she could just remain there on the bathroom tiles until she knew whether she'd be sick again and how on earth she was going to explain this to Cam but she knew she couldn't.

"I'm all right now," she said. "Thanks for your, uh, help."

"It was no trouble," he said, with a crooked smile. "I was right here."

She felt a rush of heat and humiliation.

"We've gotten awfully intimate, awfully fast," she muttered.

"I didn't mind," he said, smoothing the hair off her forehead. "It feels right."

Her heart twisted. It wasn't right. There were too many secrets between them. Too much betrayal. And it was all on her side.

She realized he'd been naked when she burst in before. Now he was wearing jeans and nothing else and he looked sinfully sexy. Not that she was in any condition, physically or emotionally to do anything about that.

"C'mon," he offered her a hand. "Let's get some clothes on you."

She felt a rush of heat. *Good grief.* She was naked, too.

"You know," he said, as he lifted her to her feet and put an arm around her waist to help her out to the bedroom, "over the past twelve years, I've spent a fair amount of time imagining us, you and me, in various settings. None of those was a bathroom."

She started to smile but another wave of nausea punched her. She hurried back to the toilet, balanced on her sore knees and gripped the sides of the porcelain bowl. Once again he held back her hair. Afterwards, he got her a cool washcloth and a glass of water. She sipped just enough to clear the taste out of her mouth.

"Thanks. I think I can make it back to bed."

He helped her to her feet and out into the bedroom where he eased her into a nightgown.

"Looks like you picked up a touch of the flu."

It was a natural assumption and almost certainly wrong. She felt a surge of guilt.

"You're pale again," Cam said, quietly. "Feeling sick?"

Not in the way you mean.

"No. I'm all right."

"Does your head ache? Your throat hurt?"

She shook her head.

"Well, maybe it isn't flu," he said, in a light voice. "Maybe you're pregnant."

It could have been a joke. Or not. He probably suspected her of a recent affair with someone else. For some reason that hurt terribly.

Nausea boiled up again and she made a gagging sound.

"Hang on," he said. He disappeared and returned moments later with a plate of soda crackers. "We need to settle your stomach."

Soda crackers, the best known remedy for morning sickness.

"Try them," he said, as she stared at the food. "They always worked for Elise."

When she was pregnant with Daisy. Molly's heart hurt. She picked up a cracker and nibbled on it.

"Is there any chance?"

The question seemed innocent enough but Molly knew that it was not idle curiosity. She was going to have to tell him the truth. She wished she had more time to figure out how to do it.

Here's the deal, Cam. I found out about your sperm sample at the Spotwood Fertility Clinic and I had myself inseminated so, yes, I could be pregnant.

She stared into his hooded blue eyes. She couldn't do it.

"I haven't been with anyone but you," she said, tiredly. The blue eyes flashed.

"Since when?"

She hadn't expected the question but she wasn't going to lie.

"Since the last time I was with you."

"You mean at the casino."

She closed her eyes and leaned back against the pillow.

"Since the spinney."

"What?"

It was time to tell him. At least some of it.

"You were married, for Chrissakes."

"Daniel married me to protect my parents and my reputation. I was seventeen and pregnant."

"WHAT?"

"There's no easy way to tell you this." She knew she should choose her words more carefully but she was too tired, too sick and she'd waited too long. "You aren't sterile."

"All but."

He hadn't yet grasped the essential point so she took the opportunity to probe.

"What made you get tested in the first place?"

"Elise wasn't getting pregnant. Her father wanted a grandson and she was very anxious to provide him with one.

"She set up tests for both of us at a fertility clinic in Boston and they discovered the low-motility. The problem was with me."

Molly didn't understand. She knew perfectly well Cam was capable of siring a child.

"Was Elise's father disappointed when Daisy turned out to be a girl?"

"They both were."

"Elise just wanted to try again. She even considered gender selection."

Molly winced. As far as she knew gender selection, a process sometimes called 'designer babies' consisted of aborting fetuses of the 'wrong' gender.

"What happened?"

"Elise was killed in a car accident. Her father got involved with a younger woman with the intent of providing himself with a male heir but nothing came of it and he's back with Elise's mother."

Molly felt a surge of sympathy for everyone involved.

"What a miserable family,"

Cam said nothing and she felt guilty. She was talking about the family he'd married into, the parents of the woman he'd loved.

"I talked to her once, you know."

"When?" The one-syllable word was infused with tension.

"She was in your dorm room when I called. She told me not to contact you again because she was your girlfriend."

"When was this?"

"That fall. A few months after you'd left for school."

His tanned face suddenly looked pale and drawn.

"You called me? Why?"

She sighed. She'd already given him part of the story. It was time to tie up the loose ends. She wished she could do it without hurting him. She wished she could do it with a clear conscience. In any case, she had to do it.

"I called to tell you I was pregnant."

His eyes darkened and he lost what little color he had left.

"I found out about a month after you'd gone. I didn't know what to do. I knew we were too young to get married but James and Muriel had done so much for me. I couldn't shame them. I called to discuss it with you. That's when Elise told me she was your girlfriend."

"And you believed her?"

Molly shrugged her shoulders.

"I didn't know what to believe but you hadn't contacted me and, like I said, I knew it wouldn't work between us. I didn't try to call again."

"Goddam you," he muttered. "Goddam you, Molly."

She probably deserved that. In the thirteen years that had passed since she'd failed to tell him, she'd come to realize that the father always deserves a chance to know.

"I did the wrong thing," she admitted, "but it turned out for the best, Cam. I lost the baby. If you'd left school and come back to marry me we'd have ended up divorced, too. We were too young for all that responsibility."

"You mean I was too young."

She looked at him steadily. "Yes. That's what I mean."

His glittered like hard, blue diamonds. "I will never forgive you."

She recognized helplessness, guilt, frustration and pain but still the words hurt.

"I know."

She waited while he worked out some of his agitation by pacing the small floor of her bedroom. He thrust his fingers through his thick, dark hair and rubbed his palm against the back of his neck.

"You lied to me by omission."

"Yes."

"And, apparently, Elise lied."

"I don't know. It's possible the test revealed slow motility."

"For God's sake, Molly! You and I had sex once. I'd say that makes my sperm hale and hearty."

"But why would Elise lie?"

His shoulders slumped and all the fight went out of him, like a helium balloon on the morning after. She realized, suddenly, he'd just suffered a double blow.

"I don't know. Maybe she didn't. It hardly matters now." His eyes came up to her face again. "But if I am potent, you have something new to worry about."

His eyes were hard and accusing.

I will never forgive you.

She couldn't tell him what she'd done. Not now.

"It was only once."

"Twice. It was twice, Molly. That time at the casino might have been clumsy and fast but I came inside you just like I did last night. There's no five-second rule in fucking."

She winced at the harsh word.

"That would be a real déjà vu for you, wouldn't it? For the second time you'd be pregnant without a husband, stuck with a baby that didn't belong on the rez. Think Grey Wolf would marry you again? Or would you just cut to the chase and have an abortion?"

The cruel words cut at her like knives. She knew they were borne of his frustration and his anger with her. She shook her head.

"I wouldn't have an abortion and I wouldn't marry Daniel. Not that he'd have me again. Let's not borrow trouble, Cam. Let's part as friends."

He stared at her a long minute.

"It wasn't just that we were too young, was it? It was that we were too different. You didn't want to give up your place on the rez."

She met his harsh glare.

"That's right."

"Damn, Molly." This time he sounded more hurt than angry. "If there'd been a child would you have let him believe Grey Wolf was his father?"

She'd never thought that far ahead. Nausea roiled through her, this time caused by guilt and regret.

"I suppose so."

It wasn't strictly the truth. She'd never intended to stay married to Daniel nor he to her. The point didn't seem particularly relevant now.

Emotions flashed in the blue eyes.

"When, exactly was the miscarriage?"

Technically it hadn't been a miscarriage but a premature birth. She didn't want to tell him.

"Come on, Molly. No more lies."

"At five months."

Pain flashed across his face. Of course. Cam knew something about pregnancy. He'd know that it hadn't been a typical case. She needed to explain. "Placental abruption. The placenta detached too early."

His face retained its pallor but lost some of its harshness.

"I'm sorry, Tiger Lily. It must have been hell."

It was all hell—losing the baby, losing Cam. It had happened a long time ago but it had never stopped hurting.

She didn't have to tell him. He'd always been able to read her thoughts and emotions with ease.

"That's why you became a midwife, isn't it? That's why you got behind the casino. You wanted the income to build a clinic so this would never happen to anyone else." Cam dug his finger and thumb into his eye sockets. "Christ. I should've been here."

"You were eighteen. You wouldn't have known

any better than I what was going on, Cam. It wouldn't have made any difference."

"It would have made a difference. You'd have been living near a hospital, not out on the godforsaken rez."

She held very still trying to absorb the pain. He'd hit on the chief source of her guilt about the baby. She should have been closer to good medical care. His face was a hard mask.

"I've got to get out of here."

She knew it was time for him to go and she wanted that, too. She also wanted him to stay.

"Yes," she said.

"You'll be all right?"

Her heart squeezed. Right now she was his worst nightmare but he was still concerned.

"I'll be fine. I'll call my mother if I need anything."

The pain of watching him leave was making her hear things, specifically an odd pounding.

"Damn," he said. "there's someone at the front door."

Molly closed her eyes.

"It's okay. I'll get rid of whoever it is and then I'll go."

A moment later Molly heard a jumble of voices and then the bedroom door burst open.

"Hi, Molly!" Daisy's high-pitched voice rang through the air. "Hallie and me camed-ded to see you." She pulled on the leash in her hand. "Wilbur, too."

"Daisy and I heard about the excitement at the Tall Tree's," Hallie explained. Her eyes looked a quiet question and Molly knew the curiosity was as much about Cam's presence in her home as about the events at the *sagama's* house. "We wanted to make sure you were okay."

"Can I get up on the bed?" Daisy asked.

"No," Cam said.

"Sure," Molly said.

Hallie lifted the child up onto the bed but she had the final word.

"Wilbur stays on the floor."

****

Cam watched the woman and the girl together and his heart exploded. Not, he realized, for the obvious reasons, that Daisy might have been *their* child although he'd always wished it were true. Molly's hair, dark, like his, contrasted sharply with Daisy's sun-colored curls.

It was because of Tiger Lily's smile.

Without even trying, Daisy had elicited Molly's magical smile, the one that had, long years ago, been reserved only for Cam. He hadn't realized until this minute that she'd been holding back.

Jealous. He was jealous of his own daughter. *God.* He was a sad case.

"You need to get off the bed," he said, more brusquely than he'd intended. "Molly's sick."

Molly's dark blue eyes met his but she didn't contradict him. She just brushed a blonde curl behind Daisy's ear.

"I'm so glad you came to see me, darlin'," she said to the child. "But I don't want you to get sick, too. Will you go to Daddy and talk to me from there?"

Daisy disregarded the request. She slithered right back to Molly's arms. Despite Cam's irritation his heart softened. Daisy had a mind of her own. Just like him.

And they had something else in common, too.

They both loved Molly Whitecloud.

Cam balled up his fists. It was past time to face that particular truth.

He understood now, finally, why she'd abandoned him all those years ago to marry Grey Wolf. He could feel the last of his resentment evaporate. She'd been a teenager, desperate to save her position in her adopted family, desperate to save that family's reputation. Cam imagined there was even more to it than that. Cam's father had not been thrilled with his son's obsession with the Indian girl. Had Jesse Outlaw said something to her? And then there had been her fear. She'd been afraid to leave the safety of the Penobscots, the safety of the rez. How could he blame her? She'd been in an impossible position.

He'd relived over and over the moment he'd arrived at her parents' trailer that long ago December only to be told she'd married Daniel Grey Wolf. He'd held onto the sense of injury for so long. He probed his psyche like he'd test out a sore gum after surgery.

The anger was no longer there.

The relief was acute and tempered only by the knowledge that she might not have forgiven him. It was he who'd abandoned her, who had failed to call after their first and only intimacy, who'd let her cope with the frightening situation alone.

No. Not alone. She'd had Grey Wolf.

"Hallie and me and Wilbur brung you some bread," Daisy was telling Molly. "Asia made it and some soup and we didn't bring Robert."

"I appreciate the food," Molly said, gently, "but you could have brought Robert. You know I care about him, don't you, Daze? He's your cousin so that alone makes him very important."

A new pain sliced through Cam's battered heart. Molly loved Daisy, too but she was choosing her words carefully. She didn't want him to think she was presuming with his daughter.

When he'd fallen in love with Tiger Lily all those years ago he'd thought he'd be happy for the rest of his life. Somehow, he'd made that life into a train wreck.

"Jeez, Molly," Hallie said. She collapsed in the chair. "Big night for you. First you delivered the baby at the casino then you saved Sandra Tall Tree's life. You deserve a lot more than soup!"

"Cam was the real hero," Molly said. "He kept Winston from shooting Sandra."

Cam frowned. He still wasn't sure what had happened on the Tall Tree's stoop. A thought occurred to him.

"How do you know all of this already," he asked his sister-in-law.

"You didn't come home last night," she said, "so I called Sharon and she mentioned the call from Molly. Apparently she talked to Jake."

Cam winced. Everyone still thought he was almost engaged to Sharon and here he was in Molly Whitecloud's bedroom.

"Daniel and Sharon are here, by the way," Hallie said, eyeing him. "They were concerned about you and Molly."

Cam met Molly's gaze. He'd told her it was over between himself and the innkeeper but maybe she didn't believe him. And why the hell did Grey Wolf keep showing up? He thrust his fingers through his hair again.

He needed to get out of there.

He needed time to think.

"I'll go talk to them," he said. A minute later he was in Molly's driveway.

"How is Molly," Sharon asked, leaning toward the driver's side.

"Sick," he said. "I'm going home."

Daniel Grey Wolf's dark eyes studied Cam's face.

"Take Sharon home," he said, quietly. "I'll look after Molly."

Emotions welled up in Cam and he realized he'd been wrong.

He was still jealous of Grey Wolf. He was still angry at Molly.

Chapter Twelve

"Cam spent the night here?"

It was a personal question but Hallie was a good friend. Molly knew she cared about her and she cared about Cam.

"I fell apart after the shooting. He waited to make sure I was all right."

"I wanna go see the garden," Daisy announced. "Hallie said there would be daisies and lilies and forget-me-dots."

****

At lunchtime, Daniel prepared a meal for Molly, Hallie and Daisy. He sliced the bread and warmed up the soup made of harvest vegetables. The foursome sat at the table. Wilbur, in a nest of blankets, watched a taped episode of Emeril LaGasse as the chef prepared a pork-free Cajun specialty. Molly tried to focus on her visitors but she couldn't stop thinking about how she had told Cam about the lost baby and then he'd left, abruptly and with Sharon Johnson.

She hoped he'd told her the truth, that his relationship with the red-haired beauty was over. Molly hated to have hurt the other woman. She hated even more the prospect of Cam's marriage to Sharon.

For the first time she wondered whether she could stay on the rez. Even if she wasn't pregnant, a possibility that seemed less and less likely, she didn't know whether she could spend the next thirty years watching Cam raise his family with Sharon.

Daniel insisted on washing the dishes with Daisy while Hallie visited with Molly. The two women had always gotten along well but today their conversation dwindled to silence.

Molly saw the concern in Hallie's eyes.

"You look like you could use a nap," Hallie said. "It's time for us to leave. I need to get back to Robert."

Minutes later she and Daisy were heading back to town in Daniel's truck.

"You didn't have to stay," Molly told him, for the third time. "I'm just going to sleep."

"I've been meaning to check on the wiring," he said. "This is a good opportunity to do it."

"Daniel, if this really is my house, that should be my responsibility."

"I don't mind, *nizwia*. Go get some rest."

She wished he would leave because his presence reminded her of past mistakes and because it reminded her that she belonged on the rez as did he. Cam and Hallie and Sharon were friends but they belonged to a different world.

She went to bed and buried her head under a pillow that smelled like barf and Cam. Hell and heaven.

She might be sick or she might be pregnant or she might be tired.

She certainly was depressed.

She awoke when the late afternoon sun filtered through the blinds on the window that faced the west.

Molly got up, ran a brush through her tangled hair, dressed in jeans and a blue plaid flannel shirt. She found Daniel in the garden snipping the dead heads off the summer roses and bundling the stalks of irises and tulips that had bloomed in mid-summer.

"Wow," she said. "I've really let things go around here, haven't I?"

"You've been preoccupied," he said, mildly.

"I know. But no more. I'm ready to get my real life back."

He looked at her, compassion in the dark eyes.

"And the baby?"

Her heart tripped as she remembered the morning sickness.

"I'll deal with that if it happens," she said, firmly.

"You know I'll be around," he said. "Whatever you need."

For once his willingness to set aside his own needs in favor of hers, annoyed her.

"You've sacrificed enough for me," she said. "It's time for you to have a family of your own, Daniel."

She'd never spoken to him like that and he looked faintly surprised.

"I didn't see it as a sacrifice."

"I know. But it was. And now you have a chance for happiness."

He dug up a bed of weeds as he answered. She saw his broad shoulders tense.

"You're talking about Sharon."

"I can see that you care for her. I think it's mutual."

He shook his head.

"It wouldn't work, *Kolokhas*." Raven.

The word made Molly wonder, again, if Sandra Tall Tree had left the dead bird on her doorstep. Had she been a party to Big Eddie DiMarco's murder? Was Davey harboring a viper who would turn on him? She wondered whether Jake had found any proof that Winston had shot the casino manager.

Molly turned her face to the horizon and watched the setting sun play hide and seek with the colorful autumn leaves. Yesterday at this time she hadn't even received the ominous shoebox, the shooting hadn't happened and the magical night with Cam Outlaw was still ahead of her.

Now everything was all over.

"Sharon and Cam have broken up," she said, abruptly.

"I know. It doesn't matter. I'm not right for her."

"Why? Because she's not an Indian?"

"That." He spoke without rancor. It was almost impossible to make Daniel lose his temper. "And I'm too old to start a family."

"That's ridiculous."

He shook his head.

"You think she still loves Cam?"

It was a ridiculous question. What woman wouldn't love Cam Outlaw?

"They are from the same world. I don't know whether they'll get back together. I imagine that will depend, in part, on you."

"This isn't about me or Cam. It's about you, Daniel. You love her, don't you?"

"That's neither here nor there, Molly. And, I'd like you to change the subject."

Molly felt a terrible emptiness under her heart and this time it was for her friend. He'd spent all these years taking care of everyone else and when personal happiness finally showed up in the person of a tall, red-haired innkeeper, he intended to turn his back on it.

Molly got up slowly and moved toward Daniel. She took his callused hand and held it.

"Don't do this. Tell her how you feel. I wouldn't be a bit surprised to find out she loves you back."

He squeezed her hand and then disentangled his own.

"Next summer you should plant some daisies."

****

Cam turned onto Rural Route Two and left the rez behind without speaking. He was lost in his thoughts and, when Sharon spoke, he glanced at her in surprise. He'd forgotten he wasn't alone.

"How long have you cared about Molly?"

He didn't pretend to misunderstand. What was the point?

"Forever. All my life. Thirteen years."

"Oh, wow. That explains so much. Was it just a matter of bad timing?"

"Something like that."

They rode in silence for a few minutes, each thinking their own thoughts.

"Do you think Dwight Winston shot DiMarco and then himself?"

Cam frowned. "Why?"

"Well, it doesn't exactly make sense, does it? I mean, if Winston was such a crack shot that he could make it look like a professional hit on DiMarco, how could he have lost control of his own gun?"

The same thought had occurred to Cam.

After he dropped Sharon at the inn he stopped at the sheriff's office but his brother-in-law was out.

Well, hell. He went to his own office and put in eight hours of badly needed work and finally he went home.

Daisy was there and Hallie, Baz and Robert as well as Asia nevertheless the big Victorian seemed less like home than the small cottage on the rez.

Over the next few days Cam compared notes with Jake and with Grey Wolf. They found proof of fraud on the part of Ed DiMarco on the purloined laptop but no provable mob connections.

Nothing on the laptop indicated that Dwight Winston had been any more than what he'd appeared to be—the manager of the Blackbird Spa. An autopsy provided the rest of the information. He'd been shot in the heart with the pistol registered to him.

"It seems incredible that he'd have shot himself," Cam said to Jake. The two had met in the sheriff's office.

"The bullet came from that gun and it was the only weapon on the scene."

"Right. But neither Molly nor I saw the pistol in his hands."

"And Sandra Tall Tree claims she never touched it."

"Think she's telling the truth?"

Jake shrugged his big shoulders. "There are no fingerprints and she wasn't wearing gloves, right?"

Cam nodded.

"Makes a nice tidy case," the sheriff said, leaning back and stretching his long arms over his head. "There's no one left to prosecute. Of course, the money's not accounted for."

"Maybe Big Ed or Winston hid it somewhere."

"That's our working theory." Jake's voice was dry. "That was a pretty traumatic scene out at the Tall

Trees," Jake said, changing the subject, slightly. "How's Molly?"

"Fine. I guess. I haven't seen her."

Jake nodded. "You never did tell me how you happened to be out there."

Cam had avoided thinking about Molly for the past few days. Her explanation about the past had made him take another look at what had happened all those years ago. He knew now that he loved her. That he'd always loved her. He just didn't know whether it was too late or whether she would be willing to live off the rez.

He forced himself to tell Jake about the dead raven in the shoebox. And the daisy.

"So you thought your daughter was being threatened and you went out to the rez to check things out. In the dark. And rain."

"No." Cam gritted his teeth for a moment. "I was afraid Molly would do something crazy."

"Like casing the Tall Trees."

"Or like marching up to the door and demanding to speak with Sandra."

"I'll bet she didn't expect to see Dwight and Sandra standing on the front stoop."

"No."

There was a brief pause.

"Hallie told Lucy you stayed out at her cottage all night. Again." Cam had stayed there several months earlier the night his partner in the casino, Nate Packer, had been killed. His reluctance to reveal his whereabouts had led to his continued position at the top of the suspects list.

"Anything illegal about that?"

Jake lifted his big hands. "Not a thing. I'm just

saying the women know."

Cam nodded. At the moment, that was the least of his problems. He needed to figure out what he wanted from Molly. And he needed to find out the truth about his late wife. Had Elise lied to him?

Suddenly Cam knew that the two problems were connected. He couldn't proceed with Molly until he knew whether or not he was infertile.

That night, after he put Daisy to bed, he hunkered down in his study. After the move from Boston, he'd filed most of his business papers but he'd dragged his feet on his personal ones. He had not been ready to re-live the painful years with Elise.

He hauled out several boxes. It took only a few minutes to find the eight-by-eleven envelope with the Spotswood Fertility Clinic logo. His heart accelerated as he leafed through the half dozen sheets of paper and he frowned when he came to the one with his signature. *Damn.* He'd given the clinic permission to use the leftover sample. He remembered now. They'd called just after Elise had died and, still in shock, he'd signed a Faxed consent form.

Why? Why had he done it and why had they wanted lazy sperm?

If it was lazy. He'd gotten Molly pregnant the first and only time they'd made love.

He picked up the phone to leave a message for the clinic director. Whether it was sluggish or not, he wanted to withdraw his sperm from circulation. He no longer saw it as a viscous mass of seminal plasma but as part of two beloved souls, Daisy and the child who'd died.

****

The morning sickness that had struck with such violence did not return. Molly told herself it didn't mean anything. As a midwife, she was something of an authority on morning sickness and she knew that it followed no rules. It would probably attack again when she least expected it.

She used the period of good health to check on her patients and her parents. She refused to think about the night she'd spent with Cam Outlaw. It was a relief to have told him the old secret. It had been gratifying to know that he still wanted her. It was clear, if unsurprising, that he did not want her again. She reminded herself nothing had changed. She'd never expected a second chance with him. That ship had sailed.

Molly stopped by the community center to talk to Davey. She'd been worried about him after the shooting. He told her Sandra seemed to be all right, if somewhat subdued, and that she'd gone to New York for a few days for what he called "retail therapy."

It seemed a little insensitive to have watched your lover shoot himself and then go shopping but Molly knew Sandra was an unhappy young woman. Maybe a new pair of shoes would help. She decided against mentioning the dead raven to Davey.

"Say, Molly," he said, as she stood to leave, "did the sheriff ever find that money?"

"Not as far as I know."

He nodded. "That Dwight Winston probably hid it somewhere." He sighed, dolefully "I think Sandra and I will be all right," he said, "now that the casino's closed. It was the casino that was the bad influence on Sandra. She's very young, you know. And she was an orphan.

She never had anything."

"I know."

The pinched look on his pudgy face pulled at her heart. As far as his marriage was concerned he was the Pillsbury dough boy headed for the oven.

"I like for her to have nice things," he added. "And it's important that the wife of the sagama look good."

She thought about that. No one on the rez ever dressed to impress. It was the first time she'd even heard anyone discuss the importance of clothes.

"Sandra always looks nice," she pointed out. "When she gets back I'd like to talk to her about the crafts co-op." Maybe Sandra would find some happiness at getting involved in a charitable project with other young woman.

"Sure," Davey said

Molly stopped in at the Trading Post, the market attached to the community center but she couldn't concentrate on shopping. She kept thinking about Davey's odd marriage. Why had the beautiful half-breed woman married a dumpy, middle-aged man like Davey? He'd been a tribal cop in a place where there was little to no crime and he'd been elected chief, mainly because no one else raised his hand.

Was Sandra the deprived orphan Davey made her out to be or was she playing a deep game? Had she known Dwight Winston before her marriage? Had she known Big Eddie?

Molly was almost certain that Sandra was behind the dead raven. Was that threat neutralized now? Or was Cam's young daughter at risk?

She wished she had the right to keep an eye on Daisy but she didn't and she had to trust Cam.

Suddenly she missed the child and her father so much it was like a pain in her heart. She tried to shake it off as she searched for groceries. She needed bananas and oranges. She was definitely low on vitamin C. On her way to the fruits and vegetables she passed the shelf devoted to personal hygiene and there, between the lip gloss, cotton swabs and toothpaste was a lone pink-and-white box. Molly picked it up. It was time to face the truth.

There was no reason to be self conscious about buying an early pregnancy test, still, Molly was relieved to see silent Hank Deerkill behind the counter instead of Maggie "Magpie" Woods, the cashier who considered it her personal mission to keep everyone on the rez informed about everyone else's business.

It was a good sign.

She'd reached the vegetable aisle in her progress toward the counter when the little bell over the door jingled.

"Hey, Molly," called out Maggie. "Tell me all about the shooting out at Davey's place, will ya? I've been waiting forever for you to come in." The older woman's sharp black eyes glittered with curiosity and Molly reacted without thinking, snatching the E.P.T. box out of her basket and thrusting it behind a can of creamed corn.

When Molly had finished a brief recital of events, Maggie produced a basket of deerskin bracelets.

"Think you could sell these in Eden?"

Molly examined the hand-tooled, leather jewelry. It was rustic but striking in its way.

"I'm almost sure we can. Eventually we're hoping to set up an online storefront. That way we can sell to people all over the country. Can I take these with me?"

She was, in fact, heading into town to deliver to the co-op Ellen Waters's hand-woven baskets, Gwen Racer's beaded necklaces and the carved totems created by Charlie Watson. She stopped at her parents' trailer to pick up the dream catchers Muriel fashioned out of hemp and beads and feathers.

The Indians believed if a dream catcher was nailed to the wall above a bed, positive dreams would slip through a hole in the center then slide down to the sleeper below. The bad dreams, not knowing the way, were supposed to get tangled in the knots and feathers and expire with the first rays of the sun.

Molly, who had one of Muriel's dream catchers above her bed, believed in the tradition, just as she believed in the other Native rituals. She knew her family's ways had startled Cam when she'd first met him all those years ago. He'd thought them quaint but she knew the life he wanted to share with Molly would be based on concrete reality and it would be centered in town.

Molly hadn't worried about the discrepancy between them—not until she'd discovered she was pregnant.

Farrell's Pharmacy on Eden's Main Street was empty except for Agatha Farrell, the mother of the present proprietor. The matriarch, sixty, plump and inquisitive, squinted at the E.P.T. kit through her thick bifocals. Molly knew the older lady would assume the kit was for a patient as the midwife was unmarried.

"How's the baby business?"

"Booming," Molly replied. "We had a bumper crop at the last full moon."

Mrs. Farrell chuckled. "When will it be your turn, dear?"

It was a friendly question and one Molly had heard often enough. She found a smile for the older woman and delivered her stock answer.

"I should probably find a husband first."

Mrs. Farrell nodded. "Don't wait too long, child. Life goes by fast."

Molly swallowed around the lump in her throat as she climbed back into the Jeep and deposited the brown bag containing her purchase on the passenger's seat. She'd turned into a leaky faucet lately. The probability that her rampant emotions stemmed from pregnancy did not comfort her.

The crafts cooperative called the Maine Event was located on Main Street in the space previously occupied by the family-owned White's Department Store, an institution that had closed its doors years earlier, after Eden lost its last textile mill.

Sharon, Hallie, Molly and several others had chosen the spot for its central location and its luxurious floor space. They'd opted to set it up as though it were actually someone's living room with bookshelves filled with handcrafted items, pictures on the wall, handwoven rugs on the floor and handmade wooden furniture. One alcove held the display of silver jewelry and another, the colorful Norwegian sweaters Mrs. Cat had made. As Molly pulled into a parking space behind the co-op, her heart sank as she spotted Sharon's forest green SUV. It looked like she was going to pay for her good luck at the pharmacy with an awkward encounter here. Whatever the relationship between Sharon and Cam, Molly felt guilty about sharing intimacies with a man the other woman had cared for so recently. And she wondered about Sharon and Daniel. Did the innkeeper feel anything for Molly's own ex?

She lectured herself as she climbed out of the Jeep. It was an unfortunate coincidence that she and Sharon had the same taste in men. What was important, she reminded herself, sternly, was that she and Sharon were both colleagues and friends and nothing would alter that.

The scent of peppermint tea, the soothing sounds of a recorded string quartet and Sharon Johnson met her met her just inside the back door.

"Molly! I didn't expect you today."

Sharon looked lovely, as usual, in a pair of designer jeans, a dashing emerald-colored poet's shirt with her brilliant hair tied back in a matching emerald scarf. Her hazel eyes sparkled and there was a faint flush under her freckles. She really was the most striking woman.

"Are you feeling better?"

Dang. The reminder that Sharon had been at her cottage when she was sick, that she'd gone home with Cam Outlaw and that she, Molly, hadn't heard from him in the subsequent five days, stung.

"Much better," Molly said, pleasantly. "Thank you for asking." She set a load of baskets down on the front desk.

"Got anything else in the Jeep?"

"A few things."

"Great, I'll go get them."

Molly flashed on the pink-and-white early pregnancy test in its brown paper bag. Sharon would think it, too, was a craft for sale.

"No! I mean, no thanks. I can carry the rest. Is that peppermint tea?"

"It is. Will you join me in a cup?"

Molly didn't love peppermint tea and she felt more awkward than she'd thought possible with Sharon. It wasn't just guilt, she realized. She felt jealous. *Good grief.* She was annoyed with herself and her mood didn't improve when the tea tasted like the dregs of the Penobscot River.

"You know, I love your mother's dream catchers," Sharon said. "I plan to buy one for each room at the *Garden of Eden.* I like the tradition behind them and I think they really reflect the Native American culture of this area."

Molly was surprised. Most of the business owners in Eden were tolerant of the reservation's residents but few actively sought out ties to the Blackbird community. The redhead seemed to read her mind.

"I've learned quite a bit from Daniel's research," she said. "He's been kind enough to share it with me."

Molly nodded. "Daniel's a kind man. I have to say, though, as long as I've known him, he's never offered to share any research with me." She smiled at Sharon. "It sounds as if you two are getting along."

The lovely smile faded and the bright light went out of Sharon's light brown eyes.

"We are good friends," she said. "That's all."

"That's a shame." Molly spoke impulsively. "Oh, I beg your pardon. I didn't mean to get personal."

"It's okay. I think it's a shame, too. He doesn't think we'd suit."

"Men," Molly said, with asperity, a comment that made her companion laugh.

"What about you and Cam? I understand you knew one another a long time ago. When I realized he'd spent the night at your cottage I couldn't help thinking maybe something was starting up again."

A familiar lump formed in Molly's throat and she shook her head.

"You know how it is with your first love," she said, lightly. "There's always a fantasy that it was the most important relationship. We spent a little time together at the casino and, I think, found some closure."

She couldn't believe what she was saying to Sharon. Lies, all lies. And for no apparent reason. It sounded as if things were finished between Cam and Sharon.

"Did they ever find the money that was in the casino safe?"

Molly shook her head. "Not as far as I know."

"I suppose Dwight Winston must have hidden it somewhere."

Molly had a sudden vivid memory of Winston's furious last words.

Get in the house, bitch. Get me the money!

"I don't think Winston had it," she said, thoughtfully.

"Well, maybe it was Big Ed."

"Maybe."

But if it had been Big Eddie, wouldn't someone have found the money after he died? If not for the money, why was he killed? It didn't make sense.

"I keep thinking about poor Sandra Tall Tree," Sharon said. "People are saying she was Dwight Winston's lover. Not only did she witness him shooting himself but now her husband knows all about her affair."

"I'm hoping things will settle down out on the rez," Molly said, noncommittally. "When the casino reopens we'll get a fresh start."

"A fresh start." Sharon repeated the words as if trying them out on her lips. "Molly, I'm going to ask you a really personal question and you don't have to answer me. Is there any chance you and Daniel might remarry?"

Whatever she'd expected it wasn't that.

"No. No chance at all. Daniel married me when I was seventeen to help me out of a situation. He's always been like an older brother to me."

Sharon nodded. "That's what he said. And yet, I know how much he loves you. And, Molly, again I know this is none of my business, but a family—a child—would mean so much to him. And he'd make such a fine father."

Molly ached for the other woman. She wanted to wring Daniel's stubborn neck for refusing to see the gift being offered. She realized, suddenly, that she and Daniel suffered from the same belief that the cultures wouldn't mix.

"I've always thought he'd be a good dad," she said. "I hope he'll get the chance. But, Sharon, there's no chance that it will be with me."

The hazel eyes searched hers.

"And that nausea you had last week?"

"The flu," Molly said, firmly. "Just the flu.

She could hardly explain that it might have been morning sickness without raising the question of how, exactly, she might have gotten into such a delicate state. She should never have helped herself to that sperm but she knew if she had a chance to rewrite history, she'd do the same thing again. She still wanted Cam's baby.

And she still wanted Cam.

Molly drove slowly through the small town. Preoccupied as she was, she couldn't fail to notice the commotion in the town square. People were hauling bales of hay, preparing to build scarecrows. She remembered that the first annual Harvest Festival was scheduled for tomorrow. Long tables borrowed from St. Luke's Congregational Church were set up to display home-baked pies and pastries, bushels of apples and early fall vegetables. Fat, orange pumpkins provided brilliant slashes of colors on the emerald grass. A temporary wooden dance floor had been erected near the gazebo. Molly knew the Green Mountain Fiddlers would come from Vermont to entertain the crowds.

The festival was one of Cam Outlaw's ideas and something they'd talked about during their undercover days at the casino. All of that seemed far behind her now. Even the threat sent with the dead raven. It seemed that little Daisy was safe.

As Molly waited at Eden's only stoplight, she glanced at the old Commerce Bank Building that now housed Cam's Community Bank. Since he'd returned to Eden he'd made loans available to small businesses, created jobs, helped develop the resort and casino and revived the chamber of commerce. He had turned into the pillar of the community his dad had wanted him to be. He was thoroughly respectable with a darling daughter and an extended family. The dalliance at the casino and again in her bedroom was merely closure to old, old business for Cam but he'd been honorable enough to cancel his engagement. He, like Daniel, was a good and decent man.

Molly made a sudden and momentous decision. If the E.P.T. was positive, she would have to tell Cam about the baby.

The prospect of dealing with his justifiable disappointment and anger made her shake. Tears filled her eyes and she could barely see to drive as she turned left on Maple Street on the way to Rural Route Two. As she passed Sharon's yellow clapboard inn, she spotted a tall, lean figure wearing a long, gray braid, torn jeans and an old brown cardigan with holes in the elbows. He was intent on clearing the leaves from the inn's garden. He looked so familiar, so safe, so much like home. Molly parked the Jeep intending to throw herself in Daniel's arms when she saw him turn in response to the sound of another car. His sudden grin reminded her of the Fourth of July fireworks. Molly stayed where she was and watched Daniel gazed at the tall redhead walking toward him. When Sharon reached him they did not touch but he leaned toward her, his broad shoulder curved protectively and she tilted her head so that if she had dropped it another inch it would have rested on his shoulder.

Molly pulled her car away from the curb and made a U-turn. Daniel Grey Wolf was no longer her haven. Whether he accepted it or not, he belonged to someone else now. It seemed that, like the Penobscots of old, both she and her ex-husband were making a portage to another life. She hoped and prayed he would be happy.

Chapter Thirteen

Cam sat in Sarah Lanham's empty office in the Spotswood Fertility Clinic and waited for the director to reappear with his file. He hadn't questioned her request that he drive to Boston. He had a feeling he was about to be treated to another unpleasant truth about his ex-wife and he understood Mrs. Lanham's reluctance to impart that information over the phone.

Damn. What had he been thinking to marry Elise Larkin? He'd met her that first semester of freshman year and she'd stuck around, hauling his drunken body home again and again during that nightmarish second semester after he'd found out Tiger Lily was married.

He'd dated a lot of women in college but he'd never fallen in love again and when Elise suggested that since they were "best friends" they could have a good, workable marriage, he'd agreed. It hadn't seemed to matter. He didn't believe he'd fall in love again.

What he hadn't bargained for was that he'd never fallen out of love with Molly Whitecloud. The ever present, helpful Elise of college days had turned into a demanding princess and their short marriage had been one of the worst periods of his life.

Except there had been one saving grace. Daisy. He hadn't appreciated the child at first. She'd been a disappointment to Elise and he had spent most of his time avoiding the big house on Beacon Hill. And then

Elise had died and Cam had brought the little girl back to his father's house in Maine and he'd learned, belatedly, how much he loved her.

Molly loved her, too. Would it be possible to cobble the three of them together as a viable family? Or would old hurts intrude and make life miserable for the child at the center of it?

"Thank you for waiting," Mrs. Lanham said. The well-upholstered lady was slightly out of breath. "This whole situation is rather irregular and I thought it would be better if we met, well, in person."

"I understand. You remember that I wish to withdraw my consent to the use of any, er, leftover sperm?"

"Yes." She sat heavily in the chair behind the desk. Sarah Lanham's graying blonde hair frizzed out like a halo and her kind, intelligent eyes softened her severe features. She stared at Cam.

"There is something I should tell you about that."

In spite of her words she didn't speak again immediately. Instead, she shuffled the pieces of paper in front of her. Cam waited, briefly, then took the opportunity to ask his question.

"I'd also like to see all the papers in the file, particularly the documentation on the fertility tests and issues. Until now I haven't needed to know the specifics but I've decided to remarry."

"Congratulations!"

"Thank you." The announcement surprised him but he realized he meant it. What had happened in the past had hurt Molly at least as much as himself. It was water under the bridge now. He would ask her as soon as he got back to the rez. A surge of excitement swamped him and he was anxious to get home.

The clinic director sifted through the papers, placed one on top and handed him the stack. He scanned the page to the salient line, "Sperm viability adequate."

"So they aren't lazy, after all."

An odd expression flickered across the woman's face.

"Didn't you know?"

He shook his head. He didn't intend to tell Mrs. Lanham or anyone else about Elise's lie but he suspected the director knew.

"I was under the impression that we were using the clinic to make a mixed drink, a cocktail, if you will, of sperm because mine weren't up to the job."

Mrs. Lanham frowned.

"The sperm, which was yours, was injected into a donor egg," she explained, gently. "I'm afraid your late wife had suffered a very early menopause." She studied his face. "How did you remain in ignorance of that fact?"

Cam felt the warmth of a telltale flush in his cheeks.

"I'm afraid I was inattentive. Just starting a career and, well, I left it all to her."

"I'm surprised she would mislead you on such a subject," the director said, in a slightly disapproving voice, "and even more surprised that she got away with it."

Cam did not try to defend himself. He had not been a good husband. Perhaps he deserved what he'd gotten. It occurred to him, suddenly, that Daisy hadn't been Elise's biological child. Had her father known that? Was that why he'd never shown much interest in the little girl?

Cam rubbed the back of his neck. He'd come down here intending to be disgusted with Elise and wound up disgusted with himself.

"How old is your child now, Mr. Outlaw?"

"Five. Her name is Daisy."

"Lovely. And you plan to give her a brother or sister?"

He nodded. "It's something of a relief to find out there're no fertility issues. My fiancée will be pleased." *I hope.* "And you will destroy any remain specimen samples?"

She looked grave.

"I'm sorry to tell you that request comes too late. Your sample was chosen by an applicant several weeks ago."

More negligence. Cam winced, knowing this was his fault, too. "Oh well. Who would have believed a child could be this much trouble before he was even conceived?"

Mrs. Lanham did not return his grin.

"The client's request matched up with your description in ninety-five percent of the categories. And she was such a sweet young woman. It occurred to me to double check with you but, in the end, I couldn't deny her. If it's any consolation I'm certain she'll make an excellent mother."

Something twisted in Cam's gut.

"And her husband?"

Mrs. Lanham looked away from him.

"We made an exception in her case. She wasn't married. But she's thirty years old and extremely responsible. She had all kinds of references and she knows all about babies. She's a midwife, you see."

A midwife? A MIDWIFE?

For an instant, Cam went completely still as he tried to absorb the damning information.

"Was she a Native American?"

Mrs. Lanham went pale.

"I can't answer that. I shouldn't have told you anything about her."

Cam's lips thinned into a straight line and his lashes hooded his eyes. He knew he had to maintain control until he was out of the clinic. It wasn't Mrs. Lanham's fault that this had happened. He'd been unpardonably careless. It was his fault. His and Molly's. He recalled Molly's graceless lunge at the toilet bowl the morning he'd been at her cottage. It wasn't necessary to ask the question but he did, anyway.

"Just tell me one thing," he said. "Is the sperm recipient pregnant?"

"Well, we don't know." Mrs. Lanham was nervous now. She'd probably detected the hint of a lawsuit in his hiss. "The clients usually call to tell us but often not until the second trimester because of the risk of miscarriage."

Cam shut out the memory of Molly's long ago miscarriage. Nothing excused this. She'd found out about his sperm and she'd swiped it. It would be funny if it wasn't such a betrayal. Cam gritted his teeth.

"Thank you," he said, getting to his feet. "I won't take up any more of your time."

She got to her feet.

"I hope you don't mean to take legal action," she started to say. He waved away the words.

"No. It's not your fault. If you'll excuse me, I'll be on my way."

Red, yellow and orange leaves lined the sides of the road and provided brilliant, flaming color against the clear, blue sky. It was scenery worthy of an Oscar-winning movie but it might as well have been the unrelenting black of a dungeon cell for all that Cam cared.

During the entire duration of the drive north Cam fed his fury. He fought the temptation to look at this from her point of view. She was trying to replace the baby she'd lost. But what about him? What was he, a stud bull? It was Elise all over again trying to manipulate circumstances to fit her dream. Whatever happened to the old custom of a couple sleeping together and getting a child as a byproduct of that pleasure?

He couldn't shake the notion that Molly had acted no better than Elise. Worse, in fact. They'd both lied but at least Elise had been married to him.

Pain shot up his forearms and he realized he was gripping the steering while tightly enough to turn the hard plastic into liquid.

Fury pounded through his blood combined with a soul-deep regret. They'd been so close to a happy ending. He slammed his fist against the steering wheel of the Mercedes, heard the horn shriek and admitted to himself what was really bothering him. She'd wanted the child without the complication of a man who didn't belong to the rez. His eyes closed, briefly, in anguish.

Tiger Lily.

****

The sun was low in the sky.

Molly stood in her bedroom and contemplated the pink-and-white cardboard box.

Why had the manufacturers made it pink? Shouldn't it have been yellow or green? Something neutral? Half the babies born were boys. Pink seemed like a ridiculous color to choose for such a product. Probably somebody in some marketing department decided it was a color that would appeal to the prospective customers, all of whom were women.

She realized she wasn't just stalling. She was babbling. In her head. She was stuck in the mental weeds of irrelevance.

Who cared what color the box was? What did it matter?

Molly felt her heart beating like a hummingbird's wings. In another minute she'd hyperventilate. The outcome of this test would change her life. Maybe. If it were negative nothing much would happen except she'd be honor-bound to tell Cam what she'd done. If it were positive, she'd be tied to him for the rest of their natural lives. In either case he'd hate her.

And he'd be right to do so.

She'd been insane. She could have tried to adopt a child or gone through an ethical insemination. She'd have loved any child who came into her home. Why had she done this? It was a question she'd asked herself a lot lately. She was not proud of the answer. She had wanted to hold onto a part of Cam. Despair welled up in her heart and leaked down her cheeks. Hormones. *Dang.* She was almost certainly pregnant.

She wiped her eyes with her hands, opened the box and dumped the contents onto her unmade bed. The same bed she had shared with Cam only a week earlier.

She glanced at the sheet of instructions typed in an ant-sized font and read them carefully. She'd administered plenty of early pregnancy tests in the past ten years but reading the directions would give her a few more minutes of protection against the future. She held the featherweight plastic wand with a tiny empty window that, minutes after she peed on it, would give her the news in plain English: "pregnant" or "not pregnant". She wondered if the words would be capitalized. They should be. They were such important words, such life-changing words.

Life changes. A picture of Sandra Tall Tree flashed into her mind. What an absurd moment to think about the confused young woman who was not nearly as innocent as her husband believed. Sandra had broken her marriage vows and broken Davey's heart and, very probably had broken the law. It seemed more and more likely to Molly that Sandra had the stolen money. There simply wasn't anyone else who'd been near the casino that night. No one else who could have scooped the money out of the safe after Big Eddie was killed.

Molly had pitied Sandra Tall Tree for her rough upbringing and she'd judged her for her behavior. Now she compared Sandra's sins to her own. Was it worse to steal a man's money or his sperm? What a no-brainer. Money could be replaced. Even infidelity could be forgiven.

There was no way to make restitution on a stolen child.

Suddenly, she couldn't do it. It was no longer just her life that would be changed forever but that of a man who had done nothing to deserve this. She threw on a jacket and stepped out to her garden.

The vision of the dying sun on the radiant leaves of the hardwoods in the forest behind her home stole her breath. She sat on her back stoop and watched the sun's light move upward, spotlighting sections of the trees as if they were entertainers in a nightclub. When the sun finally reached the horizon only the crowns of the trees were still on fire.

Already leaves were falling like flakes in a storm. In a few weeks they would cover the ground, the branches would be bare and maybe, if they were lucky, they'd get a week of Indian summer before the bitter cold set in for the season the ancient Abenakis called, "the moon that provides little food grudgingly."

Molly contemplated the months ahead. Would she spend another winter alone? It seemed likely. But what about the spring? Would it bring new life?

She spoke to the ancients, Molly Mathilde, the peacemaker, Molly Ockett, the healer and Molly Spotted Elk, the lady who loved to dance. She asked them for strength to handle whatever lay ahead today, in the spring and in the distant future. She felt the curious warmth that always followed this exercise. She might be an orphan and a foster child but she was not alone. She had not been alone since she'd come to Blackbird Reservation. She sucked in a long breath.

It was time.

Moments later butterflies carousing in her stomach turned to circling buzzards as she waited for the test results. The box suggested a five-minute wait. She decided to give it seven and to use the extra time to make a phone call.

"I took a pregnancy test," she blurted into the receiver.

"And?"

"I don't know yet."

"Ah," Muriel said. "I'll be right over."

****

Cam got home late, exhausted from the drive but more particularly, from the emotions that had been jerked around as if he were a kite in the March sky. Ever since Molly had walked into the honeymoon suite he'd felt like an emotional punching bag. He realized now his heart had been encased in ice for a long time. Seeing Molly, being with her, had thawed it out. She'd made him vulnerable.

He wasn't sure he liked it.

Cam stared into the bathroom mirror and noted the dark bristles on his jaw.

What the hell was he going to do about the woman?

He'd like to put his hands around her slender neck and squeeze. He'd like to settle her under him and thrust himself home. He'd like to hold her against his heart and tell her everything would be all right.

Dammit.

Cam clenched his fists as he realized he was dithering again. He *hated* to dither.

In this case it was a useless exercise. Molly had stripped away his decade-long defenses and, as if she'd given him a magic kiss, she'd brought him to life. And to love. He was going to forgive her. He was going to get down on his knees and beg her to marry him. And it had nothing to do with the potential baby. It was the woman herself. *His* woman.

The bathroom door opened without warning as it always did. Daisy climbed up onto the covered toilet seat as if it were her throne. Cam remembered the way Molly had burst in on him a week earlier. Apparently, bathroom privacy was a thing of the past. He grinned. It was a small price to pay. His daughter crossed her arms over her small chest like an irritated schoolteacher.

"Daddy, Wilbur 'n me need to know if we're really gonna marry Miss Johnson."

He slapped some water and soap on his face and picked up the razor.

"Why do you and Wilbur need to know?"

"Cuz she would be our new mom. An' Wilbur is gonna have to adjus."

"Adjust?"

"That's what Asia says."

"Well, the two of you might have to adjust but not to Miss Johnson. We aren't marrying her." He stroked the razor along his jaw. "I mean, I'm not marrying Miss Johnson. Or, more accurately, Miss Johnson isn't marrying me."

"Why not?"

He shrugged and pulled his mouth to one side to get a better angle on his right cheek. "We aren't in love."

"Oh." She was silent for a moment, apparently considering that development. Out of the corner of his eye he saw her nodding. Her yellow curls bounced against her soft cheeks. "Me and Wilbur are in love with Molly. Are you in love with Molly, too?"

She sounded so hopeful, so wistful. Cam paused, his razor in the air.

"Cause if you love Molly," she said, encouragingly, "we can marry her, right, Daddy?"

Moisture from the razor ran down his bare forearm.

It tickled.

"Daddy?"

He stared at his small daughter. He wasn't going to lie to her and, anyway, she deserved to know. She'd been motherless long enough.

"Yes," he said. "Yes."

She cocked her head to one side. "Yes?"

He almost smiled at her attempt to pin him down. A successful attempt, as it turned out.

"Yes," he repeated. "If she'll have me. We'll marry Molly."

Daisy's grin stretched across her small face. "She will. She loves me an' Wilbur. I'll go tell him now."

Cam hoped Daisy and Wilbur would be just as thrilled when the new baby re-drew the boundaries of their family circle next summer. He felt a warmth in his soul that had been missing a long, long time.

****

Molly's nerves were shredded. The stick rested on the bathroom sink where she'd left it. She and Muriel sat on opposite corners of her bed.

"It's been thirty-two minutes," her mother said, finally. "That's long enough. I'm going to take a look."

Molly closed her eyes and waited for her mother to emerge from the bathroom. A moment later Muriel stood before her holding the stick at arm's length as if it were a wiggling snake. The woman's normally open countenance was inscrutable.

Molly waited for the words. It couldn't have been more than a second or two but it seemed like a decade.

"*N'onon?*"

And then Muriel opened her mouth and the unthinkable happened.

"I'm sorry, *nizwia.*"

"Sorry?"

Muriel's dark eyes were sad. She shook her head. "Not."

Molly didn't believe it. She'd hadn't the morning sickness. She hadn't imagined the over-the-top emotions. Was it possible her mother had misread the test? It was a ludicrous thought. Muriel wasn't a Rhodes Scholar but she was an excellent reader. She even belonged to the Blackbird Ladies Reading Society that Molly had started several years ago. Muriel was more than capable of telling the difference between "pregnant" and "not pregnant."

As if she knew that Molly had to see the proof, Muriel handed her the stick. She stared. Only three letters to make such a difference. She thought of all the unmarried women in the world who would welcome that message. Molly was unmarried. She should have felt relieved. This gave her a chance to clear her slate. She could confess to Cam without seeing the grimace acknowledging that he was caught in her deception. She could return to the work that she'd found satisfying all these years. She'd taken her shot at motherhood and she'd lost. It was out of her hands.

It wasn't meant to be.

It felt like the end of the world.

She didn't realize she was crying until Muriel gently wiped away her tears with a tissue. Her mother gathered her into her warm, welcoming arms but Molly felt none of the heat.

"It isn't fair," Muriel murmured. "You wanted this so badly. It isn't right."

Molly closed her eyes. "I wanted the baby for the

wrong reasons," she murmured.

"Will you tell him? The boy from town?"

Cam Outlaw might be past the age of thirty but Muriel would always think of him as that boy from town. The one who broke her daughter's heart.

"I'll tell him." But not yet. She wanted to be alone with her grief first.

Muriel understood. She hugged Molly.

"Call me, *nizwia*."

"I will." Molly wandered to her living room and watched through the front window as Muriel climb into the family's Chevy pickup. She stood there long after the truck disappeared down the road. After awhile her gaze wandered until she noticed a cobweb attached to the bookcase that contained volumes about pregnancy and childcare, books full of information she needed in her work, information she'd hoped to use in her own life. The cobweb looked ghostly, magical in the soft glow from the moon. How long had it taken the spider to spin the web? And where was that spider now? Had she abandoned her home? Would she return? Molly decided to find out. She slid down to the floor, circled her knees with her arms, rested her face on her knees and prepared to wait.

When the phone clanged in her ear she jerked awake, immediately aware of aching joints and bones caused by a night spent on the hard-wood floor. She tried to stand to get to the phone but her knees refused to obey so she fell back in a heap and listened to the answering machine.

"Ms. Whitecloud, this is Sarah Lanham from the Spotswood Fertility Clinic in Boston. I'm sorry to bother you so early but I wanted to let you know that your donor turned up yesterday and, well, to put it plainly, I revealed a bit too much information about you. I believe he knows your identity and I'm afraid he is not pleased." She paused. "Just for my own peace of mind I need to know whether or not the insemination was successful."

Molly heard the awful tension in the woman's voice. She was probably afraid of being sued by her for revealing her identity or by Cam for giving away his sperm.

Molly lurched toward the phone and picked it up. "You can relax," she said, in a kind voice. "I took a test last night. The results are negative."

"Oh." The woman couldn't quite restrain her relief. "Oh, I'm sorry for you, dear. I know how much you wanted this but perhaps, all things considered, this is the better outcome."

"Yes."

"Well, I'll let you go, Miss Whitecloud. Best of luck in the future."

Molly said goodbye and hung up. So Cam knew what she'd done and probably Mrs. Lanham would inform him of the "better outcome."

Molly stretched her back, glanced out at the dawn and back at the web. The spider hadn't come back. She slid back to the floor and hugged her knees with her arms.

She'd wait a little longer.

Chapter Fourteen

Daniel Grey Wolf applied the last strokes to the thick piece of vellum on his desk then leaned back in his chair and held the drawing up to get a better look at it.

God, she was beautiful. He drew his thumb over the high cheekbones he'd sketched, and for just a minute, allowed himself to drown in her clear eyes. A sense of emptiness coalesced inside him.

She'd told him she was free and he believed it. Molly Whitecloud had Cameron Outlaw's heart whether he acknowledged it or not. Sharon had said she wanted him and Daniel believed her. And yet he'd said no to the most precious gift he'd ever been offered. He told himself she needed someone younger but he wondered if he was being honest with himself. Was the truth that he was afraid? He had stayed on the sidelines for a long time. Maybe too long. Did he lack the courage to get into the game?

And Sharon wanted a child. Years ago, he had wanted a wife and child but he'd waited and then Molly's trouble gave him the perfect excuse to play the safe role of protector. Was it too late? Could he make himself vulnerable enough to be the man Sharon needed?

He would never forget the look on her face after he'd rejected her offer. Deep, quiet sadness that had made his throat ache and his chest feel hollow.

Had he made the right decision for the wrong reasons? Or had he made the wrong decisions with the reasons merely irrelevant?

Daniel crumpled the drawing and pitched it into the wastebasket and got wearily to his feet. Today he felt every hour of his forty eight years. He'd dressed carefully in a chamois-cloth shirt and buckskins in order to escort her to the harvest festival. He wore his long, straight gray hair in a braid. As long as he kept a neutral expression on his face he knew he looked like a cigar store Indian. He was an alien to Sharon Johnson. He wanted them both to remember that.

The sound of fiddle music infiltrated the room. The harvest festival had begun. He waited to hear her knock. As always, it reverberated in his chest and he felt that rush of excitement he hadn't experienced in decades until he'd met Sharon.

She gave him her usual friendly smile but her face was pale beneath the freckles. She wore a pair of plain jeans and old Keds and a blue-plaid flannel shirt.

"I can always tell what mood you're in," he said, with an attempt at levity, "by your wardrobe. When you wear the red flannel shirt, you're feeling upbeat, the yellow, you're happy."

"And this one?" Her hazel eyes were luminous with unshed tears but he refused to use the adjective that came immediately to mind.

"Pensive," he said. He couldn't resist cupping her face in his hands.

"You've been crying."

She nodded.

"Is there anything I can do?"

"I could use a cup of tea."

He smiled at the small request, slid one hand down the length of her arm and twined her fingers in his in a gesture of friendship. Giving comfort to disappointed women was one area in which Daniel had a yeoman's experience.

He started to lead her toward his kitchenette but she resisted.

"Daniel, I don't really want tea. I want... I want..."

He sensed the danger but was helpless to draw back.

"What?" He murmured. "You want what?"

She moved against him and Daniel felt her soft breasts mound against his chest. She wasn't wearing a bra. Daniel shivered.

"Could you just hold me, Daniel? No strings, I promise."

He shouldn't do it. His body was hardening faster than the speed of light. He felt his control slipping and knew he had to move away.

His mind listened. His body did not.

He tightened his arms around her. He knew she couldn't mistake the insistent arousal under his trousers. She didn't. She pressed closer.

"Tighter," she said, "could you hold me tighter?"

Daniel damned himself for a fool even as he tightened his arms around her soft curves and let one palm slide down to her shapely hip. She shivered and rubbed against him and he groaned. She placed her own hands on his hips and pulled him closer, driving his erection against her soft belly. He buried his face in her auburn hair.

"Kiss me," she whispered. It was an unnecessary

directive. He'd already lowered his head. Her lips were warm and pillow soft and she made needy little noises. Daniel's pulse throbbed in his throat, in his temple, in his groin. The wet, warmth of her mouth nearly sent him into a coma. She tasted as sweet as Penobscot fry bread. His body kicked and he went crazy, feasting on her like a starving man. He couldn't break the contact with her mouth, not even to breathe. She finally came up for air and he pulled away.

"No," she protested. "Don't stop. I just need some oxygen."

Before he could object she rose to her tiptoes and began to press small kisses against his cheek, his ear, down the column of his throat. She pulled the soft fabric of his shirt out of his pants and slid her fingers up the hot skin of his torso.

Daniel wondered if his heart would leap out of his chest and into her hand. He grimaced. Something was leaping at her and it wasn't his heart. She felt it, too. And then she was touching him, cupping him. He laid a big hand over hers. He was fast approaching the point of no return. A shudder of longing racked his body.

"Sharon," he ground out. "No."

"You're right," she whispered. "Not here. On the bed."

"No." His voice sounded weird. High and cracked and desperate.

"No strings, remember?"

How could he tell her he wanted strings? He wished he knew the right thing to do. He wished he could think clearly enough to figure out the right thing to do. He wished he had the courage to tell this woman how he felt about her.

"Life is short, Daniel. I want you and, at least now, I know you want me, too."

The earnest hazel eyes warmed his blood, his soul. They dispelled his fear. Without another word he scooped her up in his arms and carried her to the pull-out sofa that was also his bed. She twined her arms around his neck, released the leather band that held his braid and threaded her fingers through his hair then she brought her soft mouth to his and, again, he tasted heaven.

"People will say I'm too old," he whispered.

She gave him a smile as beautiful as the dawn.

"People," she said, "will be wrong."

****

What a tangled web we weave when first we practice to deceive.

Sir Walter Scott's words fit her perfectly. She stared at the entry on her computer. She'd thought it had come from Shakespeare, which only showed that her education was sadly lacking. That's what she could do this winter, she thought. When the snow kept her bound to her tiny cottage, she could read the classics.

There was some comfort in the picture of herself wrapped in a warm quilt reading *The Canterbury Tales.* It would be lonely but peaceful. And safe.

First though, she had to see Cam Outlaw one last time. His sky blue eyes would be accusing even if his words were not. She'd deceived him again about a child. And this time it had been no accident but a deliberate betrayal.

Molly stared over at the deserted web and wished she, too, could run away from the tangled mess she'd woven.

233

But she couldn't. She wasn't a spider.

The telephone jangled and she jumped. It would be Cam. It was the morning of the long knives and she wasn't ready. What could she say to him? Nothing. There was no excuse. She'd just let him have his say and then she'd tell him she was sorry.

She sucked in a long, fortifying breath and picked up the receiver.

"This is Molly."

"Oh, thank goodness you're there," said Nancy Dove. "Lenaya's bleeding again. This time it's something awful."

A reprieve. Molly snapped into professional mode. She could tell Nancy was on a cell. "Where are you?"

"On Route Two."

"Good. I'll call ahead to the hospital and they'll be expecting you. And, Nancy, I'll be there as fast as I can but be safe. She'll be all right."

Minutes later, without even brushing her teeth, Molly hopped into the Jeep. Lenaya would have the miscarriage with or without her and whoever was on duty would take care of the girl but experience had taught Molly that folks from the rez were more comfortable at Eden Memorial when she was there, too.

This natural termination of the pregnancy was best for Lenaya and her mom but Molly felt a twinge at the thought of the life that would never be. Impatient to get to the hospital, she stomped on the gas and the Jeep squirted forward. Luckily, there was little traffic on the road. She barely paused as she reached the intersection of the rez's main road with Rural Route Two. Moments later though, she heard the wail of an approaching train. *Dang.* Could she beat it? She knew it would take the lumbering freighter about thirty seconds to reach the crossing. She stomped hard on the accelerator but the little Jeep had limited horsepower and the guardrail dropped into place when she was still twenty feet away. She braked like a crazy woman, causing the small vehicle to fishtail on the highway.

Dang.

Well, maybe it would be a short train.

The big, boxy, black engine chugged past and she ground her teeth as the conductor waved, lazily, to the occupants of the car stuck on the westbound side of the crossing.

The freight cars rumbled by at a snail's pace. Molly noted the logos: *Maine Eastern, Burlington Northern, Penn Central, National Steel, Siemens.* She winced. *Siemens* reminded her of semen. She shook off the thought. She'd make sure Lenaya was all right and then she'd find Cam. She'd apologize and the whole, misbegotten adventure would be over.

Except for the guilt.

And the regret.

And the loss.

Molly vowed to consign all three emotions to the dream catcher.

She drummed her fingers on the steering wheel and peered through the chain of cars, surprised to spot the red Porsche.

It was only about nine a.m. It was conceivable that Davey Tall Tree could be on the road heading to Eden but coming back toward the rez? What could have taken him to town at this hour?

Her attention caught, Molly tried to see if it was Davey driving the sports car. Yep. Davey at the wheel and a dark-haired woman next to him. Probably Sandra.

Had they dropped in at the harvest festival then recalled some previous engagement on the rez? It seemed unlikely. Molly tried to make a mental list of the reasons they could be on the east side of the railroad tracks this early but she came up blank.

A flatbed car clattered past affording Molly a clear view of the *sagama* and his wife. Davey's normally jovial face looked drawn and Sandra's dark eyes were stark above her high cheekbones. Neither seemed to be aware of Molly. Was she getting a bird's eye view of a marriage falling apart?

Poor Davey. Poor both of them.

Molly's thoughts turned to the Doves. She hoped they'd made it to the hospital by now. At least they weren't stuck at the crossing. Another dozen boxcars passed. Finally the caboose was in sight. Before it arrived though, there was another flatbed. Molly chanced to look across the tracks at the Porsche. This time she couldn't see Davey's expression. His head was turned as if he were checking on something or someone in the backseat.

Molly's curiosity was piqued. As soon as the caboose cleared the crossing, she took a closer look. Just as the gate lifted, the morning sun glinted off of something bright. Hair. It was blonde hair. What on Earth? A tremor that owed nothing to the brisk morning air rippled down her spine. She glanced at the slowly disappearing caboose and saw the brakeman wave to the Porsche. Suddenly it all came together like pieces of a jigsaw puzzle. Someone blonde in the backseat, the waving brakeman, the fact of the sagama's car heading back toward the rez, the tension on the faces of both

Sandra and Davey.

There was a child in the backseat of the Porsche. Molly caught her eye as the truth dawned.

It was Daisy.

They had Daisy.

Molly's heart stopped. The threat of the squashed flower had come true. The Tall Trees had kidnapped the child, probably as a hostage. Did this mean Davey was Sandra's partner? Suddenly Molly understood. Sandra had had the money all along and Davey, lovesick fool that he was, had offered to join her after Dwight Winston's untimely death.

Oh, Davey.

The thoughts flashed in her head but she didn't wait to think them through. Davey and Sandra had Daisy and there was no telling whether anyone else even knew it. Davey Tall Tree's eyes met hers as he powered the Porsche across the tracks. His face was set, his mouth, a straight line. No longer the lovable teddy bear, he looked determined. Intent. *Deadly.*

Molly's tires squealed as she executed the world's clumsiest U-turn. There was no time to waste.

She had to rescue Cam's daughter.

As soon as she'd stabilized vehicle, she thrust her hand into her purse to fish for the phone which was, as usual, underneath her wallet, traveling thermometer, blood pressure kit, sunglasses, notebook and bottle of aspirin, and other paraphernalia.

Molly's own blood pressure rose as she watched the Porsche widen the distance between the two cars. She used her thumb to punch in the emergency number. The sheriff's department dispatcher patched her through to Jake's cell.

"Langley,"

Molly could hear voices laughing and fiddle music in the background. The sheriff must be at the Harvest Festival. She told him quickly what was going on.

"I think they're heading to the border."

"I'll call a state unit," he told her. "And I'm on my way. Listen, Molly, I know you want to keep Tall Tree in sight but don't take any unnecessary chances."

"They've got Daisy." She hoped he hadn't heard the wobble in her voice.

"I know. Calm down. There's no reason for Tall Tree to hurt her. She's no good to them dead. What's that fool up to, anyway? Sandra's not gonna be charged with anything. Something's got them spooked. Don't worry, Molly, Daisy's their insurance policy. She'll be okay."

Molly wished she could be sure of that. Jake hadn't seen the snarl on Davey's face. Daisy was at risk and not just from the speed of the Porsche. Molly caught her breath on a sob. If anything happened to Daisy it would kill Cam. *Good grief.* He wouldn't even be involved in this—or his small daughter, either—if Molly hadn't tried to fix things by going under cover at the casino.

This was her fault.

She stomped on the gas so hard the old Jeep rattled and creaked. What if they turned off before the sheriff could get here? What if she somehow lost them? No, no, she assured herself, Davey wouldn't turn off. He had to be heading to Canada and this was the fastest, most direct way. He must think he could lose himself on the other side of the border.

Molly tasted blood and realized with surprise, that

she'd bitten her lip.

She should have *listened* to Davey. He'd told her he wanted a good looking wife. He'd told her Sandra wanted pretty things. She should have heard the implicit message: he needed money. As she bounced and jolted along the road another thought barreled into her.

Davey had been on the porch the night Dwight was shot. Was it possible he'd shot Dwight with the man's own pistol? Was it possible he'd been in on this all along? And what about Big Eddie. Molly strained her memory to recall that night at the casino. Had Davey been there? She remembered Daniel excusing himself to talk to the former tribal cop.

Had the answer to this been under their noses all along? Had Sandra just been using Dwight? Had she been Davey's accomplice all along?

A modern day Bonnie and Clyde.

And no one had suspected him. Davey, with his big, woebegone eyes and his terrycloth robe. Davey, with his stories and over-the-top pride in being elected sagama. Davey, who, until his mother had died, had lived in her shadow.

If true, this was another black mark against the rez but that hardly mattered. The thing that mattered, the *only* thing that mattered was the child in the speeding Porsche.

Please, Molly prayed, *I'll spend the rest of my life working for the good of the rez, I'll give up my dreams of a husband and child if only Daisy is safe.*

The getaway car was way past the rez now and heading due north. It had become a dot on the horizon. She willed Jake to hurry. She willed the Porsche to run out of gas. She willed Daisy back to safety in Eden with her father.

Molly leaned forward in a hopeless effort to make the Jeep fly.

The road bent sharply to accommodate a hill and for the distance of a mile or so Molly lost sight of her quarry. There was no turn off here, no major road at any rate but what if Davey knew of a shortcut? What if she lost them? And then the road straightened out and the Porsche was there, no longer a sleek, beautifully engineered machine speeding along but a beached creature, like a horseshoe crab. It listed on two punctured tires like a fat kid pushed over by a bully. Orange cones littered the highway. An earthmover and a dump truck sat, empty, several yards away on the grass shoulder.

Davey must have blown out his right side tires in the construction zone.

Molly held her breath and, without thinking, she jerked her Jeep to a halt and sprinted toward the other vehicle.

****

Cam slipped the wide, plain gold band into the pocket of his charcoal flannel shirt. It had belonged to his grandmother. He'd never thought of giving it to Elise who'd wanted a large diamond and he hadn't considered giving it to Sharon Johnson, either.

Molly would love it. She would know that it represented a welcome to his world, an invitation that was long overdue. Several days of reflection had convinced him that what he wanted was Molly and the new baby. And Daisy, of course. They would start over again and the glow of happiness from their instant family would wipe out any hard feelings left over from the past.

He smiled to himself. He'd always wanted Molly. The baby she was carrying would be the cherry on top of the sundae.

Cam grabbed his car keys and, on his way to the back door, glanced at Wilbur who was lounging on his Miss Piggy pillow in the kitchen.

"Get ready, son," he said. "Everything's going to change. For the first time, everything's going to be perfect."

He heard the fiddles well before he arrived at the park. The Harvest Festival was in full swing. Hallie and Asia had taken Daisy early and he'd promised to stop by to take the little girl through the corn maize and on the moon bounce after which he'd head out to the rez. He'd ask Molly the all-important question of whether she wanted to elope to New Jersey or plan a wedding in Eden. He wouldn't give her a choice about marriage.

That was a done deal.

He felt a rush of emotion that left his heart light and his blood hot as he pulled onto Main Street and parked behind Jake's white Blazer. The sheriff was at his window before he turned off the Mercedes. Cam flashed his brother-in-law a cocky grin. "This an illegal zone?"

Grim lines bracketed the sheriff's mouth and Cam's gut tightened.

Something was wrong.

"Davey Tall Tree was evidently behind the robbery at the casino," Jake said, tersely. "He's heading out Route 15 toward Quebec and he's got Daisy."

Cam cursed and jerked the ignition.

"Come with me," Jake said.

"Merc's got more horses."

"Yeah, but I've got the lights, the sirens. And the guns."

Guns. Cam forced back the fear, leapt out of the Mercedes and vaulted into the Blazer.

****

Daisy's eyes were giant cornflowers. When she saw Molly they became giant wet cornflowers. Molly leaned over the door and worked at loosening the child's seatbelt.

"Get away from her, Molly. Don't think I won't shoot."

She glanced up into the barrel of a blue-gray revolver in Davey's hand. Everyone on the rez could handle a rifle and Davey had been a tribal cop. Still it was strange to see the easygoing *sagama* brandishing a handgun.

"He'll do it," Sandra whispered. "He killed Dwight."

"I said get away from that kid," Davey growled, ignoring his wife. Molly forced herself to take a step away from the Porsche and Daisy let out a howl of protest.

"It'll be okay, Daze," she said, in what she hoped was a comforting voice.

"It'll be fine," Davey bit out, "if you follow my instructions. Here's what we're gonna do now. We'll take your Jeep. And you're gonna drive."

Molly was surprised. "You want me to drive? Why?"

"He's sick," Sandra muttered.

"He 'frowed up, already," Daisy put in.

Molly's medical instincts kicked in at once. He did look a little white around the gills. "What is it? Flu?"

"Shut up. Just listen."

Molly had known Davey Tall Tree for Two years. He'd always been a bit of a hypochondriac and a mama's boy. He'd always reveled in sympathy. That dimension of him probably hadn't changed even if, as seemed likely, he was now a cold-blooded killer.

"Get Sandra into the back of the Jeep. I'll bring the kid, then I'm riding shotgun."

"No-o-o!" Daisy screamed and kicked and generally gave a performance worthy of a two-year-old.

"Jesus." Davey's face had turned the color of winter wheat and he was breathing hard. Probably getting ready to puke again, Molly thought. That flu gave her a slight advantage. All she had to do was figure out how to use it.

"I'll get her," she said, diving for the little girl's seatbelt before Davey could object. "You get Sandra over to the Jeep."

"I'm not leaving you here."

"C'mon. What am I gonna do? There's no way I could outrun that gun even if I were willing to leave Daisy behind," she said, reasonably, "which I'm not. And I'm not interested in risking an accident with the child. I'll get Daisy and meet you in the Jeep."

Davey didn't answer. Molly got the feeling he was using most of his concentration to keep his guts from hurling out of his mouth. He grunted as he staggered out of the Porsche. Sandra looked as if she couldn't move. Her slender body remained huddled in the front seat of the sports car and she shook like an aspen. Davey jammed the nose of the gun into her shoulder.

"Go ahead, Sandra," Molly said, hoping that man who used to be her friend wouldn't hurt his wife. "Davey won't hurt us if we cooperate."

Molly heard a harsh retching sound and realized that while Davey had made it to his feet he was now doubled over vomiting all over the hood of the cherry-red Porsche. He managed to keep a grip on the weapon.

"He's crazy," Sandra said, in a dazed voice. "I told him I could make good money from Dwight but he didn't care. He was crazy jealous."

"I imagine so. He loved you."

"He didn't understand," Sandra mumbled. "We could've been rich. It was just sex."

It was the young woman who didn't understand, Molly thought. Davey might have wanted her to have nice things, but one of those things wasn't another man.

"Get a move on," Davey rasped. He held the gun on Sandra while she climbed out of the Porsche and into the back of the Jeep. "Put the kid in the back," he told Molly.

"We don't need her," Molly argued. "She's just gonna slow us down, Davey."

"She's my insurance policy."

The words were slow, halting and Molly knew the *sagama* was about to be sick again. She tried to think fast. Jake would be here soon. If she could just keep Daisy out of the Jeep, the child would be all right.

"You don't need her," Molly said, casually. "You want protection from pursuit, right? I can give you that."

"Like hell. She's Outlaw's kid. The sheriff's niece. You're nothing but a rez midwife."

"That's not true. I'm engaged to marry Cameron

Outlaw. And I'm pregnant with his child."

Davey made a derisive sound.

"You're lying, Molly. Outlaw dumped you years ago."

"That's right. I found out that he and his late wife used a fertility clinic and I managed to get a sample of his sperm."

He looked at her, a glint of respect in his dark eyes. "You're crazier than hell, you know that?"

At least he believed her. It helped that he was almost completely disabled from the combination of nausea and stress. Still, she couldn't afford to wait for him to agree to her terms. She had to act.

"They won't come after us if we leave Daisy here," she said, firmly. She bent over to put the child back in the Porsche. She kissed Daisy, who had started to squawk.

"Just wait here," Molly said, in a low voice. "Uncle Jake will be here in five minutes." She straightened. "C'mon, Davey."

"Get Sandra in the Jeep."

The directive came out in little gasps each word separated by a retching sound.

Molly crossed her fingers and headed back to the Jeep.

"Let's go," she said. "You want to make the border before the sheriff catches up with us."

"Sandra," he puffed.

"She'll just slow us down."

"Fine." Retch. "Then I'll just—" he paused to retch again, "—shoot her."

Sandra shrieked and got out of the Porsche. An instant later she was in the backseat of the Jeep with

Molly in the driver's seat. Davey struggled over to the car, gasping and retching and cursing. He fell into the passenger seat and held the gun on Molly.

"I'll take you to Canada, Davey," she said, forcing back the fear. It was terrifying to look down the barrel of a pistol. "But if you hold that gun on me I'll roll the Jeep. I can do it, too."

Davey knew she was telling the truth. Everyone on the rez knew it. She'd flipped the Jeep once on ice—not on purpose—but how hard could it be? Fortunately the chief's brain was too nauseated to remember that she was supposedly pregnant and unlikely to risk the baby. He rested the pistol on his thigh and Molly pulled onto the road. She watched Daisy's bright blonde head disappear in her rearview mirror.

Chapter Fifteen

"There it is," Jake said, as they pulled out of a blind spot and back onto the highway.

Cam's heart jerked as he glimpsed the red Porsche. An instant it turned over when he recognized the head of blonde curls just visible over the sides of the convertible. Daisy was alone in the car. As soon as Jake skidded to a stop, Cam hit the ground running. He lifted his daughter out of the sports car and crushed her against him.

"Easy," Jake said. "Don't want to scare her."

The sheriff, father of twins a year older than Daisy, probably knew what he was talking about. Cam loosened his grip, fractionally.

"You comed to get me!"

"Of course, baby." He inhaled her fresh, powdery scent and sent up a prayer of infinite thanks. "Are you okay? Does anything hurt?"

She frowned. "I'm not sick. The bad man's sick. He frowed up all over the place. Look." She pointed to the puddles of vomit on the car's hood and on the road.

Cam and Jake exchanged a look.

"Where'd he go, sweetie," the sheriff asked.

"Went off in the Jeep with that Indian lady with the mean eyes."

"Sandra Tall Tree," Cam muttered to Jake. "They must've been in it together. Fooled the hell out of me."

Jake's focus was on the child. "What car," he asked.

"Molly's car," Daisy said. "The bad man was really sick but he had a gun."

"Molly's car?" Cam's whipped around. He stared at Jake. "What's Molly got to do with this?"

"She's the one who called. She spotted them at the railroad crossing and tailed them. Tall Tree must have blown out his tires. She probably stopped and he commandeered her Jeep."

The explanation made too much sense. Cam looked at his daughter.

"Where's Molly now?" His voice sounded remote, as if he were speaking in an echo chamber.

"She went 'stead of me," Daisy reported. "And he maked her drive so's he could frow up."

"You stay here with Daisy," Jake said.

"Not on your life." Cam buckled the little girl into the backseat of the Blazer and slid into the passenger seat. "Okay, sheriff, let's ride."

"Tall Tree needs a hostage to keep us at a distance," Jake said, as he drove. "Molly must have gotten him to take her in exchange for Daisy."

Cam could barely hear over the pounding of his heart and he could barely swallow past the lump in his throat. She'd put herself at risk for his daughter.

Jake glanced at him.

"It'll be all right. He has no reason to hurt her."

"He's got a gun. And they're in a high speed chase."

"I know. If it relieves your mind at all, I happen to know Molly's a damn good driver. She told me once she'd flipped the Jeep on ice."

"Did you ask her whether it was on purpose?"

Jake looked startled. "No. But she knows how to do it."

"So she flips the Jeep and he shoots her."

"It's a light vehicle and Molly's got a good head," Jake said, reassuringly. "She'll wear her seatbelt and there's an air bag."

"You don't understand." Cam could barely form the words. Fear had turned into a boulder in his gut. "She's pregnant."

Jake grimaced. "Damn."

****

Several miles from the border between Maine and the Province of Quebec, another state road fed into Route Two. As Molly zoomed past she glimpsed a cop car paused at a Stop sign. A moment later she heard a siren, checked her rearview mirror and found herself staring into a pair of baby blue eyes in a pleasant, pudgy face. An instant later a siren's bleat filled the air and Davey snapped to attention. He turned the gun on his wife.

"If you so much as slow down, I'll kill her."

Molly kept the pressure on the accelerator and replied in a calm tone.

"I won't slow down but don't expect me to believe you'd kill either one of us. She's your wife and I'm your friend."

"Believe it, Molly." His pudgy face shone with sweat. "I've gone too far. Done too much. None of the pretty girls on the rez ever paid me any attention, including you. I figured if I got myself elected *sagama* I'd get more action and it worked. I met Sandra. When I found out she'd cheated I just went bat shit." He used his free hand to wipe the sweat off his face. "You don't know. Betrayal wrecks a guy."

Sympathy flooded her even as she fought to keep the speeding Jeep under control, to ignore the cop behind her and to think about how to save herself and Sandra.

"I'm sorry," she said, meaning it. "But, Davey, if you killed Dwight Winston because you thought he'd brainwashed Sandra, you'd have a real case. A good defense lawyer could get you a plea bargain."

"And when I told him I killed the fat man for the money in his safe?"

Molly was silent.

"That's what I thought. Like I said, I've done too much." He groaned and clutched at his stomach.

"That might be an ulcer," Molly said.

"Jesus, Molly. Who the hell cares? That's the least of my problems right now."

"You'd get that taken care of if you turned yourself in. And it would look better."

"Look better? I can't go to jail. I'm the sagama. Don't you care about the rez?"

The accusation seemed exceedingly unfair considering that, ever since she'd come to Blackbird, she'd chosen the rez above anything else. She didn't say that. Neither did she point out that it would not exactly be a public relations coup to have the world find out that The Penobscot chief had killed two men in cold blood.

The countryside flew past the windows in a volley of brilliant colors. The young cop on her tail stayed a safe distance behind. She could almost sense his indecision. People were supposed to stop when they heard sirens but if they didn't, there wasn't much an officer could do about it.

Molly wrenched her mind away from the chase and tried to focus on her options. The highway had been built up on a trestle like a railroad track so there were ditches on either side of her. If she turned the wheel sharply, she'd plummet into a gulley. The problem was she was driving over eighty miles an hour and such a maneuver would create a deathly impact.

Another plan was to wait another mile until the terrain evened out and just drive off the pavement. Unfortunately, the row of trees was no more than thirty feet away. The chance of hitting one of the white pines that stood along the highway like well-disciplined sentinels was somewhere around one hundred percent.

They were fast approaching the border. She knew she couldn't make herself plow through the guard station. It was much too likely she'd kill a guard. And she couldn't just stop. Davey had promised he'd shoot Sandra and her and she believed him.

He'd probably shoot the downy-faced cop, too.

There was only one viable possibility. She had to jerk the car hard and hope that, when Davey's treacherous stomach turned on him, he'd drop the gun.

The ditches disappeared and the landscape evened out and Molly thought she heard a second siren. *Jake.* But it was too late. The sheriff couldn't help her now. She was on her own and she had to act quickly. This would be her best—and only—chance to avoid a horrendous crash and almost certainly more deaths. She prayed Sandra was buckled in, sucked in a quick breath then she switched her foot to the brake. The vehicle shuddered and jerked and Davey screamed, trembled and retched like Mount St. Helens. Molly glanced at the gun. *Damn.* It was still in his hand.

She narrowed her eyes, jumped on the brake then quickly stamped on the accelerator and whipped the steering wheel hard to the right. The Jeep fishtailed wildly just before it left the pavement. The whole thing seemed to be happening in slow-motion. Molly had time to brace herself against the steering wheel. She had time to think of Daisy back at the disabled Porsche. She had time to think of Cam and to regret the trick she'd played on him one more time. *Betrayal wrecks a guy.*

She heard the pistol discharge and felt the little car lift into the air. She heard the shriek of metal against pavement and felt the explosion of pain as she slammed her forehead against the steering wheel.

In the midst of the carnage she felt an odd sense of peace.

Daisy was safe.

****

The presence of a searing white light convinced her she was either dead or in the hospital. Molly cracked one eyelid and winced. "Light," she whimpered.

She heard a sharp snap and the blinding glare disappeared. She felt like one big bruise. She tried to sit up and a million knife points attacked her. *Jeez.*

Someone placed a firm hand on her shoulder. "Don't move, honey."

She wanted to tell whoever it was she had no intention of trying to move again. And she was not his honey. She opened her eyes and peered into pieces of the summer sky.

"Cam."

"I'm here."

But it didn't sound like Cam's confident baritone. This voice was higher, thready. She closed one eye and squinted. The man with the blue eyes had lost his tan. He was a pale as a corpse.

Molly's heart constricted. Had something happened to his little girl?

"Daisy?"

"She's fine," he said. His face twisted and she wasn't sure she believed him. "She's home with Hallie and Baz getting a hero's welcome."

That sounded reassuring but Molly wasn't allowed to enjoy the feeling very long. Something gripped her right hand in a bone-crushing vise and pain shot through her fingers and up her arm. She moaned.

"What is it? What hurts?"

"My hand."

Instantly the grip was loosened.

"Sorry," he muttered.

Another voice cut in. This one sounded more normal.

"You're back with us." Stan Schmidt grinned at her. She peered into friendly light brown eyes magnified by strong lenses. Eden Memorial was a small hospital. As a midwife with privileges, she'd met most of the staff including Stan, a middle-aged surgeon who had, apparently, drawn E.R. duty today. He repeated Cam's question. "Anything hurt?"

Molly shifted and winced. "My shoulder," she said. "And my hip. My head. My eyelashes. Take your pick."

The doctor smiled at her. "I wanted to wait until you'd regained consciousness before I gave you something for the pain. You'll be sore for a couple of days but I can't find any breaks. You had a lucky escape, lady. There's a lot of bruising but there shouldn't be any lasting damage."

"Sandra? Davey?"

It was too much effort to form a sentence but her listener seemed to understand the question.

"Tall Tree's got a busted sternum and contusions. His wife suffered a concussion and broken leg."

Molly thought about that. "I think he has an ulcer."

Dr. Schmidt chuckled. "I'll check for it. In any case, they'll both live."

"For the moment," Cam said, softly.

Molly's eyes riveted on his. She knew he'd go after them with single-minded intent. With his determination, to say nothing of his wealth and influence, he'd win, too. For once Molly couldn't fault him for lowering the boom on members of the tribe. They'd kidnapped his daughter. She remembered the tyke's stoic expression when Molly left her in the Porsche. She was a chip off the old block.

"Don't smile," Cam ordered. "Just lie still."

An instant later Dr. Schmidt slid the cold stethoscope under Molly's hospital gown and pressed it against her heart. A shiver ran through her and she heard Cam's voice again. It was curiously thick.

"Go easy, doc."

Molly's heart constricted. Cam felt responsible for her because she'd gone after the child. She wanted to point out that, if not for her, Daisy would never have been at risk. It would take too many words. Instead, she said, "I'm fine. You should go on home."

"I'll go when you're ready to come with me."

Sir Galahad. For some reason his determination to rescue her made her sad. Even her sperm heist had not made him abandon her. Not yet.

"Daniel can pick me up."

Even before the words were out of her mouth she remembered that Daniel had other interests now. For a moment Molly felt like Superman in his fortress of solitude—completely alone.

"Feel up to talking a little business?"

Stan wrapped the black compression band around her upper arm to take her blood pressure.

She winced. "Sure."

"We admitted one of your patients a few hours ago." He handed her a couple of tablets. She put them in her mouth and reached for the paper cup of water. Cam snatched it and held it to her lips.

"Lenaya Dove."

Good grief. She'd forgotten all about the girl.

"Was it a miscarriage? Is she all right?"

"Yes to both questions. Doc Watson did a D&C and sent her home."

A dilation and curettage was a common procedure after a miscarriage. It was an operation, though, and something Molly wasn't qualified to perform. Just one more reason the rez needed a clinic with an M.D. on duty.

So Lenaya had lost the baby. Molly felt another wave of sadness. And then she felt warmth…someone—Cam—was stroking her fingers. Her heart filled with gratitude for his understanding. She wished she hadn't betrayed him at the Spotswood Clinic. She wished she could deserve his comfort and she wished she didn't hurt.

"I want to go home," she said.

"Give it a few more hours," the doctor said. "We'll

see how you feel. You were unconscious briefly after the accident, then the medics put you out during the drive to the hospital. Believe me, you would've felt every bump in the road from the border back to Eden. If you still want to leave, I'll dope you up for the ride home. And then I'd like someone to stay with you."

"My mother will come." She remembered the Jeep. "My car?"

"It did a three-sixty," Cam said. His voice sounded strained. "The airbags deployed and your seatbelt held. The other two weren't wearing belts. Jeep's banged up but drivable. I took it to Charlie Styles' garage in Eden."

"Thanks. Are the Tall Trees in the hospital?"

"At the moment. We're sending them both to Portland. They've got better recuperative facilities there. After that, my guess is they'll go to jail."

She felt a flash of sympathy for Davey, the insecure tribal cop and Sandra, the misfit, who had tried to straddle two worlds. It hadn't worked for Sandra. It wouldn't work for Molly, either. She had made the right decision thirteen years ago and she'd made the wrong one earlier this month. She looked at Cam Outlaw's lean face and the unreadable blue eyes under the dark brows and she said a last, silent goodbye.

"All right, Miss Molly," Dr. Schmidt said. "You get some rest. I'll check in on you in a few hours. With any luck you'll be back home by tonight. Got any questions?"

"No." She gave him a smile and noticed her face didn't hurt as much as it had a few minutes earlier. Thank God for pain meds.

"I've got a question," Cam startled her by saying.

"What about the baby?"

Molly's eyes widened and the doctor stared at Cam then at Molly.

"You're pregnant?"

"Yes," Cam said.

"No," said Molly, and for some reason, tears formed in her eyes and trickled down her cheeks.

"How 'bout it, Molly? This is no time to be coy. Which is it?"

"I'm not." She kept her gaze on the doctor and kept her tone bright. "It was a possibility but I took a home test last night. All clear."

The doctor patted her arm. "It's just as well. A battering like you took today could have caused some damage. Give your body a chance to heal before you try again."

It was a kind and generous comment considering he knew perfectly well she wasn't married.

She waited until the doctor had left the room then she forced herself to meet Cam's intense gaze.

"I'm so sorry. About the clinic and, well, how you had to find out about it." She was so tired every word was an effort but she needed to let him know he was off the hook. "I told him the truth. There's no baby." For some reason the tears kept coming. Cam squeezed her hand, gently.

"Get some sleep. We'll talk later."

She didn't want to talk about it later. She wanted to apologize and be done.

"I just want you to know I'm sorry," she said. "I'm so sorry."

"I know," he said, quietly. "I'm sorry, too, Tiger Lily."

Much later in the day Cam used a wheelchair to transport her to curb in front of Eden Memorial and then he scooped her into his arms and deposited her in the backseat of his Mercedes so she could stretch out on the way home. The irony of exiting the hospital in the new-mom mode wasn't lost on Molly. She felt an ache inside that rivaled every outer wound. She promised herself that this would be the last time she'd indulge in self pity. In a day or two, when she felt better, she'd go back to her father's reservation. She'd find out what she could about John Wind and about the woman who was Molly's mother. After that, she'd come back to Blackbird, to James and Muriel, and to everyone else who belonged to the rez, including the mollies who had always served as her strength. She'd redouble her efforts to get a clinic and, perhaps, a school.

At least, she thought, as sleep claimed her, she had a plan.

It was always good to have a plan.

When they arrived at the cottage she awoke to find herself, once again, in Cameron Outlaw's arms. He carried her into the bedroom and placed her on the bed. Then he stood back, for a moment, gazing at her. She closed her eyes, willing him to leave. He seemed to understand.

"I'm going, Molly. Is there anything I can do for you first?"

She opened her eyes and glared at him, perversely wanting him to offer to stay. And then she heard the front door open.

"Molly?" It was her mother. Molly looked at Cam.

"You called Muriel?"

His lips twisted into a half smile.

"Better her than Grey Wolf."

Or you. "Thanks."

He feathered her cheek with his fingertips. "Feel better," he said.

She closed her eyes, unable to watch him leave for the last time.

****

Another day like this one and they could just dig a hole and drop him in it.

He'd practically stroked out when he'd learned Daisy was kidnapped. He'd thought nothing could be worse than the fear that his child was in danger until he'd watched Molly's Jeep turn a cartwheel. *Jesus.* The output of adrenalin had left him without any resources, physical or mental. If he stayed at the cottage he'd have forced her to agree to marriage and he knew it would have been a mistake. It was the wrong time and the wrong place and, besides, he needed to do some work on his sales technique.

He needed to do more before he'd be worthy of claiming this woman.

But it was damn hard to walk away. He'd stayed a minute to speak with her mother.

"Will you let me know if she—or you—needs anything?"

Muriel White Cloud's black eyes seemed to study his face.

"My Molly," she said, in a low voice, "she means something to you?"

He shook his head.

"She means everything to me. She always has."

He realized it was true. He should never have married Elise. He'd never had anything to offer her. He was, and always would be, a one-woman man.

His cell phone rang as he turned off Route 15 on his way to Eden. The caller I.D. said *Grey Wolf.*

Cam stiffened. What the devil did he want? He punched the phone with his thumb.

"Is this about Molly?"

There was a low chuckle. "You've got it bad. No. It's about Sharon."

"Sharon Johnson?"

"I'm going to marry her."

"You need my blessings?"

"I thought you should know."

"Well now I do. Anything else?"

"Yeah, there is. What're you gonna do about Molly?"

Cam's first instinct was to tell Molly's ex to go to hell but he stopped himself. Instead, he consciously thought about the past and what he owed the man. Grey Wolf had married a pregnant girl to protect her good name, a girl he, Cam, had abandoned. Okay, so he hadn't known. He also hadn't cared enough to find out. He owed the shaman the truth.

"I probably don't deserve a second chance but I'm taking it."

"You're going to ask Molly to marry you?"

"It won't be a question." He paused. "But I may need a little help."

Grey Wolf chuckled, softly. "Whatever I can do."

****

Molly slept nearly around the clock.

By late the following afternoon she felt considerably better. She could hear someone working in the kitchen and she smelled Muriel's chicken soup.

"Mother?"

An anxious round face appeared at the door.

"How are you feeling, *nizwia?* "

Molly moved her neck and arms, gingerly. And then her legs.

"I'm much better. I think I needed the rest." She let out a sigh. "It takes a lot of energy to live a lie."

"Don't be so hard on yourself, sweetheart."

She shook her head. "I am so ashamed. I want you to know I'm glad I'm not pregnant.

"Really?"

"It would have been a bad way to start a new life."

Muriel nodded. "Daniel called to check on you. He is going to marry the red-haired woman, you know."

Molly smiled, happy for her friend. Daniel, it seemed, was able to cross the bridge into another culture, but then he'd had practice. He'd lived in Washington D.C. for years.

"He'll be a good husband and father," Molly said. "Over-protective, neurotic and loving."

"I've made soup. Are you hungry?"

"Starving."

"And there's fresh bread. Maybe you should shower first."

"Mother! Are you telling me I smell?"

"You'll feel better with clean hair." Muriel grinned and the two women exchanged a look of relief. Finally, after what seemed like the longest, dark night, Molly was back to her old self. Or, at least, nearly.

The shower, meal and her mother's warmth felt wonderful but when she'd finished, Molly decided to go for a walk in her woods. She intended to move forward now despite the emptiness in her heart. She needed to gather strength from the generations of women who had preceded her, from the nature that surrounded her. She needed time and solitude to regain her harmony so she could continue on her solo journey. She reached into her coat closet for an old gray windbreaker to slip on over her navy sweater and jeans but Muriel stopped her.

"I won't go far," she promised, assuming her mother was going to caution her about walking in the woods at night. "I just need a little fresh air. It's the Moon of Ripening Berries. My favorite season, you know."

"Please wear this." She handed Molly a breathtakingly beautiful white jacket decorated with porcupine quills and beads.

"You made this?"

"For you," Muriel said.

It was on the tip of Molly's tongue to protest. The garment was clearly meant for a special occasion. But Muriel's solemn expression dissuaded her and, in a way, it was a special night. The first night of freedom from the awful secrets she'd harbored in the past. The first night of the rest of her life. She repressed a pang of longing. She would face the future alone.

"Thank you, n'onon. This is the most beautiful piece I've ever seen. "

"Warm, too. And wear your boots." Molly pulled on the tall moccasins Muriel had made the previous year. Half an hour later, as she watched the sun's last rays slant horizontally through the trees and glance over the fallen leaves, she was glad of the warmth. The temperature had already dropped and it wasn't even fully dark. It would drop again, shortly. After all, it was late October. The jacket and boots kept her warm, inside and out. She felt like a real Penobscot. She felt like a real daughter. She thought about the love she'd received from her adoptive parents. Perhaps one day she would find a child to adopt, too. The thought lifted her spirits.

At home in the woods, Molly wandered about, inhaling the fragrance of pines, the scent of the earth, and gathering the sense of peace around her. It was out here that she felt most strongly connected with generations of Miqmaq and Maliseet and Passamaquoddy and Penobscot. She accepted the forgiveness implicit in the night and she accepted the elements of herself including the pain. Tonight all the parts came together.

She was the child, Raven Wind.

She was the midwife, Molly Whitecloud.

She was the woman who'd loved and lost Eden's golden boy.

She was Tiger Lily.

Chapter Sixteen

The sky had turned indigo by the time Molly's ramble took her to the spinney by Blackbird Pond. The familiar scent of the woodlands and fresh air mixed with something unexpected. Molly sniffed the air. Tobacco.

Someone was here.

Someone who smoked a pipe.

Molly felt a flash of concern. The woods were dry at this time of year. A dropped pipe, a lit match, any flicker of fire could destroy her beloved forest. She'd find the offender and give him a lecture. She turned down a small path that plunged into inky darkness. It would have been smart to bring a flashlight but Molly wasn't worried. She knew the layout of the woods as well as she knew her own cottage. She inhaled deeply to locate the source of the pipe smoke then stopped in her tracks as a struck match revealed a human face.

Molly smiled. It was a familiar and beloved face, the face of one of her favorite people in the world.

"*N'dadan*," she said. Father.

James Whitecloud's eyes were black buttons in his wrinkled face. Between his strong teeth he held the flat, narrow end of a traditional peace pipe and in his gnarled fingers, the bowl.

Before Molly could ask why her father had come to the spinney to smoke, she heard a series of scraping sounds. Other matches flared and the scent of tobacco grew stronger. And then, as if directed by some unseen hand, the glowing pipe bowls moved into a configuration.

She was so busy trying to identify the individuals in the faint light it took her awhile to get the significance of the formed circle. Suddenly, she understood. It was a Medicine Wheel sometimes used for a native marriage ceremony.

Who was getting married?

A glimpse of another familiar and dear face on the circle brought understanding. *Daniel.* Molly didn't even have to consult her feelings. She felt a wave of gratitude and happiness for her friend. He'd waited a long time for this. He deserved it. She smiled but there was a catch in her throat as her eyes became accustomed to the dark and she recognized Lynn Brown Bear, Nancy Dove, Maggie and other friends from the rez along with Hallie Outlaw and her husband Baz, Lucy Outlaw Langley and her husband, the sheriff, Sharon, of course, and a smiling Daniel.

Cam had not come. Her heart squeezed a little. She couldn't blame him. The rez was the last place in the world he'd want to be.

And then she felt a warm hand on her shoulder and he turned her toward him.

"Molly Whitecloud," he said, in a deep, serious voice that turned her insides to oatmeal, "I have loved you nearly half my life. Will you marry me?"

She gazed into the chips of blue sky. Tonight she saw something in them she'd never seen before. Uncertainty.

"Marry me, too," chirped a small voice. Molly

tilted her head back surprised to see Daisy Outlaw perched on her father's shoulders.

"Well, Tiger Lily?" Cam's voice was soft. "What do you say?"

"Daddy, you silly," Daisy said. "Molly's not a tiger."

Cam's eyes, morning glory blue even here in the dark forest, glittered.

"She was a tiger when rescued you, Munchkin. And she was a tiger when she rescued me."

Molly lifted her fingers and stroked them down the little girl's cheek but her eyes never left Cam's. She thought about living in Cam's house in Eden, away from the rez. She'd always thought it would be impossible. But not now. She'd have moved to the moon if he'd asked her.

"We won't leave the rez," Cam assured her, reading her thoughts. "We can live in your cottage so you can continue your work."

"I can't ask you to do that."

"You didn't ask me, love. I want to do that. There are no emergencies at the bank. I can live wherever I want and I choose to live where you are."

"Me, too," Daisy chimed in.

Suddenly Molly thought of something. "Where's Wilbur?"

"I couldn't get him to wake up," Daisy said. "But he sended you a kiss." She leaned over and delivered it.

"Are you ready, nizwia?" It was James's voice.

She was about to get married. She couldn't get married in jeans! Then she remembered the beautiful jacket. Like any loving mother, Muriel had prepared her for this.

She smiled at Cam.

"I'm ready."

Cam handed Daisy to Hallie and gripped Molly's hand and James Whitecloud pressed ashes on each of their foreheads. Then Muriel handed Molly a cedar-lined basket that contained an ear of corn, which, as Molly knew very well, signified fertility. A moment later Muriel covered them with a hand-woven blanket. Molly heard a childish giggle. It was Daisy but Molly wondered, suddenly if the others, especially Cam, found the Native American ceremony silly.

Once again he read her mind and squeezed her fingers.

A tall, thin man detached himself from the Wheel and moved next to James.

"Elgin Cantwell," Cam whispered. "He's a justice of the peace from Bangor. I was so careless before. This time I'm covering all the bases."

Soon the formalities were over and, with the blanket still symbolically separating them from the rest of the world, Cam pulled her into his arms. His kiss was full of forgiveness and promise and deep, abiding love. When it was over he murmured against her lips.

"*Behanem*."

Tears pricked the backs of Molly's eyes. He'd learned the Penobscot word for wife. Suddenly, she knew the wedding was a message. He wanted her to know how completely he accepted her heritage. How he embraced it.

"*Sanoba*," she replied. Husband.

His smile warmed the corners of her heart. He bent to her lips again.

"*Wajemi*."

Kiss me.

James began to chant the Apache Wedding Prayer and the words drifted over them like the first flakes of the Moon of Blinding Snow. A benediction.

"Now you will feel no rain, for you will be shelter to each other. You will feel no cold, for each of you will be warmth to the other. There is no more loneliness, for you will be companion to the other.

"Now you are two bodies," James continued, "but there is only one life before you. Soon you will go to your resting place, to enter into the days of your togetherness. May your days be good and long upon the Earth."

Their days would be good, she thought as warmth and anticipation filled her lower body. And their nights would be even better.

Hours later, after a feast of traditional fry bread and vegetables, chicken and wedding cake, Cameron slipped his arm around the waist of his bride.

"I don't know about you," he whispered, "but I'm ready to go to our resting place to enter into our togetherness."

She twined her arms around his neck and kissed a crumb on the corner of his mouth.

"Too bad the spa is closed. We could have gone back to the vanilla Honeymoon Suite."

Cam grinned. "We can. The place is opened up just for us. We've got the whole damned building."

He slipped his tongue between her lips and reduced her to a quivering mass of need.

"*Alsoda*," he whispered.

She looked into his eyes.

"I don't know that one."

"Roughly translated it means, beloved-wife-whom-I-can't-wait-to get-out-of-her-clothes."

She held him against her with all her strength and all her love and she felt his heart thundering.

"Come on," she said.

"In a second. You haven't heard the full extent of my vocabulary yet. I have one more word that should come in handy in very soon."

She grinned at him. "I didn't think the People had a word for 'sex.'"

Cam's fingers tightened around her waist and she felt every inch of his masculine heat.

"Not that soon. Next year, in the Sowing Moon or maybe the Moon of Ripening Berries."

Her heart was full of happiness as she anticipated the word.

"*Deidis*," he whispered.

Baby.

Epilogue

Some nine months after the wedding, Cam settled himself in a chair at Eden Memorial and cradled his black-haired son while he gazed at his wife holding their tiny blue-eyed daughter.

"Looks like I'll have to increase my vocabulary," he said, his eyes brimming with love. "What's the word for twins?"

A word about the author...

Ann Yost is a former newspaper reporter and freelance humorist. The mother of three children, a daughter-in-law and a brand new son-in-law, she lives in Northern Virginia with her reporter husband, Pete, and Lucy, their golden retriever.

www.ingramcontent.com/pod-product-compliance
Lightning Source LLC
Chambersburg PA
CBHW070323260626
47160CB00003B/930